MILLIE CRISWELL

THE MARRYING MAN

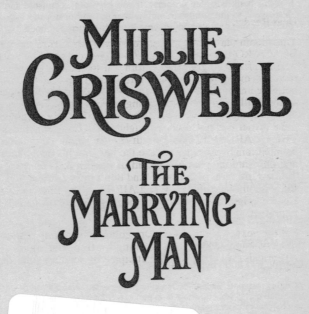

HARLEQUIN®

TORONTO • NEW YORK • LONDON
AMSTERDAM • PARIS • SYDNEY • HAMBURG
STOCKHOLM • ATHENS • TOKYO • MILAN • MADRID
PRAGUE • WARSAW • BUDAPEST • AUCKLAND

ISBN 0-373-29108-6

THE MARRYING MAN

This edition published by arrangement with Harlequin Books S.A.

® and TM are trademarks of the publisher. Trademarks indicated with
® are registered in the United States Patent and Trademark Office, the
Canadian Trade Marks Office and in other countries.

Visit us at www.eHarlequin.com

Printed in U.S.A.

Available from Harlequin Historicals and
MILLIE CRISWELL

Harlequin Historicals

The Marrying Man #508

From Harlequin American Romance

The Wedding Planner #810

Please address questions and book requests to:
Harlequin Reader Service
U.S.: 3010 Walden Ave., P.O. Box 1325, Buffalo, NY 14269
Canadian: P.O. Box 609, Fort Erie, Ont. L2A 5X3

To my soon-to-be daughter-in-law,
Staci Norman,
who's in the process of marrying the best man
I know. Welcome to the family!

Chapter One

"You need a wife, Ash, and there ain't no getting around that fact."

With the back of his ladder-back chair propped up against the exterior wall of the stone house, the dark-haired Ash swallowed a healthy dose of sour mash whiskey and screwed his face up in disgust, a clear indication of his feelings on the subject of matrimony.

The sun had just dipped into the horizon, streaking the autumn sky a reddish-gray color. In another hour it would be too cold to sit outside, so he intended to enjoy what time he had left. He'd spent too much time underground in the coal mines not to cherish the fresh mountain air and the wide-open spaces.

It was obvious his uncle expected him to comment, so he obliged the old man by answering. "I've had me two wives, Uncle Zeke. And that's about all a man should have to suffer in one lifetime."

The old man nodded and puffed his pipe. "That may be true, boy. Being a bachelor, I've never been overly fond of the whole marrying institution myself. But you got a child to think of.

"Addy's growing up wild with no woman around to tell her right from wrong. She looks like a boy most of the time, with her hair chopped off at crazy angles." The child had taken scissors to her long, brown locks, claiming her hair always got in the way when she was climbing trees and scampering over rocks. Ash hadn't bothered to take her to task for it, saying it was her hair and she had a right to cut it if she wanted. The boy was too dang permissive, in Zeke's opinion.

"That child smells worse than bear droppings downwind, 'cause she don't bathe regularlike, Ash, and I'm telling you that it's time you up and married again. For the girl's sake."

Ashby Morgan's silver eyes narrowed as he continued to gaze at his uncle. Zeke was a well-meaning man. Ash loved the old geezer like a father. But he didn't hold with any man telling him how to live his life or raise his daughter. He and Addy had been doing just fine these past eleven years on their own. And even if she was a bit of a tomboy, who was to say that was wrong? In time she'd grow out of it.

"You don't bathe regularly either, old man," Ash pointed out, "so you got no call to talk that way about Addy." The older man harrumphed, tapping the bowl of his pipe on the sole of his mud-caked boot to empty the ashes, then opened his mouth to say something else, but Ash didn't allow him to interrupt.

"And you know damn well that it's a woman's role in life to change a man. Adelaide tried it, and before her, Wynona. I loved them as best I could, God rest their souls, but I'm not sorry to have my freedom. I didn't ask the Almighty to take them from me like he did, but I took it as a sign that he wanted me to remain a single man.''

Ezekial Allistair Morgan pulled on his graying chin whiskers, as was his habit when he was frustrated or agitated about something. Ash had always been headstrong, even as a child, and it wasn't hard to tell where his daughter inherited her contrary disposition from. The stubborn young boy had grown into a damn stubborn fool-of-a-man. Young Addy, it seemed, was destined to follow in his footsteps.

All the Morgan men, himself included, suffered from thickheadedness, as his mama used to say. Ash's father, Aaron, had been particularly afflicted with the problem, which is why he'd failed to live beyond his thirtieth birthday. Morgan men had certain traits that couldn't be denied—the silvery-gray eyes for one thing, the stubbornness for another.

''What about a few years from now when the men start to call? Addy's beginning to grow up. In case you ain't noticed, boy, she's sprouting bosoms,'' he said, making Ash's eyes widen. ''Don't you wanna get that girl married and off your hands? No man's gonna look twice in her direction, unless you get her whipped into shape. She's behind in her learning, and she sure as heck ain't had no refinements. You got to admit—you ain't set much of an example for her.''

The younger man's face suffused with guilt, and Zeke took it as a sign of capitulation, plunging ahead into uncharted waters. ''I know you only want what's best for the girl. We all do. You know I love that child to death and would do anything for her. Which is why I've taken it upon myself to put a plan into motion.''

"What?" The younger man's eyes filled with suspicion and he frowned, rocking forward, the chair legs hitting the porch floorboards with a thud. "What have you done, old man? Don't tell me you've been playing matchmaker again, because I won't stand for it, Uncle Zeke. I told you none of the women in this town interest me." Attending to the day-to-day operations of the coal mine didn't leave much time to devote to romancing a woman anyway. Not that Ash was the least bit inclined. His needs could be satisfied at O'Connor's House of Pleasure when his urges got too strong to be denied.

Zeke's eyes, a shade darker than his nephew's, lit with a steely glint of determination and just a hint of satisfaction. "I figured as much, boy, which is why I took it upon myself to write this here lady." Removing a wrinkled newspaper advertisement from his back pocket, he smoothed it out and handed it to Ash, whose frown was deepening by the moment.

"Miss Dorothea Cartwright runs one of them finishing schools in Philadelphia—The Cartwright School of Finishing and Comportment. A real high-falutin sort of establishment, from the sounds of it."

His gaze drifting to the plump cardinal lighting on the spindly branch of the sycamore gracing the front yard, Ash's frown smoothed somewhat. "And you want me to send Addy to this woman?" He rubbed his chin, as if considering the idea, which admittedly had some merit. "I don't know…"

Zeke shook his head. "That weren't my thinking at all. Leastways, it wouldn't be right to do that, since you promised Adelaide on her deathbed that you'd always keep young Addy by your side."

"Yeah, I did." Ash's forehead wrinkled in confusion. "So why'd you write this woman then?" Suddenly a mischievous smile lifted the corners of his mouth. "You been carrying on some kind of romantic correspondence with Miss Cartwright behind the widow's back, you sly old dog?" His full-fledged grin made Zeke snort contemptuously.

"Very funny. It just so happens that Miss Cartwright teaches girls to become ladies. That's what a finishing school does. I asked Etta about it." The Widow Dobbins, as she was known around Morgantown, was the love of Ezekial Morgan's life, though the old man would rather die than admit that to anyone, especially his nephew, who he knew would tease him unmercifully if he learned just how sweet Zeke was on the widow.

"I wrote Miss Cartwright and told her that you was needin' a wife and a mother for your young daughter, and asked if she could recommend one of her girls for the job. Her girls are all refined types from good families. It says so right here, so I thought—"

"You what?" Ash bolted from his chair, shoving his furious face into his uncle's startled one. Zeke, who'd been leaning casually against the porch rail up until that moment, had now straightened and was ready for flight, just in case. Ashby Morgan had a mean temper when pushed, and Zeke may have pushed a tad bit too far.

"Are you crazy, Uncle Zeke? Do you actually think I'm stupid enough to marry some woman I've never met?" His eyes flashed quicksilver, and he shook his head. "That's not going to happen, so write the woman back and tell her to forget it."

Zeke's weathered face paled considerably. He decided to put some distance between himself and his nephew and moved around the angry man. Not that Ash would ever hit him, but a man couldn't be too careful. Zeke didn't have that many teeth left, but what he had, he intended to keep.

"It's…it's too late for that, boy. I already got a reply from Miss Cartwright. Said she was sending a young woman by the name of Sarah Jane Parker. Claims she fits the bill and will make you a wonderful wife. And," he added to emphasize his point, "an excellent mother for Addy."

"Well, write her back and tell her the deal's off. I'm not in the market for a bride, mail-order or otherwise."

"Can't. Already sent the train fare with my first letter, so there's nothing to keep her from coming. She'll be here any day now. The train from Philadelphia's due in to Fairmont day after tomorrow."

The pulse in Ash's temple began throbbing like a bubbling geyser, and the younger man let loose a string of curses, his fists clenched tightly at his side, as if the idea of striking out had crossed his mind. "I can't believe this!" He kicked the chair and sent it flying off the porch, and the older man's eyes widened a fraction, but he held his ground.

"I did what I thought was best for you and Addy," Zeke tried to explain. "I promised your daddy I'd take care of you when he went off to that damn war back in '61 and got hisself blowed up clear to kingdom come. I've tried to do right by you these many years." He squeezed Ash's shoulder, relieved when the angry man didn't pull away. Zeke loved the boy as if he'd sprung from his own loins.

"Morgan Coal Mining is taking off, Ash. Soon most all your time's gonna be spent at the mine. And if you expand your holdings, like we talked about, then you'll have even less time to devote to Addy's upbringing.

"You need a wife, boy. You don't have to love her. You don't even have to like her. You just got to marry her and let her be a mother to your girl."

The idea of living life with a woman from Philadelphia filled Ash with distaste. No doubt Miss Parker was some white-gloved, snooty society type. The kind of woman who ate an orange with a knife and fork instead of digging right into the meat of it, someone who quoted Bible scripture every chance she got, probably right before bedtime.

Living in the mountains was arduous. The work was hard, the winters harsh; he needed a helpmate, not a hindrance. "Miss Parker's a city girl, Zeke. She'll never fit in here."

"Your mama was a city girl through and through, boy, and she adjusted to life here in the mountains just fine. I'm not saying it's gonna be easy for her. But if Sarah Jane Parker's got smarts, which the letter claims she does, and gumption, which I hope she will, then she'll fare all right. You've got to give her a chance."

"She may be repulsed by my looks," the younger man said hopefully, trying a different tack, and was disappointed when Zeke threw back his head and laughed at the absurdity of the notion.

"It's embarrassing going into town with you and

watching the way them women throw themselves in your path. They're like bitches in heat, and you don't pay them no never mind. I ain't worried in the least about Miss Parker finding you to her liking.''

''What if she looks like the hind end of a mule?'' Not that he was planning to sleep with her, but still...a chill ran down his spine.

Reaching into his back pocket once again, the old man extracted a photograph and handed it to his nephew, a pleased-as-punch smile lighting a face mapped with lines of age and wisdom. ''She ain't no mule, boy. She's a thoroughbred, if this picture can be believed.''

Studying the likeness, Ash's eyes widened in surprise. Miss Sarah Jane Parker was blond, fair skinned, and possessed two deep-set dimples in her cheeks. Her nose was small and slightly upturned, and she had the devil's own twinkle in her eyes.

''She's a looker, I'll give you that. But she seems a mite young to be taking on the responsibilities of a wife and mother.'' She couldn't be more than nineteen or twenty, hardly much older than his daughter, and a full ten years younger than himself.

''The younger the better, I always say. She'll be like a young filly. You can break her in just the way you like before riding her.'' The old man chuckled. ''She won't be set in her ways or prone to give you any trouble, like the last Mrs. Morgan.'' Zeke puckered his mouth disapprovingly at the memory of Ash's late wife, who'd had an opinion on just about everything and drove Zeke nuts with her constant jabbering.

"A docile young woman is sure to make you an excellent wife," he concluded.

Ash considered his uncle's words, then finally smiled. He was beginning to warm to the idea of a docile wife who'd say, "Yes, Ash. Of course, Ash. You're right, Ash."

Neither of his first two wives had been all that easy to get along with. In fact, his first marriage had been nothing short of a disaster.

Wynona had been only sixteen when they'd married, and she hadn't wanted children. Or, at least, that's what she'd claimed. She'd been reluctant to bed him, fearing she'd end up pregnant and die in childbirth like her mother. Their marriage had been a constant battle of wills, up until the day she had fallen into the Monongahela River and drowned, three months after their wedding.

It wasn't until after her death that Ash had learned the truth: Wynona had been carrying another man's child, had, in fact, been in love with another man, and only married Ash out of desperation and to placate her angry parents who knew their daughter's married lover wasn't likely to leave his wife and two children.

Ash had been devastated by his wife's duplicity. He'd loved her and believed she'd loved him. Her deception had taught him painful lessons about trust, fidelity, and a woman's inclination to lie when it suited her purpose.

Then there'd been Adelaide, an earthy woman who had no problem with the marriage bed, but who'd been too damn opinionated about everything. Her daddy had been a coal miner down in Kentucky, and she thought she knew everything there was to know about the mining business.

She and Zeke had bickered about everything having to do with the mine. The old man had pulled no punches about his belief that a woman had no business in a man's domain, and Ash had been inclined to agree with him.

If Adelaide hadn't died in childbirth, Ash wasn't sure they'd have stayed married. A talkative, opinionated woman did wear on a man's nerves.

Sarah Jane Parker was supposedly docile. He liked that.

Docile. Refined. And no doubt spiritless.

She sounded almost perfect.

And that's what worried him. Ash had never met a perfect woman. He doubted there was such a thing.

So he made up his mind right then and there that, if Sarah Jane Parker proved to be even the least bit difficult or opinionated, he'd send her packing before she could untangle her corset strings.

Sarah Jane Parker wasn't much for corsets. At the moment, the one she wore was proving to be quite a hindrance as she attempted to shimmy down the sheet rope from her bedroom window, which was located on the second story of The Cartwright School of Finishing and Comportment—a pompous name that suited the pretentious, pious headmistress quite well.

The cumbersome skirt of her gown didn't help matters in the least. "Botheration!" she cursed when her knee hit the solid brick of the exterior wall, then held her breath, hoping no one had heard her outburst. She was prone to outbursts when things didn't go quite as planned, and realized she'd have to temper them, if she was going to pull off her charade.

Sarah Jane knew that it had been fate that had sent her to fetch the mail for Miss Cartwright that day— the day Ashby Morgan's letter arrived.

Not above a little snooping, especially when the notion that stiff-necked, oh-so-proper Miss Cartwright might have a suitor, she'd steamed open the envelope and read the letter, knowing in that moment that her prayers had been answered and her future preordained.

Since the missive hadn't been personal to Miss Cartwright, but more of a business matter, she hadn't felt overly guilty about stealing it, though it was doubtful her minister father would share her sentiments. And when she'd answered it, passing herself off as Miss Cartwright, and recommending herself, Sarah Jane Parker, a refined young woman of impeccable breeding, as the perfect choice for Mr. Morgan's wife, she'd told herself that what she was doing was in everyone's best interest.

Miss Cartwright would be only too happy to be rid of her. The two had grated on each other like sandpaper against bare skin since the first day they'd met, and she'd caused the headmistress nothing but trouble these past six years. Of course, the headmistress in turn had caused her nothing but heartache. Her father, too, would be spared the exorbitant expense of her tuition. And she, Sarah Jane, would be happy at last.

It was really the perfect solution, she told herself.

Only a few more feet and she'd be near enough the ground to jump. Sarah Jane knew this because she'd made this exit four times before. But on those pre-

vious escape attempts she'd been caught and sent
back to the school by her father, Reverend Seth Parker, a well-meaning man who wanted only what was
best for his headstrong, prone-to-mischief, and totally
irresponsible—in his opinion—daughter.

This time things would be different, Sarah Jane
vowed. She had purposely waited until the dead of
night when everyone, including Miss Cartwright and
her two yappy Yorkshire terriers, were asleep, and
had planned her escape route carefully. Her portmanteau, stuffed with clothing and other essentials, was
hidden beneath the bushes, and she was armed with
a train ticket to Morgantown, West Virginia, where a
handsome widower with a young daughter awaited
her.

Sarah Jane knew Ashby Morgan was handsome because he'd sent a photograph of himself along with
the train ticket. It was such a thoughtful gesture and
one she'd decided to mimic. It was no doubt a char-
acter flaw, but she sincerely doubted that she'd be
running off to parts unknown if the man in the photograph had looked like a hedgehog or been as old as
Methuselah.

Her mother had always counseled that it was just
as easy to fall in love with a rich man as a poor one.
Sarah Jane had applied that advice to looks, deciding
that it was just as easy to fall for a handsome man as
an ugly one, providing he was kind and had a pleasing
personality.

The romantic in Sarah couldn't resist the notion
that she was going to heal the widower's broken
heart, make him fall madly in love with her, and take
his sweet, innocent child under her wing and teach

her all she knew about good manners, proper comportment and living life to the fullest.

She had the latter down to a science. There wasn't anything she wouldn't try once. She had gone skinny-dipping in the Delaware River during the middle of a snowstorm—a tribute, of sorts, to George Washington's crossing—trimmed the hair off Miss Cartwright's terriers, making them look like drowned rats, and smoked a cigar in the bathing room of the gymnasium, nearly setting the school on fire.

Daring Sarah Jane to try something, even if it was slightly dangerous, was like waving a red flag at a bull. She loved a good challenge and abhorred boredom.

She also had impeccable manners when the occasion warranted, and knew that she'd be expected to set a good example for the poor motherless child. No doubt the little girl was sullen and withdrawn, but Sarah would soon have her out of her shell and up to snuff. In her opinion, unbridled optimism and a wealth of smiles were very effective weapons in handling difficult people or situations.

Heaving a sigh at the wonderful plans she was making, she lost her concentration momentarily and nearly let loose of the sheet she was hanging on to. Cursing her stupidity, she muttered, "Pay attention, Sarah Jane, or you'll be spending the rest of your life being wheeled around in a chair."

Reaching the ground in one piece, she groped blindly in the dark for her portmanteau and found it just where she'd hidden it—under the forbidding holly bushes, whose leaves were like knife points, and where few hands dared to reach.

Without a backward glance at the institution she so despised and had come to think of as a prison, she hurried off into the night toward the train station a few blocks away.

Within the hour, Sarah Jane was seated on the westbound train heading toward her new life, and feeling very confident in her plan to marry a total stranger.

Everyone in Philadelphia thought she was a flighty, harebrained young woman without a lick of sense. But she intended to prove to her family, friends and most especially to herself that she was an independent, responsible young woman who was going to make Ashby Morgan a wonderful wife.

Removing his photograph from her reticule, she gazed at it once again and heaved a deep sigh. "Mrs. Ashby Morgan," she whispered, smiling to herself, glad there was no one seated next to her who would think her addled.

She'd developed a bad habit of talking to herself while at school to stave off her loneliness. Many of her days had been spent in a solitary manner, due to her outrageous behavior, and the fact she was always in trouble over one thing or another. Miss Cartwright had used her as an example for the other children, of what *not* to do.

Well, Miss Cartwright would be in for a big surprise come morning, she thought with an incorrigible grin. Sarah Jane Parker had made good her escape!

The passenger car was relatively empty, save for a harried woman and her two bickering children, a couple of well-dressed businessmen seated toward the rear, who were engrossed in serious conversation about politics, and an elderly man asleep and snoring loud enough to wake the dead.

It was late and Sarah Jane imagined they'd be picking up more passengers as they proceeded along toward Fairmont, West Virginia, which was the train's final destination and located about fifteen miles from the city of Morgantown. From there, she'd be met by Ashby Morgan and his uncle, who would take her the rest of the way home.

"Home." She choked on the word, already missing her mother and father, but knowing that the home on Maple Avenue in Philadelphia hadn't been hers for a number of years.

Her parents had thought they were doing right by trying to stifle her natural inclinations and exuberant nature, and they'd sent her to Miss Cartwright's to be "toned down," as her mother, Xenobia, had put it. But they'd been wrong. The forced confinement and schooling had only made her more eager to live beyond the boundaries, to stretch her wings and try new things.

After she was married and beyond the reach of her parents, she would write to let them know that she was safe and happy.

She hoped they would find it in their hearts to forgive her for leaving, as she had tried to forgive them for robbing her of the past six years of her life.

Chapter Two

Wearing a groove into the pine planking of the wooden sidewalk, Ash paced back and forth in front of the Fairmont rail station, waiting for the arrival of the passenger train from Philadelphia. He tried to get his thoughts together, hoping to figure out just what in hell he was going to tell everyone about his decision to marry Sarah Jane Parker.

In the past, he had made it a point to share his views on his disinclination to marry again with just about anyone at O'Connor's who was sober enough to listen. A few of the ladies of the evening had taken to calling him "the marrying man" when they'd found out he'd been hitched twice before, figuring he might be inclined to marry again. He'd wanted to make it perfectly clear that just wasn't the case.

He had nothing against marrying a prostitute—they were merely women who were down on their luck for the most part, and they tended toward honesty. A man always knew what to expect from that kind of woman.

It was the getting-hitched-again part that bothered him. Which is why he'd made it plain on several occasions, and after too many whiskeys had made his tongue loose, that he had married for the last time and would never again enter into a matrimonial state.

And now that old fool Zeke was making him out to be a liar. And no doubt enjoying every minute of it.

If Ash told anyone how his uncle had hornswoggled him into getting hitched, he would never live it down. "The marrying man" appellation was sure to follow him to his grave. Getting married once was considered normal, twice, a regrettable episode, as you had either been widowed or divorced, but three times was looked upon as downright peculiar and excessive as all get-out. Especially when the person in question getting married was only thirty-one years old.

Hell! When he thought about it, he'd been married all of his adult life. Of course, he'd been widowed most of that time, but he'd still had the responsibility of fatherhood to adjust to. And being a father had a way of making a boy into a man in a big hurry.

Removing his stained felt hat, Ash ran agitated fingers through his hair. Zeke hadn't accompanied him to the train station after promising that he would, saying it was necessary for him and Etta to get everything squared away at the church for his arrival.

His uncle wasn't about to allow Ash the time to change his mind. The old man had judiciously pointed out that a single woman could not live in a house with three bachelors and not be married to one of them.

"Damn that old man anyway!"

"Did you say something, Mr. Morgan?"

Glancing up, Ash found Beulah Rafferty and her spinster daughter approaching and cursed beneath his breath. The biggest gossip in Morgantown was going to witness his meeting with his future bride.

Well, isn't this just peachy?

"Afternoon, ma'am. Miss Cynthia," he said, forcing a smile. It wasn't that Cynthia Rafferty wasn't attractive—she had a very nice smile and all of her teeth—but she wasn't Ash's type. Maybe he was just imagining things but she seemed eager to get married. Warning bells went off whenever he got within three feet of the woman.

Zeke had cautioned that spinsters were prone to acting peculiar because they possessed ardent and unsettled dispositions, owing to the fact that they'd never done the deed, which was widely known to have a calming effect on the female constitution. But Ash had no intention of doing the deed with Cynthia Rafferty, not even to restore her good health or calm her frazzled nerves.

"I'm surprised to see you here, Mr. Morgan," Beulah said. "I thought your brother had taken the wagon to Pittsburgh." In fact, she knew he had, because Beulah made it a point to know everything about everyone else's business.

"Yes, ma'am, he did. It's not A.J. I'm waiting on." His younger brother had gone to fetch supplies for the mine and wouldn't return for a few more days. A.J. had no inkling of Ash's plans to wed, and would most likely find the whole affair quite amusing upon his return. His brother found humor in most things, like a hyena, only smarter.

A speculative gleam entered the older woman's

eyes. "Oh? I usually hear about all the new folks coming to visit, on account of my cousin Virgil working the ticket office here."

Cynthia smiled up at him. "We've missed you at church, Mr. Morgan," she stated. Her eyelashes fluttered, as if she had dirt in them or something.

"Yeah, well—I've been busy with work and all. Guess I'll have to try harder to get there."

Mrs. Rafferty had been pushing Cynthia at him for years. For some reason the older woman had gotten it in her head that Ash was the only suitable man for her daughter, though there were plenty of men in town who would welcome the opportunity to become acquainted with the spinster.

Because of the fledgling coal industry, males far outnumbered females in Morgantown, and Ash had a lingering suspicion that A.J. might be interested in the woman. Better him than me, he thought, wondering if his younger brother would ever settle down and get married.

Being married did offer a man a measure of protection from overeager females. Not that it was going to be worth becoming hog-tied again, Ash decided.

The train whistle blew, announcing its impending arrival, and he was spared any further conversation. With the belching and puffing of clouds of white smoke and the screeching of steel on steel, the locomotive pulled into the station right on time.

Snapping his father's gold pocket watch closed, he dropped it back into his pocket. The watch, the land and Zeke's colorful tales were all he had left of his old man.

Both his parents were gone now. His mother had

died of pneumonia when Addy was still a baby, and he missed her to this day. She'd been a warm, loving woman with a keen sense of humor and a generous heart. And she'd been honest in all things and expected the same from her sons.

As the passengers from the train began to embark onto the platform, the knot in Ash's stomach tightened. He didn't know what he was going to say to the young woman, how he'd be able to convince her to go back home, if she wasn't everything her letter claimed her to be. But he'd think of something. He had no intention of jumping from the proverbial frying pan into the fire. Twice burned was enough for any reasonable man to contend with.

Two dogs snarling over a juicy bone caught his attention and he looked away for a moment. When he turned back, Sarah Jane Parker was standing on the platform, clutching her valise and looking more curious than frightened.

Like one of the porcelain dolls his daughter never played with, she was breathtakingly lovely. Beneath her bonnet her blond hair shimmered like spun gold in the sunlight.

It was clear she'd recognized him from the photograph Zeke had sent, because her face lit with a friendly smile and she waved, causing Ash's stomach to drop somewhere in the vicinity of his feet.

Slack jawed, he continued to stare as if mesmerized, until nosy Mrs. Rafferty nudged him in the arm. ''I think that young lady is waving at you, Mr. Morgan. Do you know her?'' Her grim expression clearly revealed that she hoped he did not.

The spell was broken. Gazing down at the older

woman, he shook his head. "No, ma'am, I don't."
Her sigh of relief was short-lived when he added,
"But I'm about to make her acquaintance. That pretty
lady's going to be my wife."

Beulah clutched the ivory cameo at her throat in
dismay. "This is the first I'm hearing of it, Mr. Morgan. Are you quite certain?" She intended to give
Virgil a good talking-to the first chance she got.

With as polite a goodbye as he could muster, he
made his way toward the slender blond woman with
the welcoming smile. She was garbed in a very becoming gown of blue silk, which was totally unsuit-
able for the mountains but showed off her generous
curves to perfection.

Ash had a weakness for large-breasted women.
Some men liked long legs, others a slender neck, but
Ash liked to wrap his hands around a pair of
healthy—he cursed beneath his breath at where his
thoughts had traveled: right over Sarah Jane Parker's
ample bosom.

The sun hadn't come out yet today, but sunshine
radiated with every uptilt of the woman's bow-shaped
mouth. A very kissable mouth, he observed, chastis-
ing himself again for having carnal thoughts about a
woman he didn't even know.

He had been determined to keep this marriage in
name only, in case he needed to have it annulled right
away. But that noble idea wasn't quite as palatable as
it had been before he'd laid eyes on Sarah Jane Parker.

Sarah Jane sucked in her breath as the tall, dark-
haired man strolled toward her. He walked with a
predatory swagger, shoulders wide, hips slim, and she

wondered for half a moment if she'd bitten off more than she could chew. This man reeked of masculinity, of experience, and she had none to speak of when it came to matters of the flesh.

Of course, she'd read about such things in books she'd received through the mail and kept hidden beneath the mattress in her room at school. But they'd been confiscated when Miss Cartwright had gotten wind of her illicit activity from one of the other girls.

Kathryn Baxter had a reputation as a tattletale, among other things, and she'd been jealous of Sarah Jane because Sarah had always gotten away with a lot and had become somewhat of a legend at the school.

Sarah Jane was positive that the straitlaced headmistress had read the suggestive material from cover to cover, because for the week following the confiscation, she'd walked around with an unbecoming red flush covering her face that cried out "guilty!"

Ash tipped his hat and smiled. "Miss Sarah Jane Parker, I presume?"

She swallowed with some difficulty, the deep sound of his voice sending shivers of awareness racing down her spine. He was tall, much taller than she, and his large form effectively blocked out the sun as it rose, casting them in shadow.

"Yes. Yes, I am. From the Cartwright School. And you must be Mr. Morgan."

"Afraid so," he replied, and she wrinkled her brow in confusion, wondering at his odd response.

Picking up her valise, he offered his arm and escorted her to the waiting buckboard. "We've got a bit of a ride back to Morgantown." He thought he should warn her, in case she had to use the facilities behind the rail station, her being a city girl and all.

She stared blankly at him, then her face flushed red, and she shook her head. "I'm fine." It was nice to find him so considerate of her personal needs, though that wasn't something usually discussed between strangers, even if they were sort of affianced.

They'd almost reached the wagon when the two Rafferty women hailed them, then approached. Ash bit back a groan.

"*Yoo-hoo!* Mr. Morgan! Aren't you going to introduce us to your fiancée?" Not waiting for his response, Beulah gave the younger woman an imperious nod and performed the introductions herself, before saying, "Of course, we were quite surprised to hear Mr. Morgan was getting married again." She told Sarah Jane, "He's been to the altar twice before, but his womenfolk just weren't strong enough to make it up here in the mountains. They died such tragic deaths." She tsked several times. "Such a pity."

Twice! Sarah swallowed her surprise. No wonder Ashby Morgan appeared to be so experienced. He'd done this sort of thing twice before, if that old busybody could be believed. "I'm very sorry to hear that," she replied. "I didn't know."

Beulah was pleased that she'd been the first to relate the news. The dissemination of hearsay had become her stock-in-trade, and folks in town relied on her to provide the latest fodder from the gossip mill. She likened her news-gathering and broadcast to performing a valuable service, not unlike tending the infirmed or administering comfort, like a member of the clergy.

"Little Addy's been without a mother these past eleven years," she added with a repetitive clucking of her tongue. "She's never known a female's influence, having been raised alone by Mr. Morgan and his—" she paused, attempting to disguise the contempt she felt for Ezekial Morgan "—family. Not to say they haven't tried, mind you, but—"

"We've got to be getting along now, ma'am," Ash interrupted, trying to keep his temper in check but not having much luck. He sure as heck couldn't blame his uncle Zeke for breaking off with the old busybody all those years ago. The two hadn't spoken a civil word since.

"Perhaps Miss Parker can visit sometime and you can fill her in on all the other sordid details of my personal life," he added.

Beulah Rafferty gasped. Cynthia stared in dismay. Sarah Jane merely smiled.

"I see my future husband has a sense of humor, ladies. I'll have to remember that. Good day to you, both." She waved. "Mrs. Rafferty reminds me of a woman I was acquainted with back in Philadelphia." When they were out of earshot, she said, "An unpleasant sort of person, very opinionated and rude. I don't think I shall be spending much time in her company. And I don't think her daughter likes me at all. I suspect Miss Rafferty has set her cap for you, Mr. Morgan. Am I correct?"

For some reason Ash couldn't quite figure out, he was embarrassed by the bluntness of the question and felt heat rise up his neck. "I—uh—"

Sarah Jane linked her arm through his and smiled up at him. "Not to worry, Mr. Morgan. You are mine now, and Miss Rafferty is just plain out of luck."

The trip to Morgantown was pleasant enough, though Ash hadn't said more than a handful of words to Sarah Jane the entire way there. He'd been too engrossed in the last comment she'd made before they'd departed. *You are mine now, and Miss Rafferty is just plain out of luck.*

Those simple words, uttered so matter-of-factly, and with such sweet possessiveness, had made him feel peculiar all over, almost feverish, as if he'd eaten a putrefied piece of meat or swallowed milk that had turned.

When they finally entered the town proper, Sarah Jane got her first glimpse of what was to be her new home. She was relieved to find Morgantown a bustling little city with substantial brick buildings lining the main thoroughfare, which had been macadamized, the layered stones creating a dust-free, waterproof surface. Hickory and maple trees bursting with autumn colors of red and gold shaded their route.

The town, which had been named back in 1766 for its founder Colonel Zackquill Morgan, one of Ash's ancestors, he'd informed her proudly, was bordered on the west by the Monongahela River, affectionately known as "The Mon" to the locals, and Dexter's Creek to the east.

Many of the small industries—the pottery, flour mill and furniture factory—had settled near the water to take advantage of the steam to drive its operations, though Ash assured her that coal was taking over as a major source of power.

"Is your house far from here?" she asked, anxious to see her new residence, which would give her an idea of just what kind of man she was marrying. You could tell a lot by the way a man dressed and where he lived. Both were reflections of his personality.

Mr. Morgan hadn't bothered to wear a suit to greet her, so she figured him for the informal type, though what he wore—denims and a blue cambric shirt—was clean and free from tears. And she could tell that his dark hair had been washed recently, because it shone in the afternoon sunshine like black obsidian.

He shook his head. "It's a short distance from here, in the hills above town. But we're not going directly home."

"We're not?" She was a tad disappointed, anxious as she was to see her new abode. "Do you need to pick up supplies first? I don't eat much, if that's what you're worried about."

He answered her teasing grin with one of his own, noting the dimples in her cheeks. "I'm not worried about how much you eat, Miss Parker. I just thought it might be better for your reputation if we were to get hitched before spending the night alone at the house. We're heading directly to the church."

Her heart began a strange fluttering in her chest. She hadn't even considered the wedding ceremony, or what immediately followed: the wedding night. "How silly of me not to have thought of that. My father is a minister, so I'm sure he'll be relieved that we'll be getting married properly in a church."

"Uncle Zeke and his lady friend are waiting with

Reverend Pickett, who's going to perform the ceremony. They'll act as witnesses.''

''What about your daughter? Won't she be there, too?''

Ash wondered just how much he should reveal about his daughter's less-than-enthusiastic response when he'd told her that he intended to marry again:

''I'll hate you, Daddy, if you bring another woman into this house. I'm in charge here, and you don't need no other woman, especially some sourpuss society lady.''

''Addy didn't take the news of my marrying too well,'' he explained. ''I left her at home with our neighbor, Georgie Ann Freeland, who looks after her on occasion.''

''I guess I can't really blame your daughter. After all, I am a stranger. And I know if I were in the same situation, I wouldn't want my papa marrying some woman I'd never met. Most likely she feels threatened that you're bringing another woman into her home.''

Ash's eyes widened at her perceptiveness, and he decided that the very least he could do was level with her. ''Addy's going to try your patience, Miss Parker. I may as well tell you that now, in case you want to change your mind about staying. I've tried my best to raise her right after her mama died, but she's turned out wild and unruly. Sort of a tomboy. And she's got a mouth on her that won't quit.'' She'd actually called him a horse's ass when he'd told her the news, but he hadn't had the heart to spank her. She was too old for spankings anyway.

Sarah Jane stifled a smile. Addy Morgan sounded like someone she was very well acquainted with: herself. "She's looking for attention, and I'll be able to provide that, as well as some instruction on better behavior, once we become friends." She knew how important it would be to gain the girl's trust.

At the woman's optimism, Ash's brows lifted clear to his hairline. He guessed her age had something to do with her naiveté and inexperience in dealing with an eleven-year-old. "Addy's not going to like being told what to do. Hell, she hardly listens to what I tell her."

Sarah smiled knowingly. "No. I don't expect she will. And you should probably try to curb your swearing in front of her, Mr. Morgan, if you want your daughter to curb hers. No doubt she mimics everything you do or say."

The set-down, though camouflaged with a sweet-as-molasses smile, was a rebuke nonetheless, and Ash had hardly seen it coming. Miss Sarah Jane Parker had a way about her, that was for certain. Only he wasn't quite sure what he was going to do about it. Or her.

"I guess I haven't scared you off then?" Part of him was hoping she'd hightail it back to Philadelphia and leave him be. He had a feeling his life had just gotten a whole lot more complicated with her arrival.

"Call me foolish, Mr. Morgan, but I love a challenge. It takes a lot to scare me off." And after years of surviving Dorothea Cartwright, Sarah Jane felt confident that she could handle just about anything thrown her way, including a small child.

She was so sure of herself, so composed, that Ash couldn't resist taunting her a bit. "Is that so? Well, I guess we'll have to wait and see if you're still of the same mind come evening when it's time to make our union binding."

Heat rushed to her cheeks. Her future husband was a plain speaker, and that was something that would take getting used to. But she was no shrinking violet. She wasn't afraid of what was to come. On the contrary, she was looking forward to the new experience.

"I'm a virgin, Mr. Morgan, so I'm going to allow you to take the lead tonight. Since you've been married twice before, I assume you're far more experienced in these matters than I. From what I've read, most men are."

Ash opened his mouth to say something, but then snapped it shut. Damn if the woman didn't take the words right out of his mouth with her bluntness. He'd hoped to get the better of her, put her in her place, let her know who was in charge right from the beginning, but she'd turned the tables on him with her wide-eyed honesty.

Pulling the buckboard to a halt in front of the Grace United Methodist Church, a charming stone and brick building located on High Street, he set the brake, then turned to the woman seated primly beside him. "Guess this is it, Miss Parker. Everyone's waiting inside."

She flashed a smile that fairly took his breath away. "Well, then, Mr. Morgan, what are we waiting for? I think we should stop talking and get on with the wedding." She sensed a hesitancy in him and was confused by it. After all, he'd been the one to write to her, or rather, to Miss Cartwright. But she pushed off his odd behavior to nervousness. If the man had been married twice before, he was doubtless apprehensive about what kind of wife she would make.

After a few moments, he shrugged. "I guess."

"Mr. Morgan," she said, placing her hand on his forearm. The muscles bunched beneath her fingers, and she marveled at his strength, wondering what it would be like to have those strong arms wrapped around her. The notion made her hands sweat inside her gloves. "I've never been married before, and I may be inexperienced in some things, but I'm a quick learner, and I intend to make you an excellent wife." She took a deep breath and continued, "My only request is that you meet me halfway. From your letters, I gather that you want to make this marriage work as much as I do."

Sarah Jane looked so earnest, so young, sitting there with her whole life spread out before her and her eyes reflecting innocence, that Ash didn't have the heart to burst her bubble by revealing that he wasn't the one who wanted a wife, that he wasn't the one who had written all that drivel.

Let her have her girlish dreams for a while, he thought. She'd be facing reality soon enough.

Hell! Addy was probably waiting at home with a loaded shotgun to greet her.

Chapter Three

Reverend Pickett had pronounced Sarah Jane Parker and Ashby Morgan to be husband and wife a short time ago, but Sarah Jane, who had no gold ring on her finger and hadn't been so much as bussed on the cheek by her new husband, didn't feel much like a bride.

What she felt was disappointed.

She'd envisioned her wedding day to be very different: close friends to wish her well, an organist playing "Oh Promise Me" while she marched down the aisle on her father's arm, who would then perform the ceremony. And she'd counted on a wedding cake.

Mrs. Dobbins had apologized profusely that no reception had been arranged for after the ceremony. "Too short of notice," she'd proclaimed. "But we'll have us a real nice shindig as soon as I can make all the arrangements and get the invites out."

The short, plump gray-haired woman was a motherly sort, and Sarah Jane had taken an instant liking to her, though several times during the ceremony she had looked at Sarah Jane with something akin to pity.

While the minister had droned on about love, honor and till death do us part, she had grown confused and somewhat frightened by the older woman's reaction.

Ash's uncle, Ezekial Morgan, had been far more animated after the ceremony than during it. In fact, the old man had looked almost relieved once she and Ash had said "I do," his crinkled-parchment face smoothing into a wealth of smiles. And when he'd grabbed her in a bear hug and told her to call him Uncle Zeke, there'd been tears in his gray eyes, as if he couldn't quite believe that his nephew's marriage had actually come about.

But it was her husband's behavior that had disappointed most of all. Ash didn't seem the least bit happy that he had entered into marriage with her. When it had come time for them to kiss and seal their vows, he had leaned forward, stared into her eyes, then hesitated, as if suddenly remembering some reason why he shouldn't proceed.

Sarah Jane had been sorely vexed by his behavior and deeply disturbed. She'd been looking forward to that kiss since first laying eyes on the handsome man. Plus, she'd never been kissed by a man, except for her father, and that didn't count, and she was curious to see if it was everything the poets wrote about.

As Ash pulled the buckboard into the long tree-lined driveway leading to the impressive stone house perched high on the hill, Sarah Jane sucked in her breath and reached for his arm, deciding it was time for some answers.

Better to confront a problem than worry it to death, her papa had always counseled.

''Mr. Morgan, do you think you could halt the wagon for a moment?''

Lost in thought, Ash didn't hear when she spoke, so she banged his arm with her fist to gain his attention and raised her voice an octave or two. ''Mr. Morgan! Could you—''

''Whoa, Rosie!'' he shouted to the mule, pulling the buckboard to a halt, then turning to gaze at his new wife. ''No need to shout my ears off, little lady.''

''I'm very sorry, but you seemed a million miles away.''

He hadn't actually been a million miles away, just one or two, back at the church, wondering why in hell he hadn't kissed Sarah Jane when he'd had the chance. She'd been wanting him to, he could tell. And she'd looked so damn desirable, so very kissable standing there in front of the altar, like an offering from heaven. But he didn't think he could stop with just one kiss, so he'd used all of his willpower to hold himself back. She might be heaven-sent, but he'd have the devil to pay if the marriage didn't work out.

''Mr. Morgan, I—''

Heaving a deep sigh, he tipped back the brim of his hat with his forefinger. ''Since we're married now, Sarah Jane, I think you should call me Ash.'' Hardly anyone called him Mr. Morgan, including those who worked for him.

Liking the sound of her name on his lips, she smiled. ''Thank you. I'd like that. Ash,'' she began, then swallowed around the large lump in her throat while she got up her courage. ''I was wondering...'' She toyed nervously with the folds of her skirt, staring down into her lap. "I was wondering...why didn't you kiss me back at the church? I—I wanted you to."

Heat galloped up Ash's neck to land squarely on his cheeks. He'd never been very good at lying, didn't approve of it, but he sure as hell couldn't tell her the truth—that he'd been scared of how much he wanted her, scared of forgetting all of the reasons he had for not consummating their marriage. From the first moment he'd laid eyes on her, he couldn't think beyond the bulge in his pants. He couldn't remember ever feeling so attracted to a woman before.

"I didn't want to frighten you, since we didn't know each other that well," he finally said. "I thought I'd give you time to adjust to being married."

Smiling, she squeezed his arm and gazed up, her eyes glowing with happiness. "That's very sweet of you. But I think I'm adjusted already, and I want you to kiss me." At the shocked look he flashed her, she explained quite matter-of-factly, "You see, I've never been kissed before, and I want to know what it feels like. Does it really make bells ring in your ears, like everyone says?" Kathryn claimed it did, but you couldn't believe anything a tattletale said.

She was gazing at him with those big, innocent blue eyes, so full of curiosity, waiting, wondering, and Ash found himself drowning, being pulled under her spell, powerless to resist her plea, though he knew he'd be eternally sorry for what he was about to do.

Setting the brake, he turned toward her and reached out, drawing her into his embrace and noting how soft, warm and womanly she was. "I should warn you, there's a lot more to kissing than meets the eye, Sarah Jane. A man doesn't usually stop at just one kiss, and it can lead to all sorts of *other* developments, if you get my drift.'' He cocked a brow to punctuate his point.

Sarah Jane's heart was pounding so loud in her chest she could hear it in her ears and wondered if Ash could hear it, too. Her nipples were puckered and pebble hard when she pressed herself into his chest and wrapped her arms about his neck. ''I'm nearly twenty-one years old, and I'm ready and willing to lose my virginity, if you're ready and willing to take it, Ashby Morgan.''

''Lord have mercy!'' he muttered, before crushing his mouth to hers in a frantic need to taste, to devour her. When she moaned beneath the assault, he gentled the kiss, exploring her mouth with his tongue, nibbling her lower lip with his teeth, before thrusting into her mouth again and tasting all the honey that she was offering. Sweet, sweet honey.

The sky had darkened with the threat of rain, leaves crackled and snapped in the fast-rising wind, but the only noise Sarah Jane heard was the sound of her own low, throaty moan and the distinct ringing in her ears, like joyous church bells on a Sunday morning.

They kissed for what seemed like hours, though in reality it had only been a few minutes. When Ash finally lifted his mouth from hers, she could see that his eyes had darkened to the color of gunmetal and that his upper lip was beaded with sweat. Caressing his cheek, which was lightly stubbled with beard, she heaved a deep sigh of longing and said, ''I had no idea that a kiss could be so wonderful, so very enjoyable. Thank you.''

Realizing that his hand was on her breast, and that

she wasn't protesting, he pulled back as if burned, lowering it to his lap, hoping to disguise the fact that he was as stiff as a petrified tree trunk. "You're welcome," he said simply, and felt foolish for it. But he'd never before had a woman thank him for kissing her.

But then, he'd never before had a woman quite like Sarah Jane Morgan, either. He had a feeling she was a breed unto herself. Her next question confirmed that opinion.

"Do you think we might do that again later? Now that I've tried it, I find that I want to do it again and again."

Ash shifted uncomfortably on the bench seat, reciting silently the Preamble to the Constitution, then throwing in a few lines of the Gettysburg Address for good measure to get his mind working again. When he could finally string two coherent sentences together, he said, "Just as long as you remember to never kiss anyone the way you just kissed me. And that you let me decide when the time is right to take our relationship to the next level."

"By that, do you mean sexual intercourse?"

His mouth fell open, then he snapped it shut and wondered what other questions were going to pop out of that provocative mouth. "Yeah, that's what I mean. But I don't think you should be saying that aloud. Around here, we call it something different."

"Then what should I call it?"

He heaved a sigh. "Don't call *it* anything, Sarah Jane. It's not considered polite to discuss such matters in public."

Reveling in her newfound freedom, and loosed

from the constraints of Miss Cartwright's rigid society, Sarah Jane couldn't help but explore this heretofore forbidden topic to the fullest. She'd never had anyone, including her conservative, mortified-to-the-extreme mother, with whom she could discuss such things. And she had a multitude of questions about the taboo topic of sex.

"Then I think we should decide on our own special name for...*it*...when we're in public, so I can ask you questions and no one will know what we're talking about. I'll give it some thought and let you know what name I come up with."

He fought the urge to roll his eyes. "You do that." Damn, he wished she'd quit talking about sex. Didn't she know what she was doing to him? And he not willing to consummate their union just yet. Not until he was sure. And not until he saw how Addy would respond to her.

Damn, but he hoped Addy liked her!

Addy hated Sarah Jane on sight.

So much for consummating his marriage anytime soon, Ash thought with a sigh, noting the marked hostility on the young girl's face that she didn't bother to hide as she stared daggers at her new stepmother.

Sarah Jane smiled at the child, whose hair was sticking out every which way and looked as if a stick of dynamite had recently exploded in it. She itched to take a pair of scissors to the mess to repair the damage. It wouldn't look any worse than the Yorkies she'd pruned when she got done with it.

The child was dressed in a pair of boy's trousers and a blue-checkered shirt. With the ugly mannish shoes, which were obviously too big for her, Addy Morgan looked like a little girl playing dress-up. Or a girl trying very hard to deny her femininity.

Sarah Jane realized she had her work cut out for her.

"Hello, Addy," she said, holding out her hand. "I'm pleased to make your acquaintance. My name's Sarah Jane."

The child stared at the hand in contempt, refusing to take it. "I don't give a rat's ass what yer name is. Just 'cause my daddy up and married hisself a whore, so he'd have someone to be with, don't mean I have to like you."

Sarah swallowed her gasp, her eyes widening a fraction. Though she'd been expecting a rude reception based on what Ash had told her of his daughter, she hadn't been prepared for this out-and-out hostility and hatred—hatred, it seemed, that was directed at all things female, including Addy herself.

Ash's face filled with outrage. "Adelaide Morgan! You apologize to Sarah Jane this instant or your bottom will see the imprint of my hand."

Crossing her arms over her chest, the child stared back at her father defiantly, her chin raising a notch. "I will not. I'm mistress of this house, not her, and I didn't ask you to bring no fancy lady here. I told you, Daddy—"

He took a threatening step forward. "Addy, I'm warning you—"

Sarah Jane placed a placating hand on his arm. "It's all right, Ash. I'm sure it's just going to take some time for Addy to get used to the idea that I'll be living here now with both of you." She'd handle the child in her own way, and in her own good time, not wanting her marriage to Ash to come between him and his daughter.

''That'll happen when hell freezes over, Miss Fancy-Pants! So why don't you just get the hell on back to wherever it is you come from.''

His complexion going from red to purple, the pulse in his temple ready to explode at any moment, Ash reached for the brass belt buckle at his waist. He was about to show his foulmouthed daughter that he meant business when the sound of Sarah Jane's laughter had him stilling his actions.

He cranked his neck to stare at the woman, wondering if Addy's cruel comments had rendered his new wife temporarily insane.

''My, my, Addy Morgan, but you do have a way of expressing yourself,'' Sarah Jane said. ''I think your vocabulary is the first thing we're going to work on.''

Ignoring the child's startled expression, she said to her husband, ''Now, Ash, I believe you were going to show me the house. I'd love to see what's beyond the front hallway, if it's not too much trouble.''

He turned his back on Addy, caught Sarah Jane's wink and nodded, allowing his new wife to try to deal with his headstrong daughter, and praying she'd have more luck than he had. ''I built the house myself,'' he began proudly, leading her into the front parlor.

Not used to being ignored, Addy ran toward the stairs and headed up, taking refuge in her room. ''That snooty, smiling jackass-of-a-woman is going to be sorry,'' she vowed, slamming the door to her room, then plopping onto the bed's feather mattress.

Wiping tears from her eyes with the back of her hand, she stared up at the whitewashed ceiling, noting the two brown water stains—the result of last week's big rainstorm that had ripped off some of the slate shingles.

Daddy was a traitor! And so was Uncle Zeke. The two men Addy loved most in the world had betrayed her, and all because they thought she needed a new mama.

Well, she didn't.

She was nearly grown and she could take care of herself just fine. She'd never had any use for doll babies and frilly dresses. A girl couldn't hang out at the mine, or climb trees, or play tag with Uncle A.J., when she was wearing a stupid dress. And she didn't need some woman telling her how to behave, how to talk or what to wear. Especially some woman she'd never set eyes on before.

Sarah Jane. Even her name was sissified. And she looked like a puny thing—skinny, though her breasts were big, so she guessed that's why her daddy liked her.

She knew men liked big ones cause she'd overheard her daddy and Uncle A.J. talking one evening when they'd had too much whiskey and thought she'd gone to bed, about Lula Mae Tucker, one of the whores over at O'Connor's. A.J.'d said Lula Mae's breasts were so big they'd be able to keep her afloat if she ever went over Niagara Falls. Daddy had laughed, like he'd known for a fact that they were.

Lula Mae did have some big'ns, that was for sure, Addy thought, wondering how the woman could see her feet to put on her shoes.

Gazing at her own chest, Addy frowned, not wanting her body to develop any more than it had already. She didn't want boys to say such things about her and try to put a baby inside her. Georgie Ann had a baby growing inside her, and she seemed real pleased about it, but Addy wanted nothing to do with babies. Women were supposed to breed, which is why she wished she'd been born a boy.

Boys had all the fun, while women did all the work. And they weren't supposed to swear, though she did anyway. And they weren't supposed to spit or chew tobacco, which she did when no one was looking. Though she knew her daddy would paddle her good if he ever found out. He didn't hold with a woman smoking like a chimney.

Georgie Ann said Addy'd feel differently when she got a little older and the boys started sniffing around. But she wouldn't. She didn't want no boy putting his hands on her or trying to steal kisses. That would make her puke to kingdom come and back again.

The heavy footfalls on the steps made Addy's eyes widen, and she swallowed with difficulty the lump of fear forming in her throat.

She'd never seen her daddy as mad as she'd seen him today when she'd called Sarah Jane a whore—his face had actually gone purple!—and she knew she was in big trouble. He might even strangle her, he was so mad, she thought, clutching her throat.

The door opened, and Ash entered, looking none too pleased by the recent state of affairs. His thumbs were hooked in the front of his wide leather belt, an uneasy reminder of what awaited a sassy-mouthed child.

"I'm ashamed of you, Adelaide Morgan. You embarrassed the hell—" he caught himself, remembering Sarah Jane's admonition "—heck outta me today. And I'm sure you hurt Sarah Jane's feelings, though she let you off the hook pretty easy." He crossed to the bed, noting the uncharacteristic fear on the child's face, the way her slender body was starting to fill out. His little girl was growing up, and he hadn't even noticed.

"Did she send you up here to beat me?" She leaned farther back into her pillows, not about to take any chances.

He shook his head. "No. Though I should anyway. Sarah Jane suggested that maybe you and I needed to have a talk about my marrying and all."

Addy's eyes widened a fraction. "What's to talk about? You didn't ask my permission before you went and married some fancy woman."

Seating himself on the edge of the bed, Ash heaved a sigh. He could tell his daughter had been crying and was doing her best to hide that fact by turning her face toward the window.

Addy viewed tears as a weakness. She hardly ever cried. Even as a child when she'd fallen off the roof of the shed and sprained her ankle, she hadn't let loose a tear, which was just another example of her strong-willed stubbornness, no doubt inherited from him. Zeke claimed Addy had inherited all of Ash's worst faults, which were numerous, the old man hadn't failed to point out.

"I hope you know, Addy girl, that no one will ever take your place in my heart. I love you most of all, and that's never going to change."

Wanting to believe him, she looked back, her blue eyes misted with unshed tears. "I don't need a new mama, Daddy. I've got you and Uncle Zeke to care for me. And Uncle A.J. makes a pretty good playmate when he's in the mood. We were doing okay by ourselves."

Ash smiled inwardly, seeing and hearing himself in the child's words. "You know, I used those very same words on Uncle Zeke and he told me I was wrong, Addy. I can see now that I haven't done right by allowing you to run wild. You need to study harder on your schoolwork, you need to quit cursin' and dressing like a ragamuffin, and you need to tend to more female pursuits, like learning to cook and sew. You'll be a grown woman soon."

She screwed up her face in disgust. "I don't want to learn those girlie things. When I'm old enough I'm going to work at the mine with you. Don't need no sewing skills at the mine."

He cocked a brow. "Is that a fact? And what if one of the men gets injured and slices open his arm? How will you sew him up, if you don't know how to sew a straight stitch? And how will you keep the books, if you don't know your sums and letters?

"There's a lot more to coal mining than just digging coal, honey. Learning is what sets folks apart from dumb animals. There's a lot of pleasure to be found in between the pages of a book."

"I don't like reading."

"That's because you never sit still long enough to try it. But now that Sarah Jane's come to live here, maybe you'll allow her to show you some of the books she's brought with her." He knew now why her valise had been so heavy. She'd buried five of her favorite novels between her garments.

Addy thrust out her chin; her blue eyes, so like her mother's, were hard as sapphires. "I'm not talking to her. Not never."

Ash stood, plowing agitated fingers through his hair. "Never's a long time, Addy girl. And I think you're going to find that you'll like having another female in the house." He'd already been contemplating the benefits.

"I won't. And you can't make me like her."

"Nope. I can't. But I can make you show respect to her. And if I ever hear you talk to Sarah Jane again the way you spoke to her this afternoon, you won't like the consequences. Am I making myself clear, young lady? And I use that term loosely."

She nodded, fighting back tears, feeling more miserable than she'd ever felt in her life, and wishing Sarah Jane would just fall into the river and drown, like her daddy's first wife had.

Chapter Four

Knowing that temptation waited for him on the other side of the eight-paneled door, Ash's sweaty hand rested on the brass doorknob to his bedroom and he swallowed.

Sarah Jane had probably stripped naked by now and was waiting in the center of his big four-poster bed, no doubt wondering why he hadn't come in to do his husbandly duty by her.

He'd thought seriously of taking up residence in the spare bedroom, until he could be sure that their marriage was going to work out, but he knew that if A.J. got wind of the fact that his big brother wasn't sleeping with his new wife—and he would, because A.J.'s bedroom was just down the hall from Zeke's— word would be all over town in a matter of hours. Not to mention the ribbing he'd take from the miners, which could undermine his authority.

He'd have to be strong. He'd just have to open the door and enter, as matter-of-factly as you please, and totally ignore the sight of all that creamy, smooth, naked flesh, those heavy, pink-tipped globes, the soft thatch of blond hair covering her—

Palming his face in frustration, he adjusted his pants and turned the knob to enter, finding to his very great relief that his young wife was seated before the fire, brushing her long, silky hair.

She was dressed in a very prim white lawn nightgown with tiny pink rosebuds trailing every which way. A closer look revealed that two of those buds were centered directly over her breasts, which were barely disguised by the thin material. Ash swallowed again.

At the click of the door shutting closed, Sarah Jane looked up and smiled hesitantly. Her face was flushed from the heat of the fire, or from fear, he couldn't be certain, and he smiled back, hoping to allay her worry. "Good evening, Sarah Jane."

"I undressed and got into my nightgown," she replied, looking a bit unsure of herself. "I hope that's all right. I wasn't sure what the proper procedure was." Setting down her brush, her hands went to the buttons of her gown. "Perhaps I should just take this off to facilitate matters."

He felt his face grow warm. "Uh, no! No. That's okay. You're fine just the way you are."

She released a sigh of relief. "I always brush my hair at least a hundred strokes a night. If I don't, it gets all snarly and ugly, and I did want to look especially nice for you."

"You do. You look very pretty." Her waist-length hair cascaded down her back in thick waves of golden honey, and he itched to run his fingers through the glossy mass.

She rose to her feet, and the firelight behind her rendered her gown nearly transparent. She may as well have been standing there buck naked for all the good the material did. Ash shifted once again to ease the discomfort growing between his legs, wondering if he was doomed to spend the remainder of his existence walking around fully aroused.

"The dinner your neighbor left for us was very good, and it was such a thoughtful gesture. I must remember to thank Mrs. Freeland when I see her."

Ash nodded. "Georgie Ann's a good girl. She's married to one of my miners."

"Well, I'm done with my hair, so I guess I'll climb into bed and wait while you undress." She set the brush down on the dresser. "I'm a little nervous, but I'm actually looking forward to experiencing sexual intercourse for the first time. I understand that it can be quite stimulating." If it was anything like kissing, she was definitely going to like it.

Sucking in his breath, Ash didn't know quite what to do or how to respond. He could hardly explain that he didn't intend to consummate their marriage until he was sure things would work out between them. That seemed too cold and calculating, and he didn't want her to think badly of him. And he didn't have the heart to just walk out the door and let her think that he didn't find her desirable. That kind of rejection could ruin a woman for life. It was a big fat lie, anyway. He found her too damn desirable, which was the crux of the problem.

Having no other choice at the moment, he began to unbutton his shirt, and her eyes followed his every movement. She looked so damned interested, he felt like one of those women who stripped off their clothes for a living, and was reluctant to continue. "You ever seen a naked man before?" he asked.

She shook her head but didn't avert her wide-eyed gaze. "You're my first. But I must confess that I've been curious. I understand there can be quite a difference in the size of a man's—"

"You might want to turn your head a minute," he interrupted. "I wouldn't want to offend your ladylike sensibilities. You see, I didn't have time to put on any drawers this morning, and I'm naked beneath these pants."

The sight of his naked chest had her mouth hanging open, and Sarah Jane felt an instant response to those bulging muscles all the way down to her toes. His chest was as solid as a granite boulder and lightly sprinkled with dark hairs that formed a vee and disappeared into the waistband of his pants.

"Oh, my goodness! Why, the sight of all that skin fairly takes my breath away. Please go on." She leaned back against the pillows and folded her arms beneath her breasts, causing them to push up. "I won't be the least bit offended. I promise."

Ash swore beneath his breath. Just his luck to find a woman who wasn't the least bit shy. What was he going to do now? "Sarah Jane," he began, not really sure what he was going to say.

"I'm so sorry," she said, as if a thought had just occurred to her, and she bounded from the bed. He'd almost breathed a sigh of relief, until she came to stand before him and reached for his buttons. "I bet you want me to help you with these. Here," she said, trying to undo them. "Let me—"

"No! That's all right," he said, clasping her hand and placing it over his heart instead, which was throbbing just as wildly as some other areas of his body. "I think we should take things a bit slower."

She stared at him in confusion. "Are you sure? After all, I'm allowing you to take the lead, since you're so much more experienced than I. But I want to do everything correctly. I think our first time together is so very important, don't you? And since I've never been with a man before—"

He placed his fingertips gently over her lips. "Let's go over and sit on the bed a few minutes, so we can get used to the idea of being together. The fact that we don't know each other very well makes me feel a bit awkward."

"Really? How interesting. And here I've been led to believe that the male species will copulate with just about anyone at any time. I didn't think men were all that discriminating when it came to sexual matters, because their needs are so much more intense and they—"

His eyes rounded like silver dollars. "Where in hell did you hear that nonsense, Sarah Jane?" Though it was probably closer to the truth than not. Men were definitely more randy than women. Although, after meeting Sarah Jane, he wondered if that notion held true. The woman seemed to have an insatiable curiosity about sexual matters.

"I've read several books on the subject."

Now why am I not surprised?

"And it's also a known fact that men frequent houses of ill repute to satisfy their carnal urges when no other outlets are available."

She bit her lower lip, knowing it was really none of her business, and asked, "Have you?"

"Have I what?"

"Been with a woman of loose morals? I believe your daughter referred to them as whores, though I daresay that's a very crude word. I think prostitute, or woman of the evening, or—"

"That is no kind of question for a woman to be asking her husband on their wedding night!" he blurted, his face reddening. "Men are supposed to be more experienced. You said so yourself." And there was nothing wrong with a single man sowing a few wild oats, seeking out a little comfort in the arms of a willing woman, as long as both parties were consenting. And as long as the man wasn't married. Ash felt very strongly about keeping marriage vows once taken, which was why he hadn't wanted to take them again in the first place.

"I suppose you must be right. Though I don't think it's fair that men get to experiment while women have to remain ignorant and chaste."

"That's just the way it is, Sarah Jane. Men are more proprietary about things, about their wives."

"Well, women are, too. And you'll find that out, Ashby Morgan, if you even think about setting foot into one of those places again."

He bit back a smile. "I never said I did."

"Well, that's true, but it was implied."

"You sure are pretty when you get all riled up, Sarah Jane. Your cheeks are all pink like rose petals, and your eyes all sparkly like pretty blue sapphires."

Emboldened by his compliment, which had touched her deeply, she leaned into him. "Pretty enough to kiss? I've been thinking about having your tongue inside my mouth all day. Is that naughty of me, Ash?''

She licked her lips in anticipation, and Ash's pants suddenly shrank two sizes. Sweat beaded his forehead and upper lip. ''No, no, that's normal. And I'm real happy you like it when I kiss you, Sarah Jane.''

''I do.'' The mattress dipped when Ash dropped down onto it and nestled beside her. ''I think it's terribly stimulating.''

''We're going to do some more kissing tonight, but nothing else. I think we need to take it slow, because you're a virgin and all, and I want your first time to be special.''

She tried to hide her disappointment. ''But how long will we have to wait? I feel so strange. Well, you know. And my breasts ache.'' Taking his hand, she placed it upon her breast, allowing him to feel the rigidity of her nipple. ''They're poking through the material,'' she explained, somewhat awed by the fact.

Moaning deep in his throat, Ash eased her back onto the pillows and covered her mouth with his own. Deepening the kiss, he inserted his tongue, thrusting in and out, while he gently massaged her breasts.

The feel of her plump globes and rock-hard nipples played havoc with his good intentions. He had to take a peek. Just one peek, nothing more, he told himself, and began to unbutton the front of her gown.

Spreading back the material, he let his gaze drift down to worship her perfect body with his eyes. ''You're beautiful.'' He toyed with her nipples, and heard her moan of pleasure. "Do you like that? Do you want more?"

"Oh yes! Much more."

He pushed the gown down to her waist and cupped her heavy breasts. "I want to see all of you. Take off your nightgown."

In a tortured voice, she whispered, "I want to see all of you, too. Take off your pants."

He swallowed the temptation to do as she asked, to strip her naked and have his way with her. But he knew it wouldn't be wise. "Not tonight," he said in a voice laced with regret.

Leaning forward, he trailed kisses down her chin, her throat, her chest, then settled on her breasts, where he feasted, until he heard her cry out.

"Please!"

Drawing a ragged breath, he stopped and pulled back, drawing her nightgown up to cover her. "That's enough for tonight."

"But—"

"*Shh.*" He cuddled her to his chest. "You have to trust me. I'm older than you, and I know what's best."

But as they lay side by side in the dark, staring up at the ceiling for most of the night, their hearts pounding in unfulfilled passion, each wondered if that were really true.

Chapter Five

Dressed in heavy woolen clothes, thick-soled boots and a miner's cap with a tin safety lamp attached, Ash stepped onto the wooden elevator platform situated over the mouth of the shaft and lowered himself via thick cables into the bowels of the mine. A large fan wheel whirred nearby, providing air for the men who worked below the surface.

The walls of grayish-black granite dripping with water passed by in a blur, and he plunged into the darkness, feeling as if he were diving straight into the black depths of hell.

The air grew heavy the farther down he went, the coal dust coating his lungs and stealing his breath away. Someday the dust would blacken his lungs and likely kill him, like it had killed so many others before him.

Of course, it was likely that he'd die in an explosion or cave-in long before that, and Ash had accepted that fact. Mining coal was dangerous business, and it wasn't for the weak of heart.

The strong odors of standing water and methane

gas reached him, and he knew that he was nearing his destination. He slackened the speed of the conveyance and brought it to a screeching halt at the bottom of the shaft.

The coal dust crunched beneath his boots as he made his way through the maze of three- and four-foot-wide tunnels that comprised the mine, nodding in greeting as he passed several of the crews that worked at their various tasks. He crouched when the ceiling lowered to meet the floor and stood upright when the area broadened out to accommodate the rail cars that would transport the coal back to the surface.

Zeke would be undermining the bottom of the coal deposit seam, which was nearly twelve feet thick. Ash had decided to cut his honeymoon short and join him, working off his frustrations by acting as laborer, loading the dislodged coal into the rail car. As a rule, a miner wouldn't do the work of a laborer; most felt it was beneath them, since they'd paid their dues and worked their way up to the top of the coal pile, so to speak. But Ash wasn't proud, and he needed the diversion.

Undermining was a slow, laborious process, requiring the men to work in teams of two, usually taking anywhere from four to five hours to hole in a room eight yards wide and four to five feet in depth.

He hoped the grueling work would take his mind off the woman still asleep in his bed.

The previous night had been torture. Resisting Sarah Jane's pleas to make love had been a test of his will, and he wasn't sure how long he'd be able to hold out. It had been a long time since he'd been with a woman, and his new wife was proving damn hard to resist. He had only to close his eyes to recall the feel, the taste of her, to hear her soft mewling sounds of passion when he kissed her.

"Well now, boy, you're looking a mite grim for a man supposedly on his honeymoon. What the hell are you doing here with me, when you're supposed to be spending time with your new bride?"

The whites of Zeke's eyes and the flash of his teeth were all that was visible through the thick coating of black dust covering his face. The yellow light on his cap as he faced Ash illuminated the younger man's embarrassment.

"I decided to work. It seemed stupid to take a honeymoon when I wasn't going anywhere." He set down his sledges, picks and wedges and crouched on the ground near his uncle.

"I thought you agreed to give this marriage a chance. How do you expect your new wife to react to your leaving her in a strange place, and with your daughter still so hostile?"

"I had a talk with Addy last evening, warned her to be polite." He thought he might have actually made an impression for a change.

Shaking his head, his disgust evident even through the grime, Zeke wiped his face with the back of his sleeve, which was just as grimy. "You know that youngster's not going to mind you, Ash. Hell, if she was of a mind to listen, you wouldn't have needed to find a wife in the first place."

"I figured we'd be shorthanded after laying off most of the men last summer." More coal was dug in the winter than in any other season.

"And we're putting 'em back on slowly, as we can

afford to, and as the weather gets colder. No sense mining more bituminous coal than we can ship. You know it can't be stocked without deteriorating.''

Ash looked determined. ''I'm staying for a while. Sarah Jane and Addy are going to have to learn to get along without me eventually, so they may as well start now.''

''Throwing the lamb into the wolf's den kinda soon, don't you think? Or is it that you don't like being around your new wife?

''Sarah Jane seems like a real nice gal to me. I ain't never met a woman with such a sunny disposition and pretty smile. Why it just about shines up a room. I sure do like that little gal's smile.''

Ash's frown had deepened grooves into his cheeks. ''And I sure do like it when you mind your own business, old man. I intend to go back to the house at noon to make sure my daughter hasn't done away with my wife.''

If he were truthful, he couldn't wait to see Sarah Jane again. If he'd been a superstitious man, he'd have thought she'd put a spell on him. Why else would he feel so compelled to be with her? He'd never felt that strong a pull with either of his first two wives. Of course, he'd been a lot younger then.

Zeke's cackle reverberated off the solid walls. ''Wouldn't be too sure about Addy winning that match-up. I'm betting that pretty lady can handle herself. I think there's more to Sarah Jane than meets the eye. She may look prim and proper, but I sense there's a fire banked within that little gal.''

It was a damn inferno. But Ash wasn't going to

confide that to his uncle. He quickly changed the subject and went to work.

Back at the house, Sarah Jane stood in front of the kitchen's cookstove and wondered what exactly she needed to do to get it to work. She dearly wanted a cup of hot coffee, had been overjoyed to find that the kitchen had a sink with indoor plumbing, but couldn't for the life of her figure out how to turn on the burners for the stove, which she assumed burned coal, since it was so readily available.

Mrs. Delaney had cooked all of the Parkers' meals, and Sarah Jane had been inattentive when Miss Cartwright had presented her cooking tutorial, so her skills in the kitchen were sadly lacking. Of course, she had omitted that little tidbit when replying to Ash's letter. In fact, she had made it sound as if she'd graduated from one of those famous French culinary schools.

The back door opened, admitting a blast of cold air and a very pregnant dark-haired woman. She was carrying a basket covered with a blue-checked napkin, and the tantalizing smells spewing forth made Sarah Jane's stomach grumble.

She'd always had a healthy appetite, and being married hadn't changed that. If anything, all that activity and excitement had made her hungrier.

"You must be Ash's new wife." Georgie Ann Freeland introduced herself as she came into the room, shutting the door behind her, and setting her wicker basket on the scarred pine table. "I was hoping to get here before you woke up, so I could get your and Addy's breakfast on the table.

"I've brought hot biscuits and honey and a few

slices of ham. Like most men, Ash ain't very good about making sure the larder's full, so I decided to take matters into my own hands. Hope you don't mind.''

Breathing a sigh of relief, Sarah Jane held out her hand. "I don't mind at all, Mrs. Freeland, and I'm so pleased to make your acquaintance. I've been wanting to thank you for your thoughtfulness in providing that most excellent dinner for me and my hus…husband last evening." The word tripped off her tongue awkwardly.

"The name's Georgie Ann, and I hope I can call you Sarah Jane. Most folks around here don't stand on ceremony, like they do back in Philadelphia."

"Please do, by all means. To be perfectly honest, I'm quite relieved you're here. I'm afraid that cooking isn't one of the courses I excelled in at Miss Cartwright's school, but I'm more than willing to learn, if you'd be willing to show me some rudimentary things, like how to work the cookstove."

Georgie laughed and was immediately put at ease by the lovely woman's honesty. She hadn't known what to expect when she'd heard that Ash had chosen himself a wife from Philadelphia society. It looked to Georgie Ann as if the handsome man had chosen well.

"I'd be pleased to," she said. "I was wed myself not long ago. Of course, my mama made sure I was handy in the kitchen before me and Robby got hitched," she added, before showing Sarah Jane how to load the coal into the firebox and light it.

"Why don't you sit yourself down while I fix us a pot of coffee."

"That would be lovely. Thank you."

"I'm sure you must be tired after your long train trip. And—" her eyebrows rose meaningfully "—after last night."

Sarah Jane's face turned as red as the cheerful gingham curtains hanging at the window, which had been put there by Georgie Ann only two days before, because she couldn't bear the thought of a new wife entering such a stark and unhomey room. Of all the rooms a house contained, the kitchen needed to feel lived-in.

Her neighbor smiled knowingly. "I wasn't meaning to pry. But like I said, it ain't been that long since I had me a wedding night. And boy what a night it was!"

Sarah Jane decided to keep the details of her unorthodox wedding night to herself. She wasn't proud that she was still a virgin the morning after the night before, and she didn't want anyone else to know. "You're very considerate," she said, and quickly changed the subject.

"When's your baby due? You must be very excited at the prospect of having a little son or daughter." Sarah Jane hadn't given a great deal of thought to having children, though she supposed it would be nice to have Ash's child—a little boy or girl who looked exactly like her husband. But hopefully, not until she had a chance to win over his daughter.

No doubt the child already felt threatened. It wouldn't do to introduce another rival for Addy to contend with. Having been somewhat of a daddy's girl herself when she was a child, Sarah Jane knew the special bond that existed between father and daughter. Addy needed to feel reassured that Sarah Jane hadn't replaced her in her father's affections.

The coffeepot boiled over and Georgie Ann lowered the flame. The old tin pot then began burping repeatedly, until the young woman deemed it to be done by its pungent aroma, which smelled heavenly to Sarah Jane.

"I think in about two months, give or take a week," she replied, filling two ceramic cups with coffee. "I feel fat as a cow, but mama says that's normal. And Robby's so happy that he's going to be a papa that all the discomfort's been worth it, except maybe the pain in my lower back. There're days when I can hardly stand up straight, my back aches so."

After adding two lumps of sugar and a small dollop of cream to her coffee, Sarah Jane sipped thoughtfully at the warm liquid, before saying, "Ash tells me that you look after Addy once in a while. It's very nice of you to help him out like you've been doing. It must have been difficult for them after Addy's mother died."

She nodded. "It was. My mama helped out as best she could, then I stepped in to give a hand.

"Me and Addy get along just fine. She's a good girl, just a bit mixed up about things. I think her body's changing and she don't know quite what to do about it. She'll probably be a handful for a while, but I think in time she'll straighten out."

Sarah Jane gnawed her lower lip, then finally decided to trust the kind woman seated across from her. There was something in her eyes that told her she could. "May I confide something to you, Georgie Ann?"

The pregnant woman nodded. "Sure. It's been a long time since I've had someone to share things with, besides my mama, that is. I'm going to enjoy having another woman living so close by.

"Living in the mountains ain't like living in a crowded city," she continued. "We're kinda isolated. I'm fortunate that our home is only a mile or so down the road from here. Others ain't so lucky, and during bad weather it can get real lonely.

"I'd venture a guess that the winters you've experienced in Philadelphia ain't nothing like the ones we have up here in the mountains of West Virginia."

After being confined day and night with fifty other students and Miss Cartwright, Sarah Jane welcomed a bit of isolation. She loved to read, and sharing her own company had never bothered her.

"You was going to confide something?" Georgie Ann's dark brow rose in question.

"When I look at Addy I see myself. Rebellious, mischievous, and at times hard to handle. My parents gave up trying to exert control over what they considered to be my unruly behavior and sent me to live at a boarding school when I was fifteen. I hated it. I don't think they realized that what they did only made my behavior worse. I resented every minute I spent away from home, and I did my best to get back at everyone. I'm afraid that I wasn't very ladylike most of the time." An understatement at best, Sarah Jane thought.

Georgie Ann rolled her eyes, finding it hard to believe that this proper young woman had at one time been less than an angelic schoolgirl and the bane of her parents' existence. "Does Ash know any of what you're telling me?'' She seriously doubted it. Zeke had confided that Ash was happy to be marrying a docile, easily controllable young woman. She smiled to herself, thinking that the widower was going to be in for a few surprises.

''No. And I'd appreciate it if you didn't mention any of this to him. I've matured. And I think I can make him a good wife. And if Addy gives me half a chance, I can be a good mother to her, too. I understand her better than most.''

The dark-haired woman reached out, clasping Sarah Jane's hand and squeezing gently. ''I won't breathe a word. I swear. And I thank you for confiding in me. I feel like I've known you forever, Sarah Jane, and here we just met. Ain't that the most peculiar thing?''

Laughing, Sarah Jane replied, ''I suspect we're kindred spirits, Georgie Ann. I felt the same way after meeting you, too. Maybe we were sisters in a previous life. I've always wanted a sister.''

''You wouldn't, if you had the one I've got. Martha Ann lives down in Clarksburg with her banker husband, Floyd Burgess. I've never seen anyone put on airs like that woman. Guess she thinks she's better than the rest of us, us being coal wives and all.''

''Your husband works for Ash, doesn't he?''

She nodded. ''Robby's an Englishman. He's got engineering experience, 'cause that's what he did back in England. He came to America about seven years ago to work the coal mines and make his fortune.'' She flashed a grin. ''But I'm still waiting on that.

''He's an expert at blowing things up. He works

with Ash on the drilling and blasting. It's very specialized work, and he's good at what he does. Though I do worry that he's going to blow himself up one of these days. And me with a baby on the way.'' The look in her eyes was sad but accepting, as if she'd already prepared herself for that eventuality.

Blue eyes widening, Sarah Jane was appalled to learn that Ash was engaged in very hazardous work and could actually be harmed, or worse, lose his life. ''I don't know a thing about coal mining. It sounds terribly dangerous.''

''It can be. There's swamp gas in the mine—methane gas—and if it was ever to ignite, the whole mine could blow out. It's happened a time or two, but not here, thank the good Lord. Ash keeps canaries down in the mine to make sure the air is breathable.''

And if it wasn't, the canaries would die. Sarah Jane cringed at the thought of those poor little songbirds suffocating to death, no matter how noble a service they performed.

''And then there's the black lung that most of the miners get from breathing in the coal dust,'' Georgie Ann added. ''It ruins their lungs, takes years off their lives, if it don't kill 'em right off.''

''My goodness! I had no idea. But why do they do it if it's so dangerous.''

The woman shrugged. ''It's in their blood. Most have been working the coal mines since they were young'ns. If you go down to the mine, you'll see school-age boys working at driving the mules or picking the slate. They usually start out as door boys and work their way up to laborer then miner.''

''Did Ash start out like that?''

"Yep. He worked alongside his uncle from the time he was small, after his pa died in the war. Then, when he got tired of making money for others, he decided to dig his own mine and make hisself rich. Of course, he ain't done that yet, but he's doing well, all things considered.

"It's a tough life. And it ain't much easier on the women." Her eyes filled with sadness. "We watch our men go into the mine, never knowing from one day to the next if they're going to come back out. Mama was widowed before she was forty."

Sarah Jane rubbed her arms against the chill that suddenly invaded her body. She wasn't at all prepared for the kind of life Georgie Ann was describing. Hardship and death were things she'd only read about in books and newspapers. She hadn't experienced them yet.

"You mentioned that there are young boys who work in the mines," she finally said. "When and where do they obtain their education? Is there a school nearby?"

"Here and there. I doubt most will have a formal type education. If they're lucky, they'll learn to cipher and do sums from their parents or an older brother or sister."

"But that's barbaric!" Sarah Jane declared. "I can't believe Ash would allow such a thing. Education is so terribly important. I know child labor exists in the mills and factories back East, but I had no idea that children were being used to work in the mines."

Concern for Ash's wife filled the woman's eyes. "It's just the way things are done here, Sarah Jane. The way they've always been done. Ash was fortunate. His mama was well educated and she made sure her sons were, too. I remember her saying once that a man couldn't get nowhere in life if he wasn't well-rounded in his schooling. She wanted Ash to go to college, but, of course, he refused.''

''I intend to speak to him about this appalling practice first chance I get. Maybe there's something I can do to help.''

''I can tell you right now, Sarah Jane, that Ash won't like you interfering.''

''But I'm his wife. Surely he won't mind me expressing an opinion. My conscience just won't let me ignore what I've heard.''

Georgie Ann wished now that she'd kept her big mouth shut, though she knew the young woman would learn of such things eventually. Mining was all anyone ever spoke about in Morgantown. She tried to explain. ''The boys working in the mines are happy. They wouldn't be working there if they weren't. Ash isn't forcing them to be there. And some need the work to help support their families.

''I'd be careful if I were you. You may just be opening up a can of worms best left alone.''

''I've never shied away from controversy, but I promise that I'll take your suggestion to heart and be tactful in whatever I say to Ash regarding the boys.''

Georgie Ann wished she felt as confident as Sarah Jane's smile implied she was.

Georgie Ann had no sooner departed for home than Addy entered the kitchen, and Sarah Jane forgot all about coal mining and child labor. She had bigger problems to worry about at the moment.

"Did you make breakfast?" the child asked, almost accusingly, before seating herself at the table and reaching for a biscuit, which she began slathering with honey.

Ignoring the little girl's rudeness, Sarah Jane forced a smile. "Good morning, Addy. Did you sleep well?"

She shrugged. "Okay. You must not have though, 'cause I heard a lot of moaning and wailing coming from my daddy's bedroom."

Her cheeks flushed at the memory of what had occurred the night before. Embarrassed that the child may have overheard more than she should, Sarah Jane turned to the sink and began to wash the dishes. "I thought we'd work on getting the house cleaned today. How does that sound?"

Ash and his uncle and brother were definitely poor housekeepers. The dust on the furniture nearly obliterated the lovely walnut and mahogany tones of the various wood pieces she'd seen, and the pine-planked floors looked as if they hadn't seen the bristled end of a scrub brush in quite a while. If ever.

"It sounds terrible," the young girl replied. "I ain't doing no housework. That's woman's work."

"I hesitate to point this out, Adelaide, but you happen to be heading in that direction. Womanhood will be upon you before you know it, and there's nothing you're going to be able to do to stop it. Wearing ugly clothes, cutting your hair like a man, and using foul language isn't going to make any difference."

Addy wiped her mouth with the back of her hand, her eyes narrowing at the words she knew to be true. But that still didn't mean she had to like them. "A lot you know."

Seating herself at the table, Sarah Jane stared thoughtfully at the child. Addy's resentment was almost palpable. "I know you don't like that I married your father, Addy, but I promise you that you've got nothing to fear. Your father loves you very much, and my being here isn't going to change that."

"I don't want to be turned into a sissy. I like wearing boy's clothes and having short hair. And I don't like reading."

Such an attitude surprised Sarah Jane, who looked at books as her closest, dearest friends. "Really? Because I brought some of my favorite books with me, and I was going to share them with you."

The child's curiosity was piqued. "Yeah? Well, what are they? Something stupid, no doubt."

Sarah Jane's eyes got a faraway look in them. "I've always liked fairy tales, and I brought along a book filled with wonderful ones, like Jack and the Beanstalk, and Hansel and Gretel. And I also brought *Little Women,* which is one of my favorites. They're all wonderful stories.

"I just love being transported to another place and time. Reading's like that, you know. You don't have to leave your house to be able to travel anywhere in the world, experience all kinds of adventures. One time you might be a member of King Arthur's court, and another, hunting fierce lions in Africa.

"After I read *Little Women* I used to pretend that I was one of the March sisters. Jo was my favorite, because she didn't like to conform, kind of like you. I didn't have any brothers or sisters of my own, so I used the March girls as my pretend sisters."

Though she was loath to admit that she found Sarah

Jane's comments intriguing, Addy's eyes, wide with interest, gave her away. "If I've got the time, maybe you can show me that book about the small women later. There ain't no sense wasting a good day by staying indoors and reading when you can go outside and climb trees."

Now it was Sarah Jane's interest that was piqued. "I used to love to climb trees. I was very good at it, you know."

Addy pulled a face, not believing for a second that her new stepmother had ever climbed a tree. "You're making that up. Ladies from the East don't climb trees. It might muss their hair."

Sarah Jane smiled at the child's misguided notion, wondering what Addy would think of her recent descent out of a second-story window. She thought it prudent not to tell her.

"If you'll agree to help me clean up the house first, I'll come outside with you and climb whichever tree you choose. Is it a deal?"

Temptation rode Addy hard. She sure did want to see Sarah Jane make a fool out of herself, and she had just the tree in mind to do it. All the kids called it "the devil's apple tree" because the temptation to climb it was too strong to ignore, and it was a hellish undertaking, due to its height.

She hesitated, biting her fingernail. "I don't know. I'm not much for cleaning. What do we have to do?"

"I guess we can start by stripping the sheets off the beds and putting on fresh linens. There's nothing like the smell of freshly washed linens to ease a body into a peaceful slumber."

"I guess I know where there's some clean ones.

My daddy makes us change the sheets on the bed at least once a month, whether or not they're dirty.''

Sarah tried not to cringe. "How admirable. And how often do you take a bath?" By the looks of her hair, not very often.

The child shrugged. "Only when Georgie Ann or Uncle Zeke makes me. I don't much like taking baths and smelling like a whore.''

Frowning deeply, Sarah Jane admonished the child. "You shouldn't use such language, Addy. It isn't polite. And why do you have such a fascination with ladies of the evening anyway? Have you ever seen one, in the flesh, so to speak?" Sarah Jane had not, though she'd read about their shocking behavior.

"No. Daddy won't let me near O'Connor's House of Pleasure. That's where all the whores live. But I've heard him and Uncle A.J. talk about Lula Mae Tucker's breasts and how big they are.''

"Really?" Sarah Jane crossed her arms over her own ample bosom, her lips pursing as if she'd just sucked a tart lemon dry. "Do tell.''

Noting how annoyed her new stepmother appeared, Addy took great joy in relating what she'd overheard her father and uncle say about the whore's assets, embellishing whenever she could. "I think daddy goes there most every night to take his ease," she lied. "Guess he won't have to, now that he's got you.''

A spurt of jealous anger shot through Sarah Jane as she recalled Ash's reluctance to bed her last evening. Maybe he was saving himself for Lula Mae Tucker.

"Young ladies shouldn't talk about such things,

Adelaide Morgan. And I am determined that one of these days you will be referred to as a young lady.'' Though she wasn't certain how many years that would take. Judging from the looks of the urchin before her, too many to count, she wasn't likely to live that long.

Addy's smile was pure innocence. "Well, you asked?''

"So I did. And it's doubtful I'll make that same mistake again. Shall we get on with the sheets? Time's awasting,'' she heard herself say, horrified that she sounded exactly like Dorothea Cartwright.

Chapter Six

Ash arrived home promptly at noon to find the house completely deserted. There was a large pile of dirty sheets in the middle of the front hall, but there was no sign of his wife or daughter.

"Addy, I'm home," he called out, walking quickly from room to room. "Sarah Jane, are you upstairs?" Foot perched on the bottom rung of the steps, he waited, but no one answered, and a sick feeling of dread formed in the pit of his stomach. He'd have only himself to blame if anything had happened to Sarah Jane. After all, it'd been his decision to leave the two females alone.

The lamb in the wolf's den. Zeke's words came back to haunt him.

Hurrying out the back door, he checked the rear barn. As he entered, the familiar odors of hay and leather rose up to greet him. The horses and mules housed in their stalls looked mildly interested at the interruption, but then went back to eating their grain.

More mules than horses were kept; they worked in the mine and earned their keep by hauling the coal cars. Steam locomotives could not be used because of the danger of explosion. When the mules became too aged to haul coal, Ash retired them to the barn and pasture to live out the rest of their lives in the sunshine.

Aside from the animals, there was no one else about, so he went to the chicken house in the hope he'd find Addy or Sarah Jane there, but it was empty as well, save for the hens and roosters, who let him know with their loud squawks and cackles what they thought of his intrusion.

Tension mounting, he cursed, slapping his cap against his pant leg in frustration, before hanging it on a fence post. "Addy!" he yelled again, louder this time, and a trace of fear entered his voice. "Sarah Jane! Where are you?"

Finally a voice he clearly recognized as his daughter's came to him from a short distance away. "We're over here, Daddy, in the apple orchard. Sarah Jane's up a tree and she can't get down."

His daughter sounded inordinately pleased by the whole turn of events, and Ash wondered fleetingly if the woman he married was cornered and afraid to come down. He put nothing past his daughter.

About a quarter of a mile beyond the barn, he came to a grinding halt beneath a large apple tree in the rear yard and looked up, shading his eyes from the sun.

Sarah Jane was holding on to one of the tree's thick branches, and she didn't look at all frightened of falling. He, on the other hand, was worried sick she'd break her fool neck.

"What in hell are you doing up there, woman?"

Ignoring her husband's deep scowl, Sarah Jane smiled brightly, though she felt like a complete fool for having gotten herself in such an awkward situation. "I'm just trying out Addy's favorite tree, that's all. Wasn't it kind of her to show it to me?" She'd hoped by climbing the tree that Ash's daughter would begin to see her in a different light and not so much the enemy.

Ash leveled a look at his daughter that promised retribution later. "Yeah, she's a real sweetheart," he said.

The little girl backed up a few steps, and muttered, "Uh-oh."

"Can you get down on your own, or do I need to come up after you?"

"She's stuck," Addy offered with a grin, unable to hide her pleasure.

"I've caught my foot between two limbs and can't seem to dislodge it," Sarah Jane explained. "So I guess I won't be coming down for a while." She heard Ash swear, despite his recent promise to curb his foul language in front of his daughter, then watched as he shrugged out of his jacket.

The man was covered in coal dust from the top of his ebony head to the toe of his dirty, scuffed boots, and it was obvious that he hadn't bothered to bathe after leaving the mine.

Sarah Jane grimaced at the thought of her lovely green dress becoming soiled with all that black grime.

Thus far, she'd managed to keep her garment clean and free from tears. It had been a major accomplishment, and one even Addy had grudgingly agreed was not bad for an amateur.

Like an agile cat, the exasperated man climbed the tree. A few moments later he confronted his errant wife. "I guess Uncle Zeke was wrong. He shouldn't have bet against Addy."

She stared back in wide-eyed confusion, and said, "I beg your pardon." She swallowed with difficulty when he clasped her foot. He paused, eyes lit with purpose, as if considering something, then moved his hand from her foot to her calf, stopping at the bend in her knee, waiting, for what she wasn't certain.

A fire ignited in her belly that had nothing to do with pain, and she tried to ignore it, tried to quell the rising excitement that his touch elicited. "Ash, I don't think this is the proper time for that sort of...thing."

The idea of making love in a tree was quite daring, and it certainly held some appeal. Sarah Jane wouldn't have minded, if not for the inquisitive child staring curiously up at the two of them. "Your daughter's watching," she whispered.

"Hell!" He'd forgotten they had an audience. Disentangling her small foot carefully so as not to bruise her flesh, he instructed, "Wrap your arms around my neck and I'll carry you back down papoose-style."

Sarah Jane was affronted by his inference that she couldn't handle herself. If he'd known how many trees she'd climbed, how many times she'd escaped out of her second-story window, he wouldn't be looking so smug and heroic. "Really! I am not a child that needs to be carried. My foot is just fine, and I'm perfectly capable of getting down on my own."

He arched a brow. "Coulda fooled me. You're acting every bit as unruly as my daughter. And as stubborn. Guess maybe it wouldn't be a bad idea to paddle your hide, as well as hers, for pulling this little stunt and scaring me half to death.''

Though delighted by the angry words her father directed at his new wife, Addy wasn't at all pleased to hear his threat to spank her. Turning before he could act on it, she took off at a brisk run, heading in the direction of the barn.

Sarah Jane's heart raced madly, but she wasn't certain if it was from excitement, anger, or the fact that Ash had cared enough about her to be scared. ''You'll do no such thing, Ashby Morgan! I don't agree with corporal punishment. My father never spanked me and neither shall you.''

His silver eyes flashed like summer lightning. ''Yeah? Well, maybe he should have. And often.'' He could see now that he shouldn't have spared the rod with his own daughter. Addy was growing into a rebellious creature, and the woman he'd married to help tame her seemed just as unmanageable.

''It's too bad you don't agree with spankings, because I do. And, Sarah Jane,'' he added in a voice that sounded far too provocative for someone who was supposedly angry, ''it's going to give me a great deal of pleasure to place my palm across your naked butt, and—''

Her cheeks turned red as cherries. Sarah Jane scampered down the tree. Her feet had no sooner hit the ground than she took off at a run in the same direction as his daughter.

Ash watched her go, then threw back his head and laughed, until the sobering thought occurred that he didn't have just one errant female to deal with, now he had two.

* * *

Dinner that evening was a strained affair for more
than one reason. Aside from the fact that Ash was
still piqued about his wife's unorthodox behavior, the
meal she'd prepared tasted worse than fresh horse
droppings.

Even Zeke, her self-proclaimed champion, was
having a difficult time swallowing what Sarah Jane
claimed to be beef stew with dumplings.

Addy, who didn't care whether or not she hurt her
stepmother's feelings, offered her unasked-for opinion first. "This tastes awful! What the heck's in it?"

Having taken one bite of the concoction, which she
nearly threw back up, Sarah Jane set down her spoon
and smiled apologetically, concluding that her stepdaughter was right.

Her first night as a housewife was proving to be a
dismal failure.

She explained, "I found a cookbook in the cup-
board and followed the directions to the letter. It's
supposed to be beef stew. But—well, something happened to it. I'm not sure what, but I don't think it
tastes quite like it should." That was an understatement to beat all understatements.

The stew was watery, the dumplings the size of
cannon balls, and just as hard. The meat hadn't been
browned and looked as if it had just jumped from
steer status straight into the pot. The unpeeled carrots
were only partially cooked, and the broth, which
looked suspiciously like dishwater, had the strangest
flavor, like soap.

Zeke gave the woman credit for trying, though he
distinctly remembered Miss Cartwright's effusive
comments about Sarah Jane's culinary skills—he

hadn't known what culinary meant and had to look it up in the lending library's dictionary—so he was a bit confused at the poor quality of the meal.

"It takes a while to adjust to a new stove, Sarah Jane," Zeke said, hoping to ease the humiliation on her face. "I'm sure once you get the hang of it, study those recipes some more, you'll do just fine." Smiling kindly, he attempted to kick his nephew under the table so he would wipe the nasty look off his face.

"We'll all be dead of starvation by then," Ash pointed out, staring horrified at the contents in his bowl.

Finding an opening, Addy took another shot. "You can't climb trees, and you can't cook. Don't seem like you can do much of anything, Sarah Jane."

"Addy—" Ash cast his daughter a warning look.

Sarah Jane smiled, mostly to hide her embarrassment. "You may be right, Addy, but at least I tried. And that's what matters most in this world. Whether or not a person tries his or her hardest to accomplish something."

The child thought for a moment, then said, "Well, I *tried* to eat what you served up as dinner, so I guess you won't be mad if I don't finish it."

Ash opened his mouth to speak, but Sarah Jane cut him off. "I won't be mad at all, Addy. And since you know how things should taste, then perhaps tomorrow you can assist me in the kitchen. We can learn to cook together. It'll be fun."

Zeke swallowed his smile, thinking that Ash's new wife was pretty darn clever to have beaten Addy at her own game, then he turned to stare hard at the child, who'd scooted down in her chair and shrugged, as if it was no skin off her back.

"I guess," she deigned to reply.

"Good. Then it's all settled." The young woman smiled as if the matter were already forgotten. "Now, who would like apple pie for dessert?"

Ash's stomach clutched at the thought, wondering if she'd bothered to peel and core the apples before putting them into the crust. No doubt the damn pie had seeds in it. "None for me, thanks."

Zeke and Addy claimed they couldn't eat another bite, until Sarah Jane informed them that the pie had been baked by Mrs. Dobbins and dropped off earlier that day.

"Yeah, we'd love some," they chorused, unable to mask their relief.

It was rather disheartening to hear how quickly everyone changed their minds, but it only made Sarah Jane more determined than ever to learn how to cook meals that didn't make people gag.

Later that evening after the dishes had been washed, Addy bathed—not without deliberately soaking the front of Sarah Jane's dress first—and put to bed, and Zeke having invented some feeble excuse to visit Etta—supposedly to thank her for the pie—Sarah Jane decided to confront her husband about what she'd learned regarding the children working at the mine.

If Ash was agreeable, she intended to offer her services as a tutor or teacher, something she was quite qualified to do. She may have hated school, but she'd excelled at most of her classes when she chose to apply herself.

Knocking softly on the study door, she waited a moment, then entered the pine-paneled room to find Ash hunched over his desk, leather-bound account books strewn every which way. He was frowning, like a child who'd been given the worst possible chore to perform, and looking not unlike his daughter when faced with a similar situation.

"I was wondering if we could talk."

Ash looked up, his eyes lighting at the sight of her. "Sure. What's on your mind?" He leaned back in his swivel chair, inhaling the scent of her lavender bath oil, imagining how she must have looked naked, wet and glistening. In fact, his imagination was so good that it soon became necessary to scoot farther under the desk to hide his reaction.

"Georgie Ann told me a bit about what goes on at the mine, and I'm wondering if it's entirely necessary for you to employ those school-age children?"

Ash's brow wrinkled in confusion. "What do you mean, necessary? Of course, it's necessary. The boys perform the tedious work that would otherwise have to be handled by laborers or miners, and that's not what those men are getting paid for.

"Everyone's job has a purpose," he explained, rather patiently, he thought, considering she was butting into something she had no business butting into. "The work at the mine is set up in such a fashion to be done quickly and efficiently. Otherwise, we can't make any money, which is the purpose of mining coal in the first place." None of them were doing it for their health, that was for damn certain!

Sarah Jane wrung her hands nervously, remembering Georgie Ann's words of caution. "It's my understanding that the boys don't have much time for schooling. Is that correct?"

"If you're asking if there's a school down at the mine, the answer's no. But no one's stopping them from attending the one in town, if they don't want to work at the mine. They're not slaves. They do get paid a wage."

"Why can't they do both? I mean, if there were some sort of school at the mine, then they could attend classes and still work."

Ash was not about to have his mine turned into a nursery for schoolboys, if that's what she was getting at, and he was pretty sure it was. "That's not the way we do it here."

"Well, maybe you should. Those boys are going to grow up ignorant and unable to do anything but mine coal, if they don't have the chance to better themselves."

"And what's wrong with that?" he asked, taking umbrage at her remark. "Coal mining's respectable work."

"There's nothing wrong with it, but a person should have a choice in what they do with their life. They shouldn't have to choose this way or that, because they've never had the advantage of being schooled properly.

"From what Georgie Ann tells me, your own mother felt the same way, which is why you and your brother were educated."

He made a mental note to speak to Robby's wife. The woman was a little too free with her comments.

"You're new here, Sarah Jane, so I'm not going to get angry at your trying to stick your nose into something that doesn't concern you." Memories of his dead wife's interference came to mind, and he scowled deeply. "I think you have enough to do with running this house and tending to my daughter without butting into business matters that are none of your concern."

Her eyes narrowed. "Women's work, you mean?" She sounded just like Addy had this morning. But the child had a point. Who had made up the rule about men's work and women's work anyway?

Men, no doubt!

"Well, you're a woman." He pointed out the obvious, ignoring her pique and grinning. "I've surely noticed that."

"Sounds to me like you've noticed that Lula Mae Tucker's a woman, too." The notion had festered like an open sore gone untreated.

He pushed himself up from the desk. "Who told you that?" But he knew. And he was going to tan Addy's hide the first chance he got. God only knows what lies she'd concocted...what truths she'd told.

"Never mind who told me. But I'm beginning to see why you don't want or need me in your bed."

She'd changed subjects so fast his head was spinning. "What?" He couldn't believe his ears.

"You made it perfectly clear last night that I wasn't acceptable. Perhaps if I acted more like a loose woman, you'd find me more attractive." Chin up, bosom out, she began to unbutton the front of her gown.

"What the hell are you doing, woman?" His eyes widened even farther as her intention became clear.

"Isn't this what ladies of ill repute do for their men? They strip down naked, don't they? I'm just trying to make you happy."

Jumping up from his chair, Ash nearly knocked it over as he rounded the desk. "Stop that!" He clasped her hands in his. "I told you we were going to take things slow."

"Yes, you did. And then you practically attacked me up in the tree, and then I found out that you've been going to that house of ill repute every night to take your ease with some other woman."

He opened his mouth to deny it, but she never gave him the chance.

"Well, I won't stand for it, Ashby Morgan. Do you hear me? I'm a woman, and I will not have it said that I cannot satisfy my own husband." She wasn't exactly sure what that entailed, but she was darn certain she could do it.

Freeing herself from his hold, she moved back. The dress came off to pool at her feet, and she stepped out of it, standing proudly in her underwear and daring him to do something about it.

She was corsetless, dressed in a chemise and drawers, and Ash was shocked at the surge of lust that suddenly rocked his entire existence, like a mine blowing out from within. "You don't understand," he said, his voice hoarse as he tried to remember why it was that he hadn't wanted to bed her.

"I guess I don't," she said, untying the satin ribbons of her chemise and the string tie of her drawers. "But I'm determined to get an answer."

He stepped closer, his eyes transfixed as she removed the garments and stood naked as a glorious sunrise in front of him. "Sarah Jane." Awe filled his voice; his upper lip was sweating and he wiped it with the back of his hand.

"Now tell me that you don't want to make love to me."

Chapter Seven

"Four score and seven years ago—oh, hell!"

Like a man possessed, Ash drew her into his arms and kissed her, running his hands over her naked backside, her breasts, and feeling himself being sucked under, drowning in the womanly essence that was uniquely Sarah.

"I want you, Ash," she confessed, the need reflected in her eyes as bright and pure as a mountain stream. "I want to know what it feels like to be a woman, to make love to my husband. And I want you to show me. Now." She reached for the buttons of his pants.

He had to think quickly, things were getting out of control. *He* was getting out of control, and he couldn't afford to let that happen. "All right!" he finally agreed. "But not here. Zeke could come back at any time." And A.J. was due to come home, exactly when, he wasn't certain. "We'll go upstairs to our room and do it proper."

She smiled the smile of sirens. "Pick me up and

carry me up the stairs. You didn't carry me across the threshold after our wedding.''

The words *docile, submissive* and *obedient* came to mind, and Ash almost choked on them. Sarah Jane was none of those things. She was stubborn, headstrong, impulsive and goddamn beautiful.

And she was driving him insane!

Hell, they'd only been married a couple of days. What was going to happen after a few years of living with her?

He had to take control. He could see that now, or she'd be running him ragged the rest of his life, leading him around by the short hairs.

Grabbing from the chair one of the afghans his mother had crocheted, he wrapped the red wool around his wife and lifted her into his arms. ''In case Zeke comes in,'' he explained at her questioning look.

Sarah Jane snuggled against his chest, felt his heartbeat against her own, inhaled the musty scent of him. ''I would never have taken you for someone prudish. I think it's awfully sweet of you to be so protective of me.''

Growling in response, he headed for the stairs, and was halfway up when the front door opened, allowing a cold burst of air to rush in.

''Hey, there, Ash. Who you got visiting you tonight? Is that Lula Mae? And are you sharing?''

Sarah Jane gasped at the mention of the whore's name.

Ash swore beneath his breath, then turned to find his brother standing in the front hallway, grinning like the fool that he was. ''I wasn't sure you'd be home tonight, A.J. And this isn't anyone you'd be interested in fooling with, because you'll have to answer to me if you do.''

The uncharacteristic spurt of jealousy that shot through his body surprised Ash and was reflected in the harsh tone of his voice. Over the years, he and A.J. had enjoyed a whore or two together, but Sarah Jane was not going to be someone he shared with anyone. Especially his handsome, rakehell, woman-loving brother.

The woman everyone was discussing as if she wasn't there peered over her husband's shoulder to find a younger version of Ash standing at the foot of the stairs. He was almost as handsome, not quite as tall, and he had the trademark Morgan black hair and silver eyes.

Smiling widely, she wiggled her fingers in greeting and introduced herself. ''Hello. I'm Sarah Jane.''

He winked, and the dimpled smile he presented made the breath catch in her throat. There was no doubt in her mind that Ash's brother was a force to be reckoned with when it came to the female population of Morgantown. In a word, he was gorgeous. Not quite as handsome as her husband, but then, no man was in her eyes.

''Hey, Sarah Jane. You're sure a pretty little thing. Are you new? Did you just start working at O'Connor's? Ash doesn't usually bring his paramours home, so you must be pretty special.''

''She's not a *paramour!*'' Ash practically spit the word back at his brother. ''She's my wife. And you won't be meeting her until after she's dressed properly.''

Hiding his surprise, A.J. caught a glimpse of a naked foot and tiny pink toes, and bit back a smile. "Didn't mean to interrupt your wedding activities. It woulda been nice, though, if you'd waited for me before getting hitched, big brother."

"Yeah, well it didn't work out that way. Go and wait in my office. I've got something to do first, then we'll talk."

The younger man laughed. "I just bet you do. Pleasure meeting you, ma'am."

"Same here, Mr. Morgan," she said, wondering why her husband's mood had suddenly turned sour. She decided to sweeten him up, now that Ash's brother had left the room.

Nibbling his chin, as if it were the sweetest stick of hard candy, Sarah Jane giggled as his stubbled beard tickled the tip of her tongue. "I just love the way you taste."

Swearing beneath his breath Ash carted Sarah Jane the rest of the way up to their room, silently reciting every verse and poem he'd ever learned.

After entering, he kicked the door shut with his foot, then dumped his wife unceremoniously in the center of the big bed and, with one last regrettable look, turned back toward the door.

It took her a moment to realize he wasn't staying. "Where...where are you going, Ash? I thought we were going to make love."

The disappointment he heard stopped him dead in his tracks, and he looked back. "I told you that we'll do that when I think the time's right. With my brother just getting home, now's not a good time."

Biting the inside of her cheek, Sarah Jane wondered if it ever would be, and tried to hold back her considerable temper. She didn't like being tricked or lied to. And she especially didn't like being disappointed. Which she most certainly was!

There was more than one way to get back at the arrogant man, she decided. Words could be a very effective weapon when used properly. Miss Cartwright had taught that lesson well.

Wrapping the afghan more securely around her, she feigned a look of pity and concern. "I've read about how some men can't perform their husbandly duties, so if that's why you're hesitating, I think you should tell me now. I have a right to know. And honesty has always been the best policy." *Not that she was one to talk.*

Ash's face purpled in rage and embarrassment. "There's nothing wrong with my working parts. And I'll thank you not to say such a thing again. I'm trying to be considerate for your own good." For her to think he was less than a man was...was...

"Impotence is nothing to be ashamed of, husband," she went on as if he'd never spoken, delighting in his anger, which barely matched her own. "I'm sure you're not the first man who couldn't satisfy his wife." She shook her head, tsking several times for good measure. "Perhaps it's your advanced age, or—"

"The hell you say!" He had half a mind to show her just how damn hard he was, but he wouldn't play into her hands. There'd be no consummation of this marriage until he said so. And that might be never.

Though he doubted it.

"I've got to talk to A.J." The excuse sounded feeble, even to his own ears.

"You needn't worry that I'll tell anyone about your terrible affliction. Well," she amended, and smiled apologetically, "I may confide in Georgie Ann, but definitely no one else." She nearly laughed aloud at his look of mortification.

"Sarah Jane, you will not tell a soul about what we've discussed here tonight. There is nothing wrong with me. I can perform just fine."

"You're embarrassed, Ash. But once you face the fact that you're unable to...to...well, it'll be better for everyone concerned.

"You know," she continued, just as her husband's hand reached for the doorknob, "it's really a shame that there's no place like O'Connor's House of Pleasure for women to frequent when they're not being satisf—accommodated at home."

Ash slammed the door so hard the windows shook, and Sarah Jane could hear him cursing and stomping all the way down the stairs. She smiled, feeling just a wee bit triumphant, but her euphoria was short-lived.

Soon the tears started to roll down her cheeks, because Sarah Jane knew for a fact—having felt a particular appendage pressed up against her abdomen—that her husband's private parts were in good working order, and that his not wanting to bed her could only mean one thing: he didn't find her the least bit desirable.

Relieving the tension that only a good cry could provide, she gave into it, then wiped her eyes with the edge of the afghan, finally deciding that she would look at this whole miserable situation as a challenge, instead of a defeat.

Ashby Morgan would rue the day he spurned her. She would make him want her so badly that his teeth ached. Among other things. She would hear thunder, feel lightning bolts—

Suddenly her eyes widened, and she smiled. The descriptive name she'd been searching for had just made itself known.

Sarah Jane decided then and there that she would have fierce, explosive *lightning bolts* with her husband or die trying.

A.J. couldn't contain his smile when Ash stormed into the study a few minutes later and slammed the door violently behind him, looking like a man burning in the depths of hell. "Trouble in paradise, big brother?"

Ash shot him a vicious look, then went straight to the desk, yanked open the bottom drawer and retrieved a bottle of sour mash whiskey. Not bothering with a glass, he pulled the cork and gulped, welcoming the burning liquid into his gut. The whiskey eased the throbbing ache in his groin and the anger that Sarah Jane's comments had elicited.

"Mind if I have some of that? It's been a long trip. I'm a mite parched."

Handing his brother the bottle, and a glass he kept in the drawer, Ash said, "Don't start with me, A.J. I'm not in the mood." He plopped down in his swivel chair, the old wood squeaking in protest.

The younger man took a seat in one of the burgundy leather wing chairs fronting the large desk. "I can't believe you up and married again, after all those times you swore you never would."

Ash sneered. ''Yeah? Well, ask that fool Zeke about it. It's all his damn fault. The old man took matters into his own hands, and by the time I found out about it, it was too late. Sarah Jane had already been custom-ordered, so to speak, and was on her way here.''

A.J.'s eyes, a shade lighter than his brother's, widened at the revelation, and he whistled. 'You mean, she's some sort of mail-order bride? How archaic. How romantic.'' His dark brow—though not as dark as his brother's expression at the moment—arched knowingly.

''Shut up! It wasn't my idea.'' He filled A.J. in on the details, then said in a calmer voice, ''Despite the fact that I didn't want to get married again, and despite the fact that I had nothing to do with Sarah Jane's arrival, I think Uncle Zeke may have been on the right track. Addy's been growing up wild without a mother. Sarah Jane's influence could be good for her.'' If Addy would only give her a chance, which would solve a lot of problems for everyone, and put him out of his misery by ending his forced celibacy. He made a mental note to talk to his daughter again.

A.J. sipped thoughtfully on his whiskey, knowing there was truth to Ash's words, but wondering if his brother's new wife was really going to provide the calming influence Addy needed. He'd observed the playful glint in Sarah Jane's eyes, the impish smile that revealed a nature too much like his own, and he couldn't understand why his usually observant brother hadn't seen it, too. Or maybe he had, but chose to ignore it. Now that was an interesting thought.

''How's the kid reacting to the news?'' he asked

finally. "I can't imagine someone as stubborn as little Addy accepting any of this without a fight."

Ash heaved a sigh, which spoke volumes. "Addy's being her usual pain in the butt." He told his brother about the apple tree episode, then added, "But I'm determined that she's going to accept Sarah Jane as her stepmother. I don't want her growing up without learning the niceties. Ma would be disappointed if I let that happen. And as my wife, Sarah Jane deserves to be treated fairly and with respect." Not that he'd done such a bang-up job of that himself.

"You care about the woman that much? By God, but she must be damn good in bed." A.J. grinned knowingly. All the Morgan men had healthy sexual appetites, and Ash was certainly no different, maybe even hungrier.

"That's none of your damn business! And no, I'm not in love with her, if that's what you're getting at. I hardly know the woman. And in case it's escaped your notice, I haven't been all that lucky in the love department."

"Won't the whores at O'Connor's have a field day with this news! 'The marrying man' strikes again." He laughed. "Guess you won't mind me paying attention to Lula Mae now that you're unavailable. I doubt she'll take the news of your marrying too well. I'll probably need to do some consoling."

"As if my bedding Lula Mae has ever kept you from messing with her before?"

A.J. grinned at the truth of his words. When it came to bedding women, there was an unspoken competition between them. "I'm partial to large-breasted women. What can I say?"

So was Ash, and his thoughts drifted to Sarah Jane's ample breasts. Feeling himself start to respond, he cursed inwardly, then changed the subject to a much safer one.

Reaching into the drawer once again, he procured another glass and filled it with whiskey. He took a sip, and said, "I ran into Cynthia Rafferty at the train station the other day. She asked about you." It wasn't quite a lie, since Cynthia's mother had mentioned A.J., if not in glowing terms, well, at least, in passing.

His brother's eyes lit, and Ash knew his suspicions had been correct. A.J. was definitely interested in the spinster. And that would fit his plans nicely. Misery loved company, he guessed. And it was time A.J. did something with his life, like get married.

"Is that a fact? Guess she musta been pretty upset that you were getting hitched to someone other than her."

"I've never been interested in Cynthia Rafferty. She's not my type. But I think she'd make you an excellent wife."

A.J. choked on his whiskey, the amber liquid spilling down the front of his shirt, and he wiped his mouth with the back of his hand. "Wife? I'm not fixing to get hitched. Just because you went and gave in to Uncle Zeke's crazy demands, don't think for a minute that—"

The chair creaked again as Ash settled himself into it and leaned back. "I know you're interested in the woman, A.J., so stop pretending otherwise. And I think you'd be wise to court Cynthia before someone else does. She's a pretty woman, and she's sweet."

Suspicion filled the younger man's eyes. "So, why

didn't you marry her, if she's so damn sweet and such a good catch?''

Ash shrugged. "Like I said, she's not my type. And I don't think I could put up with her mother. The woman grates on me the wrong way. But you, A.J., have a much easier-going personality. I don't think Beulah Rafferty bothers you all that much.''

The younger man hated the relief that welled up inside him to know that his brother wasn't interested in Cynthia. "She doesn't. But that doesn't mean I want to marry her daughter.''

"You're two years younger than me, A.J., still living at home with your family, and working at a job you never really cared about. Don't you think it's time you got yourself a woman and made a life for yourself?'' A hurt look crossed his brother's face, and Ash cursed inwardly his lack of tact. Hurting A.J. was the last thing he wanted to do, but sometimes you had to hurt a bit before you helped a lot. He'd learned that lesson from Zeke the hard way.

"If you're telling me to move out, that you no longer want me living here, because you've got a new wife, then—''

"Oh, for God's sake, Aaron James! I'm not saying any such thing, so get that burr outta your ass, and quick. You know damn well you're welcome to stay here as long as you want. Same with Uncle Zeke. This house is plenty big enough for all of us. Besides, I like having my family around me, you know that.

"But I still think you should consider settling down and having some kids. I don't want you growing old alone. Zeke and I could die tomorrow in a mine explosion, and then where would you be? Alone and working a job you've never really liked.''

Ash worried constantly about that happening. Though he was only a couple of years older than A.J., he'd always felt a paternal responsibility toward his brother. And he'd promised his mother on her deathbed that he would always look out for him and do what was best.

"I don't mind pulling my weight at the mine.''

"I know that. But it's not the same as loving the work. Don't think I don't know that it's farming you truly care about. Hell, it shows in every apple that grows on those trees out back, in every head of lettuce and ear of corn that comes from the garden you plant every year.

"I don't want you spending your life doing something that you feel forced to do. I chose to be a coal miner, but that doesn't mean you've got to be one, too, because of some misguided family loyalty.''

The words Sarah Jane had spoken so eloquently filled his mind. "You have choices, A.J. You're educated, thanks to Ma, and you should do what you want with your life. You only get one shot.''

The younger man was surprised by the vehemence he heard in his brother's voice, and wondered at the cause of it. Ash had always known that he preferred working the land over doing anything else, but he'd never seen fit to talk about it until now. "Why are you all fired up about this now, after all these years? I don't get it.''

Ash shrugged, wondering how much he should reveal. He didn't want anyone to think that his wife was having undue influence over him. Because she wasn't. Mostly. "Something Sarah Jane said to me this evening sorta took hold. She was going on about the young boys working at the mine, about their lack of choices in life, and I got to thinking that maybe she was right. That some people don't have a choice in what they do, because circumstances don't allow it.

"I love mining coal, always have, always will. And I know Zeke feels the same way. But I also know that you'd rather be doing something else with your life. And you should, if you feel strongly about it."

His brother's forehead wrinkled in confusion. "But I thought you needed me here."

"I welcome your help and your knowledge, A.J., you know that. But your heart's not in the work, and I worry that someday your inattentiveness could cost lives, including your own. I see how sometimes you daydream when you should be picking or shoveling."

A.J.'s eyes darkened to the color of tarnished silver, and Ash held up his hand to forestall his objection. "I'm not condemning you for it. God knows the work's tedious, and we all lose concentration from time to time. But it can be dangerous, and I'd never forgive myself if anything happened to you, little brother. I hope you know that."

Since he'd been a small boy, A.J. had loved watching things grow. He loved the smell of dirt, of tilling the soil, planting seeds, and knowing he'd been largely responsible for the end result. He'd never gotten the same feeling of satisfaction from mining coal. Ash was right about that. His ma had always claimed that her youngest boy had soil in his veins instead of blood. But A.J. had looked up to his big brother, wanted to be like him, and so had followed Ash's footsteps into the mine.

"Even if I was of a mind to take your advice and try my hand at something new, there's not much farmland around here." Too hilly, too wooded, too many damn rocks to cultivate the land properly.

"No. There's not. I'd have to agree with you there. But no one said that you had to live in Morgantown. There's other parts of the state more suitable to farming, or you could find yourself a piece of land in the western part of Virginia. You'd still be close enough that we could visit from time to time."

A.J. poured down the rest of his whiskey, then stood. Every bone in his body ached after the long ride home, and he couldn't think clearly any longer. His mind had grown befuddled with all the new possibilities and revelations being made. "I guess some of what you've said bears considering. I'm not sure about Cynthia Rafferty, but I'll think about it.

"But for now I'm beat and going to bed. And I suspect you'd like nothing better than to do the same, seeing as how you've got that pretty little wife warming your sheets." He winked suggestively.

Forcing a smile, Ash watched his brother stroll out the door and wondered what he would say if he knew the truth about his relationship with Sarah. Pouring himself another whiskey, he thought about the muddled mess his life had become and frowned.

Sarah Jane had wanted to make love with him, but was now convinced that he was incapable; his brother was at a crossroads in his life, and Ash wasn't certain he'd given him the best advice—God knows he'd miss A.J. if he actually decided to leave—and Addy was doing her darnedest to avoid growing up and accepting womanhood.

All in all, in the past two days things had gone from bad to worse to unbearable. And he had mostly himself to blame.

Chapter Eight

When Sarah Jane awoke the next morning it was to find Ash's side of the bed empty and fifty dollars in cash resting on the nightstand. There was a note attached, instructing her to buy Addy new clothing and whatever else was needed for the household.

Her eyes narrowed as she stared at the stack of bills, then at the note, which hadn't been signed. "Guilt money," she muttered, pushing back the covers and rising to her feet. The floor was cold, and she hurried to the fireplace to toss more wood onto the fire, jabbing it with the iron poker. The hot coals blazed to life, igniting the pine logs.

Warming her backside and hands, she glanced out the double-hung windows to find the sun had yet to clear the horizon and knew Ash had left unusually early this morning, no doubt to escape. The coward!

The hours that passed had not lessened her anger over the previous night's deception, though they had served to make her more determined than ever to carry through with her plan.

With that in mind, she donned her flannel robe and

hurried to Addy's room, which was adjacent to her own. The child was still asleep and looked so peaceful that Sarah Jane hated to wake her. It was difficult to reconcile this angelic face with the foulmouthed, ill-tempered urchin she'd come to know.

Shaking the little girl gently, she said, "Wake up, sleepyhead. We're going to town to do some shopping today." She hadn't figured out as yet just how they were going to get there, but she would.

There were few things Addy liked better than sleeping, except maybe going to town, or visiting the mine, which she got to do very infrequently because of the danger, but she wasn't about to let Sarah Jane know that. "Go away!" She nestled farther under her blankets, pulling them up to her chin. "Can't you see I'm sleeping?"

"I'm afraid I can't do that, sweetie. So you'd best rise and shine."

Forcing her eyes open, Addy found Sarah Jane standing beside her bed like a sentinel. Her step-mother's cheery smile was in direct contrast to her own fierce frown, and she groaned. "Go away! It's too early. I'm not done sleeping yet."

Sarah Jane grasped the quilted coverlet and yanked it back. Addy shrieked when the cold air hit her bare legs and arms. Sarah Jane said firmly, "Oh yes, you are! Your father left instructions that we were to go clothes shopping for you, and that's exactly what we're going to do. But first, we've got to take care of our chores. Business before pleasure, my papa always said."

Which reminded her that she still needed to write her parents and let them know that she was safe. No doubt they were worried about her. And now that she was a married woman, she was outside of their control and could afford to let them know her location. Her mother would likely have a fit of the vapors when she learned that her only daughter had married a coal miner.

"Pleasure, ha! There ain't nothing pleasurable about shopping. And I don't want any new clothes." Her eyes narrowed, and her voice was full of accusation when she said, "I bet you put Daddy up to it, didn't you?"

"I did mention that the clothing you've been wearing would look better on a ragpicker, but I wasn't sure it had made an impression until I woke up this morning and found his note."

Grimacing, the child grabbed her tummy and moaned loudly for effect. "My stomach hurts. I don't feel well."

Having used that particular ploy herself many times, Sarah Jane wasn't buying her stepdaughter's sudden illness and turned on her heel. "Fine. I'll just tell your father that—"

"Never mind." After the apple orchard fiasco, Addy knew she was skating on thin ice where her father was concerned, and she wasn't about to push her luck. "I'm getting up. But I'm not buying anything that makes me look stupid."

"Of course, you're not. We'll try to find items that suit you." Sarah Jane could remember quite clearly some of the hideous outfits her mother had forced her to wear, and she had great empathy for the child.

"You mean, I don't have to have bows and lace and all that fancy junk Mrs. Hodak puts on those dresses she makes?'' Her frown eased a bit, and she decided that it might not be too horrible to have a few new outfits, for church and such.

Most of the time the other kids laughed at her appearance, especially the girls, who said cruel things about her and called her names, like girly-boy. Addy tried not to care that she didn't have many friends and that people tended to make fun of her. But it did hurt her feelings sometimes, even though she tried to ignore them, like Uncle Zeke had told her to.

Assuming correctly that Mrs. Hodak was the local seamstress, Sarah Jane replied, ''I'm sure Mrs. Hodak will make whatever we want. And if she doesn't, then we'll go to the mercantile and look for ready-made dresses.''

Addy sat up, propping herself against the down pillows. ''Do you think there'll be enough money left over for ice cream?'' She licked her lips, unconscious of the gesture, and Sarah Jane smiled.

She adored ice cream, too, so it seemed that she and Ash's daughter had something in common after all. ''Perhaps. But only if you behave, and only if you wear something besides these filthy jeans and shirt.'' She kicked the pile of offending garments that lay on the floor, her distaste evident. ''I'm sure you have a skirt and shirtwaist in your closet that you could don, correct?''

The child's eyes widened in horror. ''You are making my life hell, woman!''

Having thought the very thing about Miss Cartwright on numerous occasions, Sarah Jane smiled inwardly. ''You, my girl, have a flair for the dramatic.

Perhaps we'll try our hand at writing some plays, like Jo did in that book I was telling you about.''

"Jo wrote stories?"

Noting the interest that flared brightly in the child's eyes, Sarah Jane sat down at the foot of the bed and nodded. "Yes. Writing was her grand passion. She and her sisters used to go up in the attic of their home and act out the stories she penned, taking turns playing the various parts.''

Addy was impressed. "All that's in the small women book?''

"All that and much, much more. Would you like to read it?''

Twisting the sheet nervously between her fingers, Addy's face fell and she heaved a dispirited sigh. "I'm not much good at reading. It would take me forever to finish that book.''

The child was obviously bothered by her lack of ability, and Sarah Jane's heart went out to her. She knew how hard it was for Addy to admit such a thing, especially to someone she considered the enemy. "We're going to work on your reading and writing skills, sweetie, but in the meantime, perhaps we can read the book together. Every afternoon, after your lessons are done, we can set aside an hour or so and read a chapter. Would you like that?''

The little girl shrugged, trying not to look too interested, but inside she was bubbling with excitement. "I guess that would be okay.''

Sarah Jane patted her leg affectionately, then rose to her feet. "Good. Now let's go down and get breakfast made. Remember, you promised to help me with the cooking.''

"You need help after that awful meal you fixed last night. I nearly puked." But this time the criticism was said with a mischievous grin, and Sarah Jane felt that maybe, just maybe, she was making some progress with the motherless child. She hoped so.

"We can help each other. That's what friends do."

Confusion marred the child's features. "We can't be friends. You're my stepmama."

The young woman tossed back her head and laughed, the enchanting sound filling the quiet room like lilting strains from a music box. "That's true. But unlike the wicked stepmother in Cinderella, I'm neither mean nor ugly, so that means we can be friends."

"Who's Cinderella? Is she in another one of those stories you was telling me about? You sure do know a lot of stories."

"Addy, my girl, the world is soon going to be a far more interesting place for you to live in. Just you wait and see."

Dressed in a navy-blue serge skirt and white shirtwaist, Sarah Jane hurried down to the kitchen a short time later to put on a pot of coffee. But when she entered the large room, now bathed in sunlight, it was to find Ash's brother seated at the table absorbed in the newspaper.

The delicious aroma of coffee filled her senses, and it was obvious that A.J. Morgan had made it, which meant it probably tasted a whole lot better than hers. Ash claimed her coffee tasted like burnt horse dung! Well, cooking was not going to be her favorite domestic task, she could see that quite clearly.

"Good morning," she said to her brother-in-law. "I'm Sarah Jane. We met last evening, under rather unusual circumstances, as I recall." Remembering her appearance when they'd first met, she cringed inwardly. Miss Cartwright had always stressed the importance of first impressions. Sarah Jane had made quite a memorable one—memorable, but not good, she feared.

Looking up from the paper, A.J. grinned, and there was a teasing twinkle in his eye, an indication that he remembered her state of undress. Sarah Jane was mortified.

"Yes, we did, Sarah Jane. And I didn't get to welcome you into the family properlike last night, did I? I'd better rectify that now." Rising to his feet, he crossed the room in two long strides and enveloped her in a bear hug. "Like I said last night, you sure are a pretty little thing." He kissed the top of her head in a brotherly fashion. "My brother's a lucky man."

A.J. had thought her a whore at the time, Sarah Jane remembered, smiling sickly into his broad chest, which smelled of shaving soap and leather.

Addy entered the room at that moment to witness the embrace and pulled up short, confusion turning to excitement. "Uncle A.J.! I didn't know you was home." Then she accused, "How come you're messing with Daddy's new wife, Uncle A.J.? He ain't gonna like that."

Sarah Jane blushed to the roots of her hair. "For heaven's sake, Addy! Your uncle was merely welcoming me into the family. Wherever do you come up with these outlandish ideas of yours?"

"Daddy's the jealous type," the child explained.

"He didn't like it none when Uncle A.J. messed with Lula Mae behind his back. Said only one Morgan at a time was going to be with that whore."

Sarah Jane gasped aloud, her mouth falling open, while her brother-in-law's face turned red with humiliation and outrage.

"Shut up, Addy! You've got a big mouth," he admonished, shaking his head and peering at Ash's new wife out of the corner of his eye. "Don't you know kids should be seen and not heard?" That had been a favorite expression of his mother, and it fit his impetuous niece to perfection. Addy had the unfortunate habit of speaking before thinking—a common Morgan trait, unfortunately.

"Sorry," she said, not looking at all contrite as she filched an apple from the wooden bowl sitting in the center of the table. "Didn't know it was a secret."

Flashing her stepdaughter a quelling look, Sarah Jane smiled apologetically at Ash's brother, then asked, "Mr. Morgan, if it wouldn't be too much trouble, do you suppose you could give us a ride into town today? We need to get some shopping done. Ash wants me to buy Addy some new clothes. Not that she deserves anything for her most recent unladylike behavior." Shades of Miss Cartwright crept into her tone as she stared pointedly at the little girl.

Fearing her ice cream was in jeopardy, the child thought quickly and pasted on a contrite expression. "I said I was sorry." There wasn't much she wouldn't do for ice cream, especially strawberry.

"It's A.J., ma'am. That's short for Aaron James, like my daddy. And I'd be pleased to take you. I've

got a few calls to make in town anyway, so it won't
be out of my way.''

He'd decided to test the waters with Cynthia Rafferty and see what developed. A.J. had had all night
to mull over his brother's advice, and decided that
maybe finding himself a wife and settling down might
not be such a bad idea after all, especially if he followed through with Ash's suggestion to buy a farm.
A man needed a wife if he was going to work the
land.

Of course, that wasn't the only reason he was interested in Cynthia Rafferty. She had the prettiest
green eyes he'd ever seen, and a mouth that looked
as sweet as ripe peaches and just made for kissing.

"Hey, if we go to town, Sarah Jane, I can show
you where O'Connor's is at.''

Addy's excitement was short-lived when her uncle's eyes narrowed. "Ladies, young or old, don't
hang around whorehouses,'' he told his niece. "Your
father'll beat you silly if you so much as go near the
place. And if he doesn't, I will.''

"Your uncle's correct, Addy,'' Sarah Jane agreed,
but the idea of visiting O'Connor's had already taken
root and was hard to let go of. The chance to see Lula
Mae Tucker in the flesh, so to speak, was going to
be too difficult to resist.

It was always wise to know how your competition
stacked up. Miss Cartwright used to preach that very
edict whenever her school had an academic contest
with a rival school. And the Cartwright School usually won.

Miss Tucker appeared to be her closest competitor
for Ash's affections, and Sarah Jane had no intention

of allowing some floozy to steal her husband away. Not when she'd gone to so much trouble to get him in the first place.

Waving goodbye to A.J., Sarah Jane and Addy made plans to meet him at Fletcher's Ice Cream Parlor in two hours. That would give the two females a chance to shop for Addy's clothes, and it would give Sarah Jane ample time to wander down to O'Connor's and see if Lula Mae Tucker was about. She would ask the seamstress to keep an eye on Addy while she was gone.

Morgantown's main street was bustling with merchants, shoppers eager to get their larders stocked, and freight wagons laden with merchandise. Addy waved to a few of the people she knew: Mr. Tompkins, the town's barber, Hillary Roth from the mercantile, and she introduced Sarah Jane when the occasion warranted.

They continued on until they arrived at Mrs. Hodak's establishment—a charming one-story brick building with bright green shutters and a large display window that fronted the store and featured a wide assortment of brightly colored hats and gloves.

The sun shone in the cloudless cerulean-blue sky, and Sarah Jane felt pleased with the world at the moment. She had made a tentative truce with Ash's young daughter, had a plan to win her husband to her bed, and she was back in town, surrounded by people and activity. Reminded a bit of Philadelphia, a sudden wave of homesickness washed over her.

Pushing aside the sentimental feeling, she entered

the seamstress' shop and was delighted with the large selection of merchandise.

All pretense of displeasure left Addy's face, too, as soon as she spotted the colorful display of fabrics, hats and shoes. "Can I try on some hats, Sarah Jane? I love that blue one over there, the one with the big feather."

Her face was animated as she pointed to a musketeer's type of hat with a huge white ostrich feather sticking out from the crown. It was just the type of hat a child Addy's age would adore. Sarah had had a similar one when she was growing up.

Mrs. Hodak, who had four daughters of her own, smiled indulgently at the child. "I don't mind, Mrs. Morgan, as long as her hands are clean."

"They are," Addy assured her, holding out both hands for inspection. "I washed them three times this morning already. Sarah Jane made me."

While Addy amused herself with Mrs. Hodak's latest creations, Sarah Jane explained to the proprietress just what they were looking for in the way of clothing. While the woman went to the back room in search of a measuring tape, Sarah Jane's attention was drawn to the filmy, scandalous nightwear on display.

Fingering the thin black material, her eyes widened when she discovered that she could see right through it, then a wicked smile crossed her lips. Wouldn't it be fun to wear this for Ash? A woman would be hard to resist in this getup.

The brass bell tinkled when the front door opened, and two gaudily dressed women in satin gowns entered the store. One had hair the color of pumpkins, which clashed horribly with her red apparel, while the other wore a brassy gold braid atop her head—the peculiar color coming straight out of a peroxide bottle, unless Sarah missed her guess.

Having never seen hair quite as colorful before, or ladies of the evening, for that matter—she'd certainly never been in the same room with one before!—she stared fascinated, even knowing it was rude. Sarah wondered if they worked at O'Connor's House of Pleasure.

Finally remembering her manners, and deciding it was none of her business anyway, she went back to perusing the nightwear.

Mrs. Hodak came back just then, looking clearly displeased when she saw who her new customers were. "I thought we had an appointment for later this afternoon, Miss Tucker," she said, almost rudely.

At the mention of the familiar name, Sarah Jane's head cranked around so fast she nearly cricked her neck. The orange-haired woman smiled, jabbing her companion in the side. "Guess Mrs. Hodak don't like our frequenting her place when she's got refined clientele, Josie. Well, my money's as good as hers—" she lifted her chin toward Sarah "—and I've come to pick up that nightwear she's fingering."

Sarah Jane dropped the offending garment as if it were tainted and pulled back her hand. "I'm sorry. I didn't know this had already been purchased by someone else."

"In my business, honey, fancy nightgowns and such are part of the trade, if you get my meaning." She winked, then caught sight of Addy and grinned.

"Hey, Addy. What you doing with that ugly hat? Thought you didn't like being noticed. That's what your daddy tells me, anyway. You sure enough will be, if you wear that god-awful hat.''

Addy opened her mouth to speak—no doubt to say something rude—but Sarah Jane stepped in front of her. ''I don't think what Addy or her father does is really any of your business, miss. And I'd appreciate it if you didn't disrupt her when she's trying on hats for a play we're planning.''

The blonde's eyes widened. ''You some kind of actresses, or something?''

Smiling inwardly at the notion, Sarah Jane shook her head. ''No. But we are interested in all aspects of the theater. Aren't we, Adelaide.''

''Yes, Mama,'' Addy replied, meek as a church mouse.

Sarah Jane tried to keep her face carefully composed.

''Mama? You mean to tell me you're Ash's new wife? The one he brought here from Philadelphia?'' Lula Mae looked anything but pleased by the prospect.

''I don't mean to tell you anything, miss. But since you asked, the answer's yes. Ash is my husband, and you would do well to remember that.''

''Yeah. You shouldn't be with my daddy now that he's married to Sarah Jane,'' Addy blurted, the mouse having apparently died a sudden death.

Mrs. Hodak gasped, clutching her throat.

Sarah Jane felt like clutching Addy's. ''Please excuse Adelaide. She's a bit high-strung.''

The prostitute smiled smugly. ''So I guess you know I'm Lula Mae Tucker?''

The pronouncement was made with such an air of

superiority that Sarah Jane fought to remain civil. By all accounts, she shouldn't even be speaking to the woman. Ladies of genteel breeding did not associate with women of ill repute, no matter the circumstances. Miss Cartwright would have keeled over in a dead faint right on the spot, if she'd been faced with similar circumstances.

"I assumed as much."

"Well, I'd say it was a pleasure to make your acquaintance, Mrs. Morgan, but it ain't. I was fixing to marry Ash myself one of these days, and now you've gone and ruined it all. But that don't mean I won't have him in my bed whenever I want. He likes what I do for him. And that husband of yours has staying power. Yes, he surely does."

Clenching her fists, Sarah Jane felt her composure slipping. She couldn't risk losing her temper or making a scene in front of Addy or Mrs. Hodak—the resulting scandal would be horrendous—but she desperately wanted to wrap her hands around the woman's slender throat and squeeze, giving her complexion some color that hadn't come out of a paint pot.

Josie tugged on her companion's arm. "Come on, Lula Mae. It's time we was getting back to work. You know Willy don't like it when we're late. We've probably got customers waiting."

Sarah Jane's face heated at the notion.

"Would you like me to wrap up these garments for you, Miss Tucker, before you leave?" the proprietress asked.

Lula Mae shook her head. "Nah. I don't want nothing Miss Fancy-Pants has touched."

Sarah Jane gasped at the insult.

"Don't you call my mama that!" Addy warned, even though she'd referred to her stepmother in the very same way when she'd first met her. She felt bad about that now. Sarah Jane wasn't at all fancy, and she sure as heck wasn't no whore.

"It's all right, sweetie. They're only words."

The two women walked out in a huff, slamming the door behind them with such force the brass bell nearly fell off. The proprietress breathed a sigh of relief, then glanced at the expensive French lingerie she had imported for Lula Mae and shook her head in dismay.

"I should never have tried to be accommodating to those...those women. Now I'm stuck with these garments."

Sarah Jane patted the woman's hand consolingly. "Addy, would you please go into the dressing room and try on the clothing Mrs. Hodak left there for you? I'll be right in to check on you and see how they fit."

Her eyes shining bright with something that looked suspiciously like pride, Addy nodded and did exactly what she was told for a change.

"Since I'm the one who caused the problem for you, Mrs. Hodak, I will purchase the nightwear myself. I think it's lovely, and I'd rather not see that woman putting it to use." On Ash, especially.

"If you're sure?" The older woman couldn't mask her relief, as she'd had to pay a hefty sum for the imported goods.

"Just wrap them up. And please keep the purchases between us. I wouldn't want Addy to know. She's still adjusting to the fact that I'm her father's new wife. You understand?''

"Perfectly, dear. Don't worry about a thing. I'll put these in a hatbox. That way no one will be the wiser.''

"Thank you. And wrap up that blue felt hat with the big ostrich feather, too—the one Addy was trying on. I'd like to buy it for her as a present.''

"That's very kind of you, Mrs. Morgan. I don't think Addy gets many presents. Men just don't think the same as women, and I don't believe Mr. Morgan is any exception.''

Amen to that! Sarah Jane thought, before going in search of her stepdaughter.

When they emerged from the dress shop thirty minutes later, both Sarah Jane and Addy were laden down with packages.

Two shirtwaists, both white, three skirts in navy, tan and blue, and a pair of sturdy shoes filled Addy's arms. They were practical, not fussy, and the young girl seemed pleased with the selections. She'd even allowed Sarah Jane to purchase undergarments for her.

"Do you like all of your new things, Addy?'' Sarah Jane asked as they made their way toward the ice-cream parlor.

"More than I thought I would. What did you buy?'' She spied the two hatboxes, unable to mask her innate curiosity.

Knowing what was inside each of them, Sarah Jane used some evasive tactics. "A surprise for you, but only if you're good.''

"A surprise! For me?''

Genuinely touched by the gesture, the child inserted her small hand into Sarah Jane's and smiled up at her. "Thank you."

The young woman smiled back and tears stung her eyes. For the first time since arriving in Morgantown, Sarah Jane felt like a mother.

Chapter Nine

A.J. cooled his heels in the front parlor of Cynthia Rafferty's two-story brick house, waiting while her mother, who hadn't looked at all pleased to see him, went to fetch—after it became quite apparent that A.J. wasn't going to take no for an answer—her supposedly otherwise engaged daughter.

Having never been in the Raffertys' house before, he allowed his gaze to travel over the fancy green velvet drapery at the windows, the crocheted ecru lace doilies covering every inch of the rosewood tabletops, the fancy etched-glass hurricane lamps on the mantel, and he grimaced. A.J. liked things plain and simple; he'd never been one for ostentation.

The house seemed incongruous with what he knew of Cynthia Rafferty's personality. She seemed quiet and unassuming, and not someone who would like all these fancy gewgaws. It was likely that the decor was more a reflection of her mother than of her.

Beulah did have a tendency to put on airs in her effort to be the center of attention. And she'd also been hoping to marry Cynthia off to Ash, so A.J.

wasn't sure just how thrilled she'd be to have him calling on her daughter. Apparently, not very, if her earlier behavior had been any indication.

Ash was perceived by most of the town's marriage-able women and their doting mamas to be a good catch. He had his own business, a fine stone house that he'd built from the ground up and was paid for, and a reputation as a hard worker and a fair man.

A.J. supposed his reputation was that of being Ash's little brother. Not that he minded, but it did make it a tad more difficult to attract the ladies when Ash was around. Of course, now that his older brother was married to Sarah Jane and out of the running, so to speak, A.J. wouldn't have to worry about compet-ing with him anymore. He rather liked that.

"Mr. Morgan, how nice to see you." Cynthia's scent of rosewater came floating into the room just ahead of her, and A.J. felt his gut tighten. He'd al-ways been partial to roses, and Cynthia Rafferty wore the prettiest smile on her face.

"Miss Cynthia," he said, nodding politely, allow-ing his gaze to roam over every inch of the woman's trim figure. Trim, but well rounded, he amended. "I hope you don't mind that I've come calling unan-nounced."

"Not at all, Mr. Morgan." In fact, she was de-lighted, though somewhat surprised. She'd had oc-casion to see A.J. Morgan in town from time to time, but they had never really spoken, except to exchange pleasantries. And she couldn't recall him ever smiling at her before, not like the way he was smiling now, deep enough to display dimples she hadn't realized he had.

Beulah entered the room on her daughter's heels, not bothering to hide her displeasure at A.J.'s continued presence or his persistence in seeing her daughter. "There's nothing wrong with your brother's new wife, is there, Mr. Morgan? She seemed a puny, unhealthy sort when I met her at the train station the other day." A.J. detected a ray of hope in the question and almost smiled.

"Mama!" Cynthia looked aghast at her mother, wishing she wouldn't say every little thing that came to mind.

"No, ma'am. My calling on Miss Cynthia has nothing to do with Ash or my very healthy sister-in-law. I've come on my own behalf."

The young woman's cheeks blossomed the color of sun-ripened peaches, and she smiled shyly at the handsome man. She opened her mouth to speak, to thank him, but her mother butted in before she got the chance.

"That is news, Mr. Morgan. Didn't know you was partial to my daughter. Are you here to make a formal call?"

Unsure of what proper courting procedure actually entailed, A.J. inserted his index finger between his shirt collar and neck and pulled, then swallowed. "Well, now, ma'am, I thought it might be nice for me and Miss Cynthia to get better acquainted, if she's got no objection."

"I don't," the young woman blurted before her mother could utter another word, then said, "Mama, why don't you bring Mr. Morgan a slice of that delicious banana bread you baked yesterday? I'm sure he'd love to have some. Wouldn't you, Mr. Morgan? My mother's a wonderful cook.''

''I'd be quite pleased to taste it, ma'am.'' And he'd like to have a taste of Cynthia's soft lips, as well. He knew they'd be sweeter than any banana bread the old sourpuss could cook up.

Beulah preened, just like her daughter knew she would. ''I do have somewhat of a reputation.''

A.J. nodded. ''Yes, ma'am, I know.'' But he wasn't talking about her ability in the kitchen.

Knowing exactly what the handsome man was referring to, Cynthia almost laughed. Everyone in town knew Beulah Rafferty was the biggest gossip for miles around. She'd become somewhat of a celebrity because of it, with the townswomen always asking her advice on things, or stopping by to give her the latest tidbits of news, so she could pass them along to the next person.

Her mother's avocation as a busybody was, she supposed, harmless enough, but it did grate on Cynthia's nerves from time to time. Silence was not a frequent companion in the Rafferty household, and there were days when she just wished she could go off by herself and be alone.

Getting married could solve that problem, but she needed to find a husband first. She sized A.J. up, then smiled.

''I'm very glad you came by to visit, Mr. Morgan. And I'm pleased that your brother decided to marry. I hope he'll be very happy with his new wife. Sarah Jane seems a lovely young woman.''

''She is. My brother's a lucky man.''

''Please don't take offense at anything my mother

says. It's true that she'd been hoping to pair me off with Ash, but that had never been my objective.'' And that was the gospel truth.

Though she liked and respected Ash, found him to be a very agreeable sort of man, there had never been any spark between them. Not like the spark that had jolted her composure and sent her nerves to tingling when A.J. Morgan had stepped into the room.

"No offense taken, Miss Cynthia. But do you think you could call me A.J.? I'd surely appreciate it if you would.''

Taking a seat on the horsehair sofa, she patted the space next to her. "Only if you'll consent to drop the 'Miss' and call me Cynthia. Even though we don't know each other all that well, we have been acquainted for a rather long time, wouldn't you say?''

He nodded at her assessment. One couldn't help knowing everyone in a town the size of Morgantown. There were always church gatherings to attend—weddings, funerals and the like, or holiday celebrations. The Fourth of July picnic and Founder's Day festivities were annual events, and most everyone in town turned out for them.

A.J. had seen Cynthia at those functions and others, but he'd never approached the pretty woman, thinking that her interest was in his brother. The fact that he'd been wrong pleased him to no end.

"I was wondering, Cynthia, what do you think about farming and such? Do you like it?''

Her eyes widened at the strange question. "Well, I've—I've never really thought much about it before. I was raised in town, in this house, so I've not had much to do with farm animals, crops and such. Why?''

He shrugged. ''Just wondering.'' A.J. had never had to make conversation over at O'Connor's, and he wasn't very good at it. Judging from the perplexed look on the woman's face, he wasn't very good at courting, either, and wondered if he shouldn't just cut his losses and leave, before he made an absolute fool out of himself.

Finding a wife was going to be much harder than he thought. No wonder Ash had ordered his through the mail.

He almost breathed a sigh of relief when Mrs. Rafferty came bustling into the room, carrying a silver tray laden with coffee and sweets, and setting it down on the tea table before him.

''Now, Mr. Morgan, why don't you tell me what your intentions are toward my daughter? If you're thinking about marrying Cynthia, then we need to—''

''Mama! For heaven's sake!'' Her cheeks red, Cynthia cast her mother an anguished look, made a quick, mumbled apology to A.J., then jumped up and fled the room, teary eyed and totally mortified.

''Well, my goodness! What did I say?''

Yep, A.J., thought, staring at the woman's retreating back as she disappeared out the door, this courting thing was going to be a whole lot more difficult than he'd first thought.

Sarah Jane glanced up from her dish of vanilla ice cream to find Ash's brother entering Fletcher's Ice Cream Parlor. He looked flushed, somewhat distracted, and she wondered what had happened to make him appear that way.

"Sorry I'm late," he said, winking at Addy before taking a seat at the small round table and trying to fit his long legs beneath it. "I see you've got a dish of your favorite, kid."

Licking the strawberry cream off her spoon, Addy grinned, then went back to the business of eating.

"Did you finish all of your shopping, Sarah Jane? I see you've got a few packages." They were piled on the chair next to her.

She nodded, unsure of how much she should confide about her run-in with Lula Mae Tucker. After all, the woman was a friend of A.J.'s, according to Addy. "Yes. It was an interesting experience."

"Sarah Jane was insulted by that Lula Mae Tucker. You know, Uncle A.J., the one you like 'cause she has such big—"

The embarrassed man reached across the table, placing his large hand over the child's even larger mouth. "I know who she is, Addy, and I'll thank you to mind your ice cream and stay out of adult conversations that are of no concern to you."

"Jeez. I was just trying to explain."

Sarah Jane found herself smiling inwardly at the child's irrepressible comments. Maybe, because they weren't being directed at her for a change.

"We met Miss Tucker and her companion at the dress shop. She seemed quite displeased that I had married someone whom she apparently considered hers." The blue eyes hardened. "I'm afraid I had to set her straight, and she didn't like it one little bit."

"Yeah! You shoulda seen her, Uncle A.J. Sarah Jane—"

"Addy!" Sarah Jane cautioned with a shake of her head. "Please remember our earlier conversation and tend to your dessert. I can inform your uncle of my dealings with Miss Tucker without any help from you."

With a nervous glance at the hatbox, the child nodded, clearly disappointed at having been excluded, then went back to eating.

A.J. was surprised and quite impressed by the way his new sister-in-law handled his niece. Addy didn't appear at all resentful, as he'd been expecting. Ash's daughter wasn't the type of kid who liked being told what to do; she was a lot like her father in that regard.

"Sounds like you had an interesting day. Mine wasn't nearly as exciting."

"Really? You certainly looked distracted or agitated about something when you first came in here. I thought maybe something had happened, or that maybe you'd received some distressing news."

"I—uh—" He was obviously embarrassed and reticent to reveal any particulars of his so-called unexciting day.

Reaching across the small table, she placed her hand atop his and said, "Never mind. I think you'd better go ahead and order something to cool off. You seem a bit flushed." She tried not to smile, for she was certain that a woman was somehow involved. But which woman? Surely not Lula Mae Tucker!

While A.J. was taking his sister-in-law's advice, Ash was standing on the boardwalk in front of the ice-cream parlor, gazing at his wagon and scratching his head, wondering what it was doing in town. His brother hadn't mentioned coming into town for supplies today.

Glancing into the front window of Fletcher's, he was surprised to find his daughter, wife and brother seated at a table together. Surprised and annoyed. They were laughing and eating and having themselves a wonderful time, and his gut twisted at the charming picture they presented: they looked like a family. *His* family.

When he noticed that his wife's hand rested atop A.J.'s, that twist turned into a full-fledged flip-flop, and he stepped closer to the window to get a better view. Ash couldn't hear any of their conversation, but Sarah Jane was obviously amused about something; she was laughing, her lovely eyes twinkling, and that jackass of a brother of his was hanging on to her every word.

Pearls before swine, he thought uncharitably.

"Dammit!" he cursed, marching into the store, righteously indignant. "What the hell's going on here? Would somebody care to explain?" He stood with his arms folded across his chest, accusation glittering like hard diamonds as he stared down at them.

Raising her hand, Addy licked her lips and waved her hand. "I will. We're having ice cream. Do you want some, Daddy?"

He looked from his brother to his wife. "What's the meaning of this, Sarah Jane?"

Sarah Jane smiled at first, delighted to see him, then her eyebrows arched and she shook her head. "Meaning? I don't—"

Before she could finish, A.J. threw back his head

and laughed. "You're jealous! By God, I never thought to see the day, but you're jealous that I'm sitting here having a dish of ice cream with your pretty new wife." He slapped his palms down on the table and roared, making the dishes wobble and the other two customers in the room take notice of what was happening.

Sarah Jane said not a word. The possibilities were too intriguing. Ash jealous? Now that idea required contemplation.

Knocking the packages to the floor, Ash took a seat at the table. "Don't be a horse's ass, A.J. I'm not jealous. I'm just wondering why you're all here in town when there's work to be done at home. Sarah Jane should be in the kitchen preparing my dinner, instead of sitting here stuffing herself with sweets."

The blue eyes widened, then narrowed. "I beg your pardon. It was you who left the note that said I should buy Addy some new clothes. Or did you conveniently forget about that?"

He had the grace to look sheepish. "Oh, that. Well, just because I left you some money didn't mean you had to rush off and spend the whole day shopping and carrying on with my brother. People might talk."

"People are certain to talk, Ashby Morgan. But only because you are acting worse than the hind end of a mule."

Addy burst out laughing, and her father flashed a threatening glare in her direction.

"And for your information, A.J. and I are not 'carrying on,' as you put it," the annoyed woman continued. "He just arrived a few minutes before you did. Or maybe you thought he'd spent his day hiding in the dressing room at Mrs. Hodak's shop.'' Maybe he really was jealous, she thought.

''Now, Sarah Jane,'' A.J. warned, ''don't go giving my secrets away. You know how much I love those petticoats.''

Both Addy and Sarah Jane giggled at A.J.'s attempt at humor, though Ash found nothing funny about it. ''What's a man to think when he comes home early to surprise his bride after working hard all day and finds her gone?''

''You didn't seem all that interested in sharing my company last evening, Ash, if I remember correctly. So why the sudden change of heart?''

Eyes widening, A.J. leaned back in his chair, folding his hands over a board-flat stomach, a smug smile on his face. ''Has my brother been neglecting you, Sarah Jane? No wonder you prefer my company to his.''

''Uncle A.J. and Sarah Jane were hugging in the kitchen this morning, Daddy. I told them that you wouldn't like it none, because of how Uncle A.J. had been with that whore, and—''

A.J.'s grin suddenly vanished. ''Adelaide Morgan, will you kindly shut your mouth!''

''Well, you did. And she insulted Sarah Jane, Daddy.''

''What?'' Turning to stare at his wife, Ash waited for an explanation, looking none too pleased by the child's revelations. Either one of them.

Heaving a sigh, Sarah Jane decided that she was being paid back in kind for all the outrageous things she'd said as a child. Addy was surely God's penance.

"It was nothing. Just a little misunderstanding over whose husband you actually were."

"What the hell's that supposed to mean? Everyone knows I'm your husband. I've got the certificate to prove it. What kind of nonsense is this child spewing out?"

"Apparently your recent paramour still feels very proprietary about you. I believe she said that you had staying power, or something to that effect." Sarah Jane could only venture a guess as to the woman's meaning, and judging from her husband's crimson complexion, his prowess in bed wasn't something he liked being bandied about. She wasn't too thrilled by it, either, considering that she had no firsthand knowledge of said staying power and wasn't likely to, if Ash had anything to say about it.

"Addy, go outside and wait in the wagon," her father ordered. "This conversation is not for your ears."

"Oh, jeez! I always miss out on the good stuff."

"It sounds to me, young lady, that you've learned more about life than you should have at your young age," Sarah Jane pointed out. "Now please do as your father says."

"All right. I was done with my ice cream anyway."

As soon as the door slammed shut, Ash turned to his brother. "I think you should go outside as well, A.J. This conversation is between me and my wife."

"I don't mind if your brother stays." Sarah Jane smiled sweetly, watching her husband's gray eyes darken to pewter. "I have no secrets."

"Well, I do—*mind* that is. So beat it, A.J."

"But I'm not done with my ice cream," he said in mock protest, winking at his sister-in-law and making Ash's frown deepen.

"I'll have my wife bake a pie for you. It's no more than you deserve."

Sarah Jane gasped at the snipe directed at her lack of cooking ability and her cheeks filled with color. "How rude! I'm leaving with A.J. You can just sit here and be rude to your heart's content all by yourself."

"No, you're not!"

"Yes, I am!" Pushing back her chair, she stood. "I arrived with A.J. and I'm leaving with him." Retrieving her packages from the floor, she added, "I'm not some mindless creature you can push around, Ashby Morgan. You'd do well to remember that."

A.J.'s eyes widened at the exchange, and he was pleased by the furious look on Ash's face. Big brother had finally met his match.

Across the room, Maeve Stedmon clapped in enthusiastic approval, until her husband clasped her arm and admonished her to be quiet. He then smiled apologetically at Ash and said to his wife in hushed tones, "Are you trying to ruin me, Mrs. Stedmon?"

As one of the town's two undertakers, Morris Stedmon couldn't afford to lose anyone's business. Especially someone like Ash, who was involved in an extremely dangerous profession and had to face his mortality each and every day.

Coal mining was profitable business for an undertaker.

Choking back all the obscenities floating through

his head, Ash watched helplessly as his wife and brother exited the building.

The word *traitor* came to mind when he thought of how A.J. had taken Sarah Jane's side over his, but it was *hellion* that really got his goat when he finally realized that he had been thoroughly duped.

Sarah Jane Parker was about as sweet, docile and malleable a young woman as was the most stubborn, contrary mule in his stable. She was certainly nothing like what Miss Dorothea Cartwright had purported her to be, and he aimed to get to the bottom of things by writing to the Cartwright School of Finishing and Comportment.

But first, he intended to have a little talk with his wife.

Chapter Ten

Ash found Sarah Jane in the kitchen when he arrived home. There was a dead chicken lying on the table in front of her, courtesy of A.J., who'd killed it, and she was attempting to dress it for supper. Feathers were flying everywhere as she plucked, one landing on his head, one on his lower lip as he stepped into the room. He spit it out before saying, "What the hell are you doing, woman?"

Pausing at the sound of his voice, Sarah Jane didn't look up. "I think that should be perfectly obvious. I'm making dinner, just as you demanded."

He snorted. "That's debatable." Then he shook his head at the mess she was making. "If you'd scald the hen first, those feathers would come out a whole lot easier."

Glancing down at Amelia Simmons' *American Cookery* cookbook resting on the table beside her, she perused the page. "It doesn't say anything here about scalding."

He rolled his eyes in disbelief. "Well, of course, it doesn't say anything about it. Those folks who wrote the damn book figure you're smart enough to know that you don't cook a chicken before cleaning it thoroughly.''

Tears filled her eyes, but she blinked them back. She wouldn't give Ash the satisfaction of knowing that he'd hurt her feelings, something he'd made a habit of lately. ''I'm doing my best, so leave me alone. I don't want to talk to you. You're rude and arrogant and obnoxious and—''

He walked around the table and grabbed the chicken out of her hands, tossing it into the sink. ''You and I have some unfinished business to discuss, Mrs. Morgan.''

By the coolness of his tone, she could tell he was still angry about her behavior at the restaurant. Her temper getting the better of her again, she'd said some unfortunate things. But the arrogant man had deserved hearing every one, especially after accusing her of ''carrying on'' with his brother. ''I won't be bullied, Mr. Morgan,'' she said with more bravado than she felt, ''so you may as well say your piece and be done with it.''

''Not here. We'll go upstairs where we won't be disturbed.''

Her eyes widened. ''Well, that's a switch. *You* actually wanting to go upstairs with *me*. Usually, you can't wait to leave my presence.''

He scrubbed his hand over his face. ''That isn't true.'' But it was, and he knew it. And apparently she did, too.

Trying to keep temptation at bay, he'd purposely been avoiding her. Sarah Jane was a very tempting and desirable woman, he a very hungry man.

She turned to the sink, away from the passion that burned bright in his eyes and started plucking feathers again. "Yes, it is. I'll probably be the oldest living married virgin in these United States."

"What's a virgin, Daddy?" Addy asked, stepping into the room just then and making her father's cheeks crimson.

"A—" He groaned, then muttered invectives under his breath, and said, "Please leave the room, Addy. Sarah Jane and I are having a grown-up discussion, and it's not for your ears." There was no way he was going to explain virginity to an eleven-year-old inquisitive child. He'd rather have his eyelashes plucked out, one by one.

Her chin tilted stubbornly. "That's what you said before. But I'm hungry, and I promised Sarah Jane I'd help fix dinner. She's not very good at it, you know."

At the child's honesty, Sarah Jane bit back a smile and replied, "Thanks, sweetie. You can finish plucking these feathers out. I need to have a discussion with your father, then I'll come back and help you."

"Will you tell me what a virgin is when you get done fighting with Daddy?"

"Of course, I will. It's time you knew."

The girl's father stiffened. "You'll not be filling my daughter's head with such talk, Sarah Jane. Addy is just a child. I don't want her knowing—"

"Oh, be quiet, Ash! You're giving me a headache. If you want to discuss something, I'll be up in our room."

Addy couldn't contain her smile as she watched her

father, who was cursing a blue streak under his breath, follow Sarah Jane out the door and up the stairs.

The better she got to know her new stepmother the better she liked her. Maybe, like her daddy'd told her, it would be good having another female in the house. Addy didn't feel quite so outnumbered anymore, and Sarah Jane was real entertaining.

Standing in front of the fireplace, arms folded across her chest, Sarah Jane turned and faced her husband across the bedroom. The last remnants of sunshine darting through the window illuminated the harsh expression on his face as he stood by the door glaring at her.

Stiffening her spine, she said, "I thought you wanted me to make dinner. If that's true, why is it so important to have this conversation now?"

"You shouldn't be disrespectful of me in front of my daughter. You're not setting a very good example for her."

The audacity of the man! "And you do? Where do you think she learned all those curse words, and her proclivity to just blurt out whatever's on her mind?"

He opened his mouth to speak, but she cut him off. "If you want respect, Ash, you're going to have to learn to give it first."

Her husband began to pace, and she was reminded of a caged animal, wild and unpredictable, and knew a moment of apprehension. "I do respect you. That's the reason we haven't—you know. I thought you understood that."

"What I understand is that you don't want a wife, you want a housekeeper and baby-sitter. What I want to know is—what am I supposed to be getting out of this arrangement?'' A marriage certificate was simply not enough. She realized now that she wanted the fairy tale.

He heaved a sigh. ''Oh, all right. If making love is so damn important to you—''

Her eyes widened when he began to unbutton his shirt. The insolent, arrogant gesture made her blood boil. ''I wouldn't make love with you, Ashby Morgan, if you were the last man on the face of this earth! I realize now that I was wrong in thinking that such an act could bring us closer together. Obviously, we have nothing with which to build a relationship. Making love is not going to change that.''

''What?'' Incredulity had his mouth gaping open. ''Are you telling me that you're refusing to do your wifely duty by me?''

She nodded emphatically. ''That's what I'm telling you. And I think it would be better if you found yourself another bedroom to sleep in. I've decided that I don't want to share a bed with you any longer.''

''You don't want to share—'' His eyes almost bulged from their sockets. ''Well, that's just too damn bad! You're my wife. This is my bedroom. That's my bed,'' he added, pointing to the structure. ''And I'm staying.''

''I'm surprised you know it's your bed since you're hardly ever in it.''

''By hell, but you've got a smart mouth!'' His eyes narrowed. ''And that brings me to another question. Just how did Miss Dorothea Cartwright come to write such glowing comments about your supposedly docile personality? You're not docile at all. Quite the contrary. You, Sarah Jane, are a hellion.''

A knot of fear centered in the pit of her stomach and began to grow. If Ash pressed too closely, he was going to find out the truth and the extent of her lies; she couldn't allow that to happen. He might annul their marriage, send her back to Philadelphia, and she already cared too much to leave.

"I am usually a very agreeable and polite person," she tried to explain, "but you, Mr. Morgan, have brought out the worst in me." That was at least the truth.

"Really? So you're actually quite malleable, quite willing to accede to my wishes?"

"I—I was at one time. But I now find that impossible. You have treated me with callous disregard and ignored your marriage vows in an abominable manner. I refer specifically to your alliance with that woman of ill repute, who happens to know so much about your 'staying power,' while I have no knowledge at all, owing to the fact that you were never interested in *staying* with me."

"My uncle Zeke warned me about spinsters having serious personality defects because of not—well, you know."

Ash scratched his head. Had he really created this outspoken, sharp-tongued woman, just because he'd refused to bed her? It sure as hell seemed that way.

"I don't know what on earth you're talking about," Sarah Jane stated. "And I seriously doubt that your uncle does, either. He's a dear man, but he's not exactly an expert on the female state of mind. I fear all of you Morgan men have much to learn when it comes to women. The only semi-normal one in the whole bunch is your brother.''

A spurt of jealousy shot through Ash's gut like a cannonball. He stepped toward her, closing the distance between them. ''If you think A.J.'s normal, then you don't know him very well.'' He held out his hand. ''Come here. Let's kiss and make up.''

She was tempted. Oh, how she was tempted. But Sarah Jane held her ground. If she gave in now, allowed him to have his way with her, she would seal her fate as a woman who could be taken advantage of easily. ''I'm sorry, but it's just not that easy, Ash.''

''I'm trying to make amends,'' he said, plowing agitated fingers through his hair. ''I want to kiss you. You know how much you like it when I kiss you.''

''I admit to being naive, but I've already grown much wiser in the short time I've been here. If I allow you to kiss me now, to sweet-talk me, then you'll always think that you can treat me meanly and get away with it for the price of a kiss. I can't allow that. I'm sorry.''

Her answer wasn't what he expected, and frustration filled his voice, making his words harsher than he intended. ''I could strip you naked, throw you down on that bed and make love to you, and there'd be nothing you could do about it, Sarah Jane. You're my wife. I have rights.''

The image he created sent tremors of apprehension coursing through her. And something else totally confusing: excitement. ''I'm sure you could. You're much bigger and stronger than I am. But then, of course, I would hate you with every fiber of my being, and then what kind of a marriage would we have?

Plus, I don't think you're the kind of man who would force a woman. You have too much pride.''

She hadn't known him long, but she knew him well.

"Dammit, Sarah Jane!"

"And what of my rights, Ash? You ignored them completely, after promising to love and honor me."

"Let's start over. Let's wipe away these past few days and begin this marriage again.'' The words dripped slow and sweet like honey from his mouth. He could see now that he'd made a mistake by not consummating their marriage. Because, until he did, he and Sarah Jane had no marriage.

"That's a very nice suggestion, Ash," she said with a tinge of regret. "But it's just not practical. Too much has already been said and done. I'm afraid we can't just erase it all.''

"But—but you told me you wanted me. That you wanted to have sexual intercourse with me. You said that over and over again. I just don't understand." Damn contrary woman!

"I know you don't, husband. That's the problem with the male species—you never want what is freely given, only what's impossible to have."

"Are you saying that we're never going to consummate this marriage, Sarah Jane, because I can't agree to that?'' Hell, he was getting hard just thinking about making love to her. She was right. Now that he couldn't have what he wanted, he wanted it real bad.

"Of course not. But we're going to take our time, just as you originally suggested. I think it's important to get to know each other first—become friends, if you will. From there, we can take the next step, which is courting. Then allow our relationship to progress normally. Let nature take its course, so to speak.''

His nature had already taken course and graduated, Ash thought with disgust. ''You want me to woo you, is that it?'' Just like a woman, he thought. They were never happy until they enslaved their prey. It wasn't enough that you married them, gave them a home and took care of them. No! You had to worship at their feet.

''You're catching on. I've given this a lot of thought, and I've decided that it's the only way. A man needs to woo a woman before he beds her. That's what God intended. And that's what I'm requiring of you.''

''But I've already seen you naked! Most men who go courting don't know what their sweethearts' breasts taste and feel like.''

Her nipples hardened at the memory. ''That will only make it all the more exciting for us, won't it? We have a little knowledge. We know what awaits us around the next bend, if we can just get to that point.''

He shook his head, feeling a headache coming on. He never got headaches before marrying Sarah Jane. ''It's a stupid idea. You're my wife.''

''In name only,'' she reminded him, watching his face pale beneath tanned skin. ''If you want all of me, willing and wanting you so bad that it hurts—'' and it already did ''—then you're going to have to do it my way.''

He cursed loudly, the string of epithets making her cheeks color. ''A man has needs, Sarah Jane. You can't expect me to watch you walk around naked, lie next to you every night, and not touch you. That would be cruel.''

''And isn't that just what you've done to me since our wedding day, Ashby Morgan? And wasn't that the choice you made and insisted I live with?''

She didn't give him a chance to answer but headed for the door. Pausing, she looked back. ''Now, I insist you live with mine.''

''What the hell are you doing out here, boy? It's the middle of the night.'' Zeke sniffed the air like a bloodhound. ''And drinking alone, by the smell of it.'' A half-empty bottle of sour mash whiskey was propped on the porch rail beside Ash's foot.

He turned up the collar of his sheepskin coat against the cold, noting with disgust that Ash wore nothing but a wool shirt. The upcoming winter was sure to be a harsh one when it finally arrived, because autumn was proving to be colder than a witch's tit, Zeke thought.

''Why are you sitting out here on the porch freezing your ass off, instead of lying upstairs, all snug and warm in bed with your pretty wife?'' Not that he really wanted to know why Ash was behaving so foolishly. Zeke had just come from visiting Etta, and he was in no mood to console his nephew, who obviously had marital problems.

Zeke had problems of his own. Big problems. Etta was threatening to break off their relationship if he didn't marry her soon. Ever since Ash's wedding, Etta had been after him, like a tick out for blood. And even though he loved the widow like crazy, he didn't want to get married. Why couldn't the stubborn woman just leave well enough alone?

"Sarah doesn't want me in her bed. She's playing hard to get," Ash admitted, and the old man's brows lifted.

"Hell, you ain't been married long enough for her to be tired of you yet. What'd you do, boy? That little girl is sweet and smart. I surely hope you didn't do or say something to upset her. You know what a big mouth you got."

Ordinarily Ash would have taken exception to that, but he was just a little too drunk to care. And his wife had already done a thorough job of disparaging him, so it really didn't matter. "She wants me to woo her, Uncle Zeke. She wants me to act like some lovesick fool and come acourtin' all properlike."

Rubbing his whiskered chin, Zeke considered the man's dilemma. "Hmm. Seems a mite peculiar, seeing as how you and her are already married and have done the nasty, if you get my drift."

"We haven't done it...yet. That's the problem. And if you tell anyone, I swear I'll never speak to you again."

The old man clutched Ash's shoulder, and there was pity in his voice when he asked, "So she's like Wynona, huh? She don't want to have children?"

"Sarah Jane loves children." That was obvious from the way she had taken to Addy so quickly and had gotten the child to respond to her.

Children were a lot like animals. They could smell fear, and Sarah Jane didn't have a lick of it.

Clasping the sides of his head, he moaned, as if in

agony. "She wants me to open up a damn school for the boys at the mine!"

Perplexed, Zeke scratched his head. "Some women just don't like the physical side of a relationship, son. She's young. If you're patient with her, in time—"

"It's not that! I was the one who refused to bed her after we got married." His uncle's eyes widened at that. "I thought that if things didn't work out between us, it'd be better for both of us if we didn't consummate the marriage." And he knew it would be easier to get the marriage annulled if need be.

"So what's the problem? Just go on up there and tell her real sweetlike that you've changed your mind and can't live without making her yours. An impressionable young woman like Sarah Jane will eat that up like red licorice."

Ash snorted contemptuously. "I've already tried that. She told me to sleep in another room, but I refused. She ain't kicking me out of my own bedroom, by God!"

Lighting his pipe, the old man sucked on it a few times, the smoke curling over his head like a halo before dissipating into the cold night air. "Don't seem like you've got much choice. You either woo your wife or find another.

"Guess Sarah Jane ain't as malleable as we thought she'd be." But Zeke considered that a good thing. A woman should have a mind of her own, as long as she didn't speak it too often, and on subjects that were none of her business, like running a school for slate pickers and door boys.

Rising to his feet on unsteady legs, Ash began to pace. "And that's another thing. I reread those letters

Miss Cartwright sent. I can hardly believe that she was talking about the same woman who is now my wife.''

''People change.''

He shook his head. ''Not that much. Sarah Jane's trying to say that it's me, my rude behavior, that's made her so willful. I'm not buying that.''

''Why don't you just do what she wants? Women like to be romanced. And she is your wife. What harm can it do if you're wanting to make this marriage work?

''I've already seen a change in Addy. Sarah Jane's been good for her. Why, she took a bath tonight without even being asked. I consider that real progress.''

Ash reached for the whiskey bottle and took another swallow, wiping his mouth with the back of his hand, and wondering just how much he wanted to make his marriage work.

At first, he'd married Sarah Jane for the very selfish reasons she'd thrown at him: he needed a housekeeper, a mother for Addy, and Zeke hadn't given him an out, at any rate. But now that he'd been with her, kissed her, held her in his arms, he wanted more. But just how much more, he wasn't certain.

He hadn't known her long enough to be in love with her. But she was all he ever thought about from sunup to sundown: the way her pretty blue eyes twinkled when she was happy, how tiny lines formed between her brows when she concentrated on a task, the scent that lingered in a room whenever she stepped out of it. He figured all that had to count for something.

"I don't know anything about courting, Uncle Zeke. I never had to do it before."

"Women always came too easy for you, boy. Maybe it's time you had to work for one of them."

"Maybe I'll go have a talk with Etta," Ash suggested. "She might be able to give me a few pointers on what women like."

Horrified at the prospect, the old man's face grew florid and he held up his hands. "I wouldn't do that right now if I were you, boy. Etta and me had us a few words tonight. She may not be in a very agreeable mood." An understatement. The woman had blown like ten sticks of dynamite. It was a wonder he had a rear end left after the way she'd chewed it out.

Ash couldn't believe what he was hearing. "Here you are giving me advice on romancing a woman, and you've gone and made Etta mad at you? Some help you are, Uncle Zeke."

"Women are a tough lot to know, boy. Just 'cause Etta's older and been around don't mean she ain't just as contrary and stubborn as the next woman."

"What'd you two fight about anyway?"

"I'd rather not say." Zeke turned away from his nephew's curious gaze to look up at the black velvet sky studded with brilliant stars. An owl hooted mournfully; the wind whispered softly through the dying leaves remaining on the trees.

Soon winter would be upon them, the branches bare, the ground white with the first snowfall, and the thought of being alone didn't hold much appeal.

Ash thought he knew just what it was that had put a look of misery on the old man's face. "The widow's waiting for you to make good on your promise to marry her, ain't she?''

"I never promised. Not exactly. We've talked about it from time to time, but I never actually promised.''

"Etta's a fine woman. A damn good cook, too. No one can make chicken and dumplings like her. And you're not getting any younger, Uncle Zeke. A man as crabby and cantankerous as you ought not to be too picky. You're not exactly a prize, you know.''

"*Humph!* And you are? If you weren't so all-fired stubborn and mule headed, boy, you'd see that Sarah Jane's the best thing that ever happened to you. Okay, so she can't cook worth a hill of beans. So what? She can learn. And maybe she speaks her mind a bit too freely, but that's because she's young and has never been married before.

"That girl's got a good heart and a sweet disposition. And she cares for you, Ash. I can see it in her eyes every time she looks your way. You'd be a fool to toss that away. But then, being a fool comes easy to you.''

Ash watched his uncle storm into the house, listened while he slammed the door behind him, and he heaved a dispirited sigh.

Sarah Jane was right about one thing: Uncle Zeke didn't know about women. But then, neither did he.

Chapter Eleven

Seated before the blazing fire in her bedroom, brushing her long hair with strong, swift strokes, Sarah Jane paused at the soft knock sounding at the door.

Believing it was Ash, her stomach clenched in apprehension. She didn't think she could handle another confrontation with her husband right now. Their earlier one had been draining, leaving her exhausted, but determined, nevertheless, to stick by what she'd told him.

When the door opened and Addy stuck her head in, she breathed a sigh of relief. "Can I come visit for a while, Sarah Jane?" the child asked. "I can't fall asleep just yet."

Glancing at the ormolu clock on the mantel, the young woman frowned. "You should have been sound asleep for hours by now, sweetie. It's nearly ten, and we've got to be up early tomorrow." Georgie Ann was coming over to give Sarah Jane some much-needed cooking instruction.

"Please, just for a minute." Addy padded toward her stepmother on bare feet, a hopeful look on her face. "I could help brush your hair. You sure got pretty hair." She reached up to touch her own short mess and grimaced.

Feeling herself weaken, Sarah sighed. "All right. But only for a little while. Your daddy will be coming up soon." Ash was outside on the front porch, drinking and feeling sorry for himself. Well, let him, she thought. He didn't care how callously he'd treated her, and now that the shoe was on the other foot, maybe he'd learn a thing or two. Being courted properly was a very reasonable demand.

"He's outside talking to Uncle Zeke. I heard them from my bedroom window."

She was tempted to ask what about, but didn't. The child was too worldly for her own good as it was, and Sarah Jane didn't want to encourage Addy to eavesdrop on other people's conversations, though she'd made something of an art of it herself while in school. "Are you worried about something? Is that why you can't sleep?"

Gnawing her lower lip, the young girl reached for the hairbrush in Sarah Jane's hands and began to brush the long blond curls that shimmered in the firelight like spun satin. She regretted having hacked off her own long hair in a fit of pique.

"You said you was going tell me about what being a virgin was, but you didn't. And I can't hardly sleep for not knowing. You made it sound so very important."

Sarah Jane's flash of annoyance was quickly tempered by the child's look of curiosity. She knew from experience how children could get themselves in a heap of trouble when they were determined to get answers to burning questions, like how animals and people mated, which had nearly gotten her expelled from school.

Assuming a stern expression, so the child didn't think she was an easy mark, she said, "It's a good thing you're holding that hairbrush, sweetie, or else I'd be tempted to paddle your backside with it. I guess you're just as inquisitive a child as I was at your age."

How did one begin to explain the facts of life to a child? Sarah wondered, not knowing quite where to start. She finally decided that the only logical place to start was at the beginning. "A virgin is a woman who has not yet known the touch of a man in the biblical sense. She's pure and unsullied. Innocent in matters of the flesh."

Addy took a moment to digest the information. "So that means Lula Mae ain't no virgin, and neither is Georgie Ann, 'cause she's got a baby inside her, which means—"

Sarah Jane released a deep breath, grateful the child was so astute. Getting into lengthy explanations on the specifics of mating—not that she was qualified to do so—was something she was uneager to do. "That's exactly right."

"But how does a woman not become a virgin?"

Uh-oh! Here comes the tricky part. Reaching for the brush, she drew the child onto her lap and was somewhat surprised when Addy didn't resist being cuddled. They rocked back and forth in the old rocker as Sarah explained, "A woman's virginity is a prized possession. She only gives it to the man she loves."

"Like her husband?"

"That's right. When two people love each other and get married, they make love and the woman surrenders her virginity to the man as a token of her love. It's a very special gift and it shouldn't be given lightly." But it should be given at some point, she thought with disgust.

"Is that why you haven't given yours to my daddy? Are you saving it for someone else?"

Smiling ruefully, Sarah Jane combed fingers through the child's short mop of hair, which had grown and was starting to curl. "No, sweetie. It's just...well, your father and I didn't know each other when I arrived. We were virtual strangers, and so we've decided to wait until we get to know each other better and fall in love."

"But how do you know you will? How do you know you'll fall in love with him?"

"It's just something a woman feels in her heart. Someday when you're older, you're going to meet a young man and fall head over heels in love with him."

The child wrinkled her nose in disgust. "I seen the horses doing that mating stuff and I ain't never gonna let nobody do that to me. It's disgusting."

Sarah Jane bit back a smile. "I think you'll feel differently in a few more years, sweetie. Your body has already started changing, preparing you for womanhood. Soon your feelings will start to change, too. You'll meet a wonderful man and feel tongue-tied and breathless in his presence. You'll want to kiss him so badly you think you'll faint if you don't."

"Gosh! Did you feel that way when you first met my daddy?"

She wanted to be totally honest with the child. If there was going to be trust between them, then there had to be honesty. Unfortunately, fear kept Sarah Jane from applying that same belief to her husband.

"Yes, I did. I felt I was standing on a rug and some practical joker pulled it right out from under me."

She'd fallen hard. Love at first sight wasn't just a myth or something the poets wrote about. It was real. And she was living proof.

She had fallen in love with Ashby Morgan.

"Gosh! That's terrible."

"Yes, in a way it is. When you love someone, you pour your whole heart and soul into it. You put yourself on the line, wishing and hoping that he might love you back. And if he does, then you get married and have babies and live happily ever after."

"Like in the Cinderella story you read to me tonight?"

"Exactly. Cinderella finally met her Prince Charming and lived happily ever after."

"Her stepmama and sisters were mean." Addy pulled a face. "I didn't like them. I'm glad she got to go live with the prince."

Pleased with the child's enthusiasm for the books she was reading, Sarah said, "Now when your friends come over to visit, Addy, you can entertain them with the story of Cinderella."

Easing out of her embrace, the little girl looked suddenly uncomfortable. "You might as well know, Sarah Jane, that I don't have many friends. The girls all make fun of me, and the boys do, too. Especially Gordy Peters, the grocer's son. I had to blacken his eye the last time he came over to visit."

Though she knew she'd be sorry for asking why, Sarah Jane couldn't allow Addy to beat up on the other children, especially the males. Though if Gordy Peters was only half as obtuse and unfeeling as Ash, she could certainly understand Addy's need for violence. "What did Gordy do to receive such harsh treatment?"

The little girl hemmed and hawed, toying with the edge of her newly purchased pink nightgown. "He told me I was pretty. I knew it was a joke, 'cause I'm not. So I hauled off and punched him right in the eye, told him never to say such a thing again."

Wanting to smile but unwilling to let the child think she was making light of her feelings, Sarah Jane replied, "I think Gordy's right. You're a very pretty young woman. I noticed that the moment we met."

Addy screwed up her face in disgust. "Am not! My hair's ugly, and before you came, I wore funny men's clothes, 'cause nobody cared what I did or didn't do."

"I'm sure that's not true, sweetie. Your father loves you very much. Otherwise, he wouldn't have married again." By her confused expression, it was obvious Addy hadn't considered that possibility.

"Daddy said he was never gonna get married again, so you may be right. I couldn't figure out why he wanted to, except that he liked big bosoms—" Sarah Jane blushed "—but I guess he didn't know how to be both a mommy and a daddy. And he works a lot down at the mine. He's very important, you know."

There was such love and pride in the child's voice when she spoke of her father that it made Sarah Jane want to cry. She wondered if he knew the depth of his daughter's affection.

Fathers rarely did.

"I know it wasn't easy for you to accept a stranger into your home, Addy, and I'm glad we're becoming friends. At least, I hope you think of me that way."

Addy studied her toes, wiggling them in the colorful hooked rug that graced the floor. When she finally looked up, there were tears glistening in her eyes. "I'm sorry I called you a whore, Sarah Jane. I didn't mean it. You're not as bad as I thought you were gonna be. And I like the pretty hat you bought me."

High praise coming from Addy, Sarah thought, holding out her arms and wrapping them around the child and hugging her to her breast. "I'm always going to be here for you, sweetie," she said in a voice thick with emotion, "so if you ever have a problem, or need to talk, like you did tonight, you just come and tell me, okay?"

"Okay."

"Now, I think it's time you get to bed before your daddy catches you in here and gives us both grief over it."

Having overheard much of their conversation, Ash stepped back from the door, a thoughtful expression on his face as he made his way back down the stairs as quietly as he could.

Addy's words had touched him deeply. He loved her so much that it hurt. But it was obvious from the pain he'd heard in her voice when she'd tried to express her own inadequacies that he'd let his child down miserably, and for that he felt terribly sorry, not to mention guilty as hell.

He hadn't realized how, by allowing her the freedom to grow up wild and untutored, he had been hurting her even more. A child, like a puppy or kitten, needed to know boundaries, needed acceptance and discipline, and he'd been neglectful in providing it.

Uncle Zeke had been correct: he hadn't done right by his only daughter.

Sarah Jane's tender discussion with Addy about love and marriage had really knocked him for a loop. She'd known just the right things to say to the child and, in doing so, had revealed more of herself than she'd probably intended.

Ash didn't know that Sarah Jane had developed tender feelings for him. That she loved him! They hadn't known each other that long, and he'd just assumed by her eagerness to consummate their union that she was a curious woman bent on a little experimentation. This new insight into her feelings gave him a lot to think about.

Ash was starting to sober up by the time he reached the first floor. Heading directly into the parlor in search of the fairy-tale book his daughter had mentioned, he figured it couldn't hurt to find out a little more about that Prince Charming fella the women were so agog over.

''Happily ever after,'' Sarah Jane had said.

Was it possible? he wondered.

Beulah burst into her daughter's bedroom just as the young woman was readying herself for bed. She had that excited gossip-hungry look on her face that Cynthia knew only too well. And had come to dread.

"You'll never guess what I heard today, dear. And from Maeve Stedmon, of all people."

The young woman heaved a sigh and set down the book she was about to start reading. Jane Austen was proving to be one of her favorite authors, and she wished she had someone like Austen's matchmaking heroine Emma to find her a husband.

But definitely not her mother!

"I'm not really interested, Mama. I'm reading, so—"

Ignoring her objection completely, her mother plopped down on the end of the tester bed, much to her daughter's dismay. "Maeve was in the ice-cream parlor today and overheard Ashby Morgan and his new wife arguing." She clapped her hands and beamed, her cheeks glowing pink. "Isn't that wonderful, dear? I just knew that his marriage to that woman from Philadelphia wasn't going to work out. And when he gets his divorce—"

"Mama! Stop it! I've told you many times before that I'm not interested in marrying Ashby Morgan. We're not at all suited for each other. And I wish you would quit interfering in my life this way. It isn't good for either one of us."

A hurt expression crossed Beulah's face. "I'm only trying to help, child. You're almost twenty-three years old and still unmarried. A spinster, by all accounts. Your prospects of finding a husband at your age are next to nonexistent. So what if you and Mr. Morgan aren't madly in love with each other when you marry? Few people are. Your father—God rest his soul—and

I were quite happy, although I wouldn't have called ours a grand passion by any stretch of the imagination. Still and all, we were comfortable with each other.''

Cynthia didn't want to be merely ''comfortable'' with the man she married. She wanted to feel passion—heart-pounding, blood-boiling passion. And she intended to settle for no less, despite her mother's assurances to the contrary.

She reached for her mother's hand, which was relatively free from age lines, due to Beulah's propensity for using hand cream and wearing gloves to bed every night. ''Mama, newly married people tend to argue over insignificant things,'' she said in as patient a voice as she could muster. ''You shouldn't put such stock in what other people tell you and jump to conclusions.''

''Oh, this wasn't insignificant, Cynthia dear. Not by any stretch of the imagination. Mr. Morgan practically accused his new wife of improper behavior with his brother, no less. Maeve said he was furious, and that his wife set him down good and proper, despite her young age.''

At the mention of A.J.'s possible involvement, a spark of jealously ignited in the young woman's breast, but disappeared just as quickly. She would never believe A.J. capable of such behavior. ''I don't see A.J. Morgan as the type of man who would covet another man's wife, let alone his brother's. He's a very decent man.''

''I realize he came calling, Cynthia, and he may have designs on you for a wife, but he isn't nearly the catch his brother is. Why, it's Ashby Morgan who owns the mine and lives in that fine stone house, which he built with his bare hands, I might add.''

''No one is disputing the fact that Ash is a good catch, Mama. Or was. May I remind you that he's married now, and it's Sarah Jane who's gotten herself a wonderful husband. And though he may be an up-standing individual, that doesn't mean to say that A.J. Morgan isn't just as fine a man, and wouldn't make just as wonderful a husband.''

Unwilling to concede her daughter's viewpoint, no matter how sound the argument, Beulah rose to her feet and glared disapprovingly, shaking her head in disbelief. ''Just because a man's got a winning smile and glib tongue doesn't mean that he'll make a good husband. A good husband should be measured by what he can provide for a wife. Creature comforts and monetary things matter. And the younger Mr. Morgan is still living at the largesse of his brother. He'll never amount to much. Mark my words.''

Cynthia's green eyes filled with fire, and she came to A.J.'s defense. ''That's unfair, Mama! A.J. works hard at the mine. I'm sure that fine stone house you speak of is looked upon by Ash as the family home-stead to be used by all the members of the Morgan family. And I don't doubt for a minute that A.J. and his uncle helped build it.''

''Humph! Ezekial Morgan is a lazy cuss, and I wouldn't believe anything good about him, even if it came directly from Reverend Pickett's own mouth.''

''I know you used to be sweet on old Mr. Morgan when you were a young woman, Mama—Papa told me as much—so don't try to act indifferently about him now.''

Beulah's lips thinned. "That man toyed with my affections, then when it came time to propose, he up and left me to become the laughingstock of this community. I suffered cruelly, and I will never forgive him for it. Never!"

Surprised by her mother's admission, Cynthia felt sorry for her. It was obvious that at one time she had cared deeply for Mr. Morgan, which was rather surprising, considering that the woman valued material things highly, and Zeke Morgan had never had two nickels to rub together, as the saying went.

"Well, you met Papa and married him, so it all turned out for the best, didn't it?"

Beulah had never felt the love for Samuel Rafferty that she'd felt for Ezekial Morgan, and she'd hate the miner to her dying breath for that. The man was an out-and-out cad!

Taking a calming breath, she finally said, "I suppose you must be right, dear." When she reached the door, she turned to look back and there was a haunted look in her eyes. "Will you be seeing A.J. Morgan again?"

"If he calls." And that was a big *if* considering her mother's recent behavior. "I like him very much.

"And I would be most grateful to you, Mama, if you'd avoid the topic of matrimony in the future if Mr. Morgan comes to call. I wouldn't want to scare him off, like you scared off Frank Jensen."

"Humph! A man that can be scared off that easily is not worth having in the first place. Besides, Frank has a fondness for beer and will no doubt come to a bad end one of these days."

Cynthia hoped A.J. hadn't been frightened off by

her mother's outrageous comments. She desperately wanted to see him again. But after the way she'd behaved, courting her was probably the last thing on his mind. And then there was also the matter of having Beulah Rafferty for a mother-in-law.

Correction: Courting was probably *not* on A.J. Morgan's mind at all.

"There's no need to beat the hell outta the dough, Sarah Jane," Georgie Ann said, shaking her head and making Addy laugh and her stepmother grimace. "We're making pies, not conducting a war. Here, let me show you again."

Sarah Jane stepped back from the table, wiping her floured hands on her apron and feeling totally inept. "I'm never going to get the hang of making pies. Even Addy's pie dough looks better than mine, and she's only a child."

Winking at the smug-looking child, Georgie Ann said, "Cooking's not one of them things a body's born knowing. You got to learn, just like you had to learn how to read all them fancy books you're so fond of, Sarah Jane."

Staring down at the lump of dough that resembled hard clay, the young woman heaved a sigh of defeat. "I'm hopeless. Maybe we should move on to the next lesson?" she asked hopefully, but Georgie Ann, who was bound and determined to teach her friend how to cook, wasn't buying it.

"No one said that this was going to be easy. God only knows how many pies I ruined before I managed to make one that was edible."

"Really?" Sarah Jane's blue eyes widened. "Even an accomplished cook like you had some disasters?"

"Mama used to say that I could send a man to his grave just as easily with a piece of my pie as I could with a bullet." Georgie Ann grinned at the memory, then all three of them laughed.

"I guess I don't feel quite so stupid now."

"Hope you can teach Sarah Jane to fix something decent for supper," Addy said. "The chicken she fixed last evening was raw on the inside and burned on the outside, and Uncle Zeke got a feather stuck between his teeth. Said he was gonna use it as a toothpick."

At the memory of her husband's horrified expression when he'd bit into the bloody bird, Sarah Jane grimaced. She'd been so mortified that all she'd wanted to do was slide under the table and disappear from sight. To Ash's credit, he'd said relatively little about the food, preferring instead to gag in silence.

"After we're done with the piecrust, we're going to make something really simple for supper tonight," the pregnant woman informed them.

"It better not be stew," the child warned, rolling her eyes and pretending to choke by sticking a finger in her mouth.

"Adelaide Morgan, you stop that!" Sarah Jane smiled ruefully. "I guess it was pretty putrid."

"Daddy took it out to feed to the pigs, and even they wouldn't eat it."

"Well, heavens!" Georgie Ann's eyes grew wide. "I do have my work cut out for me, don't I?"

Several hours later, two reasonably attractive apple pies graced the center of the kitchen table, while a pot roast, which smelled surprisingly delicious, considering Sarah Jane had had a hand in its preparation, simmered slowly on the stove.

Exhausted, but feeling as if she'd accomplished something important today, Sarah Jane smiled proudly at her cooking instructor seated across the table from her, while sipping a cup of hot chamomile tea, which Georgie Ann promised would restore her.

"Thank you so much for being patient with us today, Georgie Ann. I don't know how I can ever repay you for your many kindnesses."

The woman shrugged, patting her stomach. "Just invite me and Robby over for dinner some evening so I don't have to cook. Hauling this child around wears a body down." Even with her grousing about the baby, Georgie Ann looked contented, which made Sarah Jane wonder again what it would be like to carry Ash's child beneath her breast.

"I will. I promise. But I need to practice a bit more. I hate to say it, but Addy's pie looks much nicer than mine." She could admit it though, because Addy was upstairs doing her lessons and wouldn't be able to tease her, which, Sarah Jane had discovered, was one of the child's favorite things to do.

Georgie Ann covered the young woman's hand with her own and squeezed. "There's nothing easy about being a wife and mother, Sarah Jane. I used to take everything my mama did for granted. But after I got married and had a house of my own, I realized just how much work she had to do to make our home so comfortable.

"It wasn't much more than a shack—miner's accommodations rarely are—but it always seemed so much more, because Mama had pretty curtains at the windows and a tablecloth and flowers on the table.

"It's a heap of work, but in the end it'll be worth it, you'll see. And don't forget that old saying about the way to a man's heart is through his stomach." She winked.

"Maybe that's what's wrong," Sarah Jane said, not realizing she'd spoken her thoughts aloud.

"You and Ash having trouble already, Sarah Jane? I'm sorry to hear that."

Realizing she'd already said too much, Sarah Jane shook her head. "It's nothing that knowing each other a bit better won't cure. You know how difficult it is to adjust at first."

"Well, of course I do. Me and Robby had some whoppers of arguments when we was first married. It takes a while to realize that those little things that annoy you at first really aren't so very important. And that making up in bed is a whole lot of fun."

Unwilling to touch that subject, Sarah Jane quickly changed the topic. "Did you get Etta's invitation to our wedding reception? It was so sweet of her to plan a party for Ash and I."

"Saturday night can't come soon enough for me," Georgie Ann admitted, taking another sip of tea. "I just love a party. And once the baby's born, I won't be able to get out as much. And as you well know, I just love socializing."

Sarah Jane hadn't danced in so long that she wondered if she'd remember how. Learning the proper dances had been a high-priority item with Miss Cartwright, who fancied herself somewhat of an expert.

And she had no idea if her husband knew how. "Do you know if Ash likes to dance?" she asked, and was relieved when the young woman nodded.

"All the Morgan men know. Ash's mother made sure they learned. Like you, she was from the East and felt that the niceties were important."

A glimmer of amusement entered Georgie Ann's eyes. "All the Morgan men like to have a good time, too. At last year's Halloween party, Ash, A.J. and their uncle got drunk as skunks after Zeke spiked the punch with whiskey. They nearly set the place on fire when the old man toppled over a hay bale and landed on a lighted pumpkin decoration. Scorched his bottom right proper, Zeke did. Etta wouldn't speak to him for almost two weeks."

Sarah Jane's eyes rounded, and she covered her mouth. "My goodness! Well, I hope there won't be a repeat of that at my wedding reception. I don't want it turning into a drunken brawl."

"Don't worry. Etta laid down the law, and they've been on their best behavior since. Besides, Zeke's already on the Widow Dobbin's bad side, and he won't do anything to rile her further."

"Oh?" Sarah Jane was sorry to hear that. She thought Zeke and Etta made an adorable couple. "Did they have a falling out? I hadn't heard." Besides Georgie Ann, Mrs. Price, Georgie's mother, and Mrs. Hodak the dressmaker, Sarah Jane hadn't conversed with any of the ladies in the area. She'd been too busy trying to figure out how to be a wife and mother, and hadn't had much time for socializing.

"Just the same argument they've been having for

years. Etta wants Zeke to marry her, and he keeps putting her off.

"Ash is the only Morgan man who's been inclined to marry. In fact, that's how he earned the nickname 'the marrying man.'"

"Really?" Sarah Jane didn't find that at all complimentary. If you had to be known for something, it shouldn't be multiple marriages, in her opinion.

"Well, it has been three times and all," Georgie Ann pointed out. "And we may have another wedding soon. I hear A.J. is thinking of asking Cynthia Rafferty to dance at your reception." Her brows lifted at the significance.

So that's who the woman was who'd made A.J. tongue-tied that day at the ice-cream parlor, Sarah Jane thought. "Cynthia seems nice enough, though I thought when I first met her that she had designs on Ash."

Georgie's disgust was apparent. "That's her busybody mama's doing. Beulah would have loved nothing better than for Cynthia and Ash to have married, but they've never been interested in each other like that. Not that their feelings mattered to the old hen. She wants her daughter married off, though I'm not sure it's A.J. she has in mind. Beulah likes money, and A.J. ain't exactly a rich man."

"I am quite astonished by the volume of knowledge you have at your fingertips, Georgie Ann. Where on earth do you learn all of this information?" The woman was a virtual encyclopedia of facts.

Rubbing her protruding belly, the young woman smiled. "There ain't a whole lot of entertainment in Morgantown, so folks around here tend to make their own. Gossiping is just a way of life here in the mountains. I guess some might not think it's too Christian a thing to do, but it sure as heck's provided some interesting conversation.''

Though Sarah Jane smiled and agreed, she was worried that her marital problems with Ash were going to become fodder for the gossip mill. If anyone found out that she and Ash had not yet consummated their union, they'd be the laughingstock of the community.

Horrified at the prospect, Sarah Jane suddenly dreaded the upcoming reception.

Chapter Twelve

Twirling around the dance floor in the arms of her husband, Sarah Jane felt like Cinderella at the ball. She was dressed in her nicest gown, which she'd brought with her from Pennsylvania. The soft blue wool trimmed with white lace collar and cuffs showed off her figure, making her feel pretty and confident, even though she was still a tad nervous about tonight's public gathering.

So far, she hadn't heard one bit of gossip about her and Ash's marriage, nor had Georgie Ann, because she knew her loyal friend would tell her immediately if she heard even the smallest tidbit. She was starting to relax and enjoy the attentions of her husband.

Upon leaving for the reception, being held in Etta Dobbin's vacant barn, which had been cleaned thoroughly and decorated with ribbons and flowers, Ash had presented her with a large bouquet of yellow chrysanthemums and told her how beautiful she looked with her blond hair loose and curling over her shoulders. *"Good enough to eat,"* he had said, and she'd been touched by his words and gesture.

In the days preceding the party, he'd made other considerate gestures and attempts at courting. One morning she awoke to find a small bouquet of flowers on her pillow, and the other evening he'd drawn her bath and there'd been a pot of hot chocolate and scones left beside the tub. She sighed at the memories, deciding she could get used to this courting ritual.

Smiling up at her husband, who flashed her a heart-stopping grin, Sarah Jane wondered if every other woman in the room was jealous that she'd married the handsomest man in Morgantown. She felt extremely lucky, even with all the problems they'd had of late—problems she hoped were behind them now that they had a new understanding.

"You look like the cat who's just swallowed the canary. Do I dare ask what you might be thinking?"

"I'm thinking what a good dancer you are, Mr. Morgan, and how very handsome you look tonight in that suit of black superfine. I'm sure I must be the envy of every woman here."

He warmed under her praise. "No doubt I'm the envied one. I've seen how all the men look at you, no doubt wishing you were theirs." And he intended to beat the stuffing out of anyone who so much as made a move in her direction. Sarah Jane was his, and he felt damn lucky for it. Even if she did drive him to distraction most of the time.

Sarah Jane gasped and Ash, turning to follow her gaze, found Beulah Rafferty heading in their direction. The woman had a determined look in her eyes that spelled trouble.

"Oh, no! It's Mrs. Rafferty and she's heading right for us. Quick! Kiss me, Ash. I heard she's been saying rude things about our marriage, implying that we're not getting along.''

Ash grinned, grateful once for Beulah Rafferty's penchant to gossip. ''My pleasure.'' Without hesitation, he molded his lips over hers, pulling her tight against his chest. Cocking one eye open, he was pleased to see that the older woman's determined expression was now one of shock at their public display of affection. Then, because he couldn't resist, he thrust his tongue into his wife's mouth and began to taste the honey within, only pulling back when he heard her soft moan.

''Ashby Morgan!'' Sarah Jane said when she could breathe again. ''You shouldn't have kissed me like that in public.''

''You shouldn't have asked me to kiss you then. You know I can't stop with just a chaste peck on the cheek.''

Breathless and red faced, because everyone in the room was laughing and clapping enthusiastically, she bit the inside of her cheek, trying to get her heart to stop pounding so loudly. She was sure everyone could hear it.

''Well, Mr. and Mrs. Morgan,'' Beulah said, sidling up next to them when the music stopped, a sour look on her face. ''How nice to see that the rumors I heard about your marriage aren't true.''

The miner's lips thinned. ''I just bet you were crushed,'' he said.

Sarah Jane nudged him in the side as unobtrusively as possible, and replied, ''You know how *some* people like to gossip, Mrs. Rafferty. I've always subscribed to the theory that a person should believe half of what she sees and none of what she hears. Gossip can be a very destructive force, don't you agree?''

''Where there's smoke there's usually fire, my dear,'' Beulah answered, looking not the least bit apologetic, which rankled Sarah Jane to no end.

In an acid-laced voice, she retorted, ''The only fire you're bound to find here, Mrs. Rafferty, is the one smoldering between me and my husband. And those are private matters better off not discussed.

''Right, darling?'' She smiled up at Ash, whose eyes had widened, and who'd been rendered momentarily mute.

''Well, my goodness! That's certainly a blunt way of putting it, Mrs. Morgan. Folks around here don't usually speak so bluntly.''

''Folks around here don't usually speak so honestly,'' Ash corrected with a smile, squeezing his wife's waist, proud that she had stood up to the old biddy. ''I've found my wife to be a very honest and forthright person. I can't wait to get her back home and—''

The older woman gasped, covering her ears, and hurried off to share the latest shocking revelation with her cronies—the Morgantown blabbermouths—as Ash referred to them. His grin filled with satisfaction. ''Never knew the woman to be at a loss for words before.''

''Well, that should give her something to talk about, at any rate,'' Sarah Jane said, frowning as she watched the woman cross the room and stop before three of her closest compatriots. Her mouth appeared to be moving at record speed. She suddenly felt great sympathy for Cynthia Rafferty.

How horrid to have a mother who thrived on the misery of others. Beulah Rafferty must be a very unhappy and lonely woman, she concluded.

"Thank you for defending me and our marriage, Ash. You were very gallant, indeed." And she loved him even more for it, if that were possible.

"A man in courting mode has to be gallant," he said with a wink. "Now, how about we go and see if the punch bowl's spiked? I can use a little refreshment—something to take the bad taste of Beulah Rafferty out of my mouth—and I'm counting on Uncle Zeke to provide it."

"But I'm not used to drinking spirits." Though the thought of imbibing something heretofore forbidden had her curiosity piqued.

Ash's eyes twinkled with mischief. "Really? I didn't know. But a little bit won't hurt. After all, we are celebrating our marriage."

"All right. I guess one drink can't hurt."

But her husband's erotic smile said just the opposite.

Across the room, A.J. was sipping his punch and getting up his nerve to dance. Cynthia had been watching the man studying the other people on the dance floor for over thirty minutes, and she decided that if she was ever going to make any progress with him, she was going to have to take the initiative. And dancing with him was as good a way as any to start.

"Are you enjoying the party?" she asked, stepping in front of the handsome man and blocking his view. His sharp intake of breath made her smile inwardly, for she realized that he wasn't immune to her.

Cynthia's rosewater scent taunted and teased as it

circled A.J.; her enticing smile served to render him tongue-tied momentarily. She was wearing a lovely green taffeta dress that shimmered like sparkling emeralds and contrasted wonderfully with her red hair, which had been swept up regally in a braided crown. "You look beautiful!"

"Then why haven't you asked me to dance? I've been waiting for quite a long time, but you don't seem to be able to leave this punch bowl. May I have a glass, or aren't you sharing?"

"I'm sorry." Embarrassed by his lack of manners, he filled a glass and handed it to her. "You'd best be careful. It's been spiked."

"Really?" Her eyes twinkled. "Then I shall have to be very careful, indeed. I wouldn't want to drink too much and lose all of my inhibitions, now would I? Especially with such a handsome man around who might take advantage of my helplessness."

"I wouldn't. I'm a gentleman." Though he'd like nothing better than to kiss the bold woman senseless. She was asking for something. He just wasn't sure what. But he was more determined than ever to find out and give it to her.

She peered up at him beneath lowered lashes, and said, "Well, that's disheartening to hear," then moved toward the rear door of the barn. As she had hoped, he followed her out the door and into the cold night air.

It was pitch-black outside, the air holding the promise of winter, the stars blanketing the heaven with their utter brilliance. A glorious night for lovers, she thought brazenly.

They stopped when they reached the area behind

the barn, and A.J. clasped Cynthia's hand, spinning her about to face him. "You ought not to be saying such things, Cynthia. Some men might not understand that you're teasing. They might try to take advantage of your naiveté."

She rubbed her finger over his rough knuckles and heard his sharp intake of breath. "And if I'm not teasing?" Her fine brow arched. "What then?" She was being far bolder than she should, but she had little to lose at this point, except her virginity, which wouldn't be all that horrific in her opinion. Spinsterhood wasn't all it was cracked up to be.

"Then you're going to get kissed, often and well."

Her heart started drumming. "And if I protest?"

"You won't, because it's going to be me that's doing the kissing." Drawing her to his chest, he lowered his head and placed his lips over hers.

Cynthia didn't protest.

"Hi ya, Addy."

Addy spun on her heel to find Gordy Peters stepping up behind her, and though she was secretly thrilled, she forced a bored look to her face. She'd had a crush on Gordy for weeks, ever since he'd said she was pretty and she'd punched him in the face. But she didn't want him to know that.

"Hi, Gordy. I see your eye's all healed." It was still a little purple around the edges.

He touched it with his forefinger and looked apprehensive all of a sudden. "I was going to tell you how pretty you looked this evening, Addy, but I don't want you hauling off and socking me in the eye again, so I'm not saying nothing."

The young woman grinned, pleased by the almost compliment. "Sarah Jane—that's my new step-mama—says I shouldn't have hit you, so I guess I should say I'm sorry. I guess you was just trying to be nice, and I took it the wrong way."

Gordy breathed a sigh of relief and shoved his hands into his pockets, rocking back on his heels. "I see your hair's growing out. I like it all curly like that."

Addy's palms started to sweat, and she chided herself for her nervousness. *This is just Gordy Peters, the grocer's son, for heaven's sake!* she told herself. "I like it short," she lied. "It's much easier to take care of when I'm climbing trees."

"Maybe I could come over after church tomorrow and climb that big apple tree with you."

"Maybe. But won't the other kids make fun of you? I mean, most of them don't like me."

He shook his head, and she noticed how his sandy brown hair had been slicked down with pomade; it smelled rather nice, not at all sissylike as she would have thought. "That's not true! There're a few girls who think you're a bit strange, 'cause of the way you used to dress, and because they're probably jealous, but most of the guys think you're okay. I know I do."

Thump. Thump. Thump. Addy's heart started pounding in her chest. Her tummy felt all queasy and she wondered if she'd eaten too much cake. The Widow Dobbins made the best cakes of anyone.

"Thanks. I guess you can come over, if my step-mama says it's okay. Would you like to meet Sarah Jane? She's over there talking with Mrs. Dobbins and Uncle Zeke." She pointed across the room, where the small group of people stood in conversation by the makeshift bandstand.

Doyle Trotter and his brother, Drummond, had taken a break from their guitar and fiddle playing; their instruments rested alongside their now empty stools.

Gordy shrugged, trying not to appear too eager. Addy wasn't the kind of girl who liked a boy to slobber all over her. She sure as heck didn't like compliments. "Okay, I guess."

They wound their way through the throng of revelers, and when they reached Addy's stepmother, she tugged on Sarah Jane's dress. "Hey, Sarah Jane. This is Gordy Peters. Remember, he's the one I told you about—the one I punched in the eye?"

Sarah Jane's eyes widened at the sight of her usually boy-shy stepdaughter with the Peters boy. Actually, any boy would have made her eyes widen in surprise. She put out her hand and smiled at the short, freckle-faced young man who appeared to be about the same age as Addy. He was quite adorable, and had certainly put roses in Addy's cheeks.

"Hello, Gordy. It's nice to meet you."

His mouth agape, Gordy Peters stared as if in a trance, then said, "You're sure pretty, Mrs. Morgan! I ain't never seen anyone as pretty as you before."

"Why thank you," she replied, oblivious to Addy's jealous reaction.

With a loud harrumph, and a disgusted look at her companion, the young girl spun on her heel and disappeared into the crowd.

Gordy stared after her, a confused expression on

his face, then ran off after her, and yelled, "Wait up, Addy! I didn't mean that you weren't pretty, too."

Zeke laughed. "Get used to it, boy," he said. "That's what it's like being around women." Then with a weary look at his own companion, he headed off toward the spiked punch bowl.

A man couldn't be expected to get all duded up and dance all night without the benefit of a little libation, in Zeke's opinion. And when you courted a contrary woman like the widow, you needed fortification. Etta was hard on a man's ego.

"I take it you and Zeke are having a few problems, Etta," Sarah Jane said to the older woman, who heaved a frustrated sigh and nodded.

"I'm wanting him to marry me, but the old fool doesn't want to, even though he says he loves me."

"I see. Well, if there's one thing I've learned since coming here, it's that Morgan men are not only foolish, they're stubborn. It must be something in their blood."

"Amen to that. Me and Zeke have been keeping company longer than I care to remember, and I'm tired of him cozying up to me when he wants—" her round cheeks blossomed with color "—well, you know, then hightailing it home afterward as fast as his short legs'll carry him. I don't like feeling like some kept woman. I'd get a job over at O'Connor's, if I was wanting that kind of life."

She lifted her head proudly. "I may not be much to look at these days, but I've got a lot to offer that man, and it just galls me that he doesn't realize it. The old reprobate!"

Sarah Jane thought Etta had the prettiest brown

eyes and softest smile. Her plump cheeks were always rosy, and she smelled like vanilla and cinnamon and the cookies she was so fond of baking. "I'm sure he'll come around now that Ash is married and A.J. seems bent on pursuing Cynthia Rafferty. Zeke doesn't strike me as the kind of man who wants to live out the remainder of his life alone."

"I surely do hope you're right, Sarah Jane, 'cause I ain't getting any younger, and my patience has about run out where that man's concerned."

Why did all the Morgan men have to be so obtuse and difficult? she wondered, hating to see the kind woman so miserable. "Perhaps I could speak to him."

"Oh, would you?" The widow's crestfallen face lit with renewed hope. "That would be wonderful. Zeke always speaks so highly of you. I know he'd be inclined to listen. I mean, the man's fond of lecturing everyone around him, so getting talked to in turn shouldn't be objectionable, right?"

Though Sarah Jane agreed, she couldn't help but wonder if she was stepping into something she shouldn't.

Oh well, she decided, it wouldn't be the first time. After all, that's how she'd gotten married.

"You're drunk!" Ash's eyes widened when his wife removed the shawl from around her shoulders and gleefully tossed it over his head as she made her way into the house.

"Am not!" she protested, hiccuping loudly. "And it's rude of you to say so. I only had four little itty-bitty cups of punch.'' She wiggled two fingers in front of his face and smiled lopsidedly.

"I'm grateful my daughter decided to spend the night with Georgie Ann, or you'd have been embarrassed to face her."

Sarah Jane laughed, then hiccuped again. "Don't be ridiculous. Why would I be embarr—" hiccup "—assed?" Attempting to climb the first step, she slipped, but Ash was there to catch her before she fell. "Whoops. I can't seem to find purchase."

"Like I said, you're drunk!" He shook his head. "I practically had to haul you out of the party, of which you were certainly the main attraction." He'd grown annoyed when he'd come back inside after getting a bit of fresh air to find his wife dancing in the arms of Hank Groggins, then Bobby McMillan, totally oblivious to the gnawing reaction in his gut every time she smiled at one of the miners—men he'd known and worked with for years. He could hardly have made a scene without looking like a complete jackass.

She wrapped her arms around his neck and pressed up against him. "Why don't you quit scolding and kiss me? We're alone in the house, and I'm not in the mood to argue. In fact, I'm feeling quite amorous all of a sudden."

Ash groaned, wondering if he was likely to survive this latest onslaught. Scooping her up in his arms, he replied, "I don't take advantage of inebriated women," then marched the rest of the way up the stairs. "Besides the fact that you'd probably throw up all over me. You complained the entire way home—

when you weren't snoring, that is!—that you were sick to your stomach.''

She kissed his ear, felt his shiver and smiled coquettishly. "I feel fine now. More than fine, really. I feel wonderful.'' She threw her arms wide, as if she could embrace the world. "I never knew alcohol could have such a delightful effect on a person.''

"Repeat that to me in the morning when your head feels like it's about to explode.''

"You're such a stick-in-the-mud! Why can't you just enjoy the moment, instead of spoiling everything?''

Because I want you and I'm trying to be a gentleman.

After entering their bedroom, Ash crossed to the bed and placed his burden down on the coverlet, then lit the lamp on the nightstand and stoked the dying embers of the fire, tossing in a few pieces of wood and watching till they caught. "I think you should get some sleep. It's been a long evening.'' And it was going to get even longer by the looks of it.

Her bottom lip jutted out in protest. "I think I need help undressing, Ash. I can't reach the buttons in the back, and I wore my corset. The laces need to be undone.'' She stood so he could attend to her.

Impatiently he began to unfasten her gown. "Don't know why you women insist on torturing your bodies with corsets and the like. It's not healthy squishing your organs like you do.''

She glanced back over her shoulder. "How sweet of you to care. I wasn't sure you did.''

"Of course, I care, Sarah Jane. You're my wife!''

Tossing aside the offending garment, she stood before him in her chemise and drawers. "In name only, husband. But I want to rectify that tonight. It's time."

His gaze zeroed in on her stiff nipples, which were barely concealed by the whisper-thin material of her chemise, and he swallowed when she began to untie the pink ribbons. "I thought—I thought you wanted to be courted proper first."

"I loved the flowers you brought me. And I enjoyed our dancing tonight at the party. And since it was our wedding reception, I think it's only fitting that we have a wedding night, don't you? Unless you don't want me, that is." She drew open her top to reveal her breasts and he gasped audibly.

"I don't want to take advantage of your condition, Sarah Jane." *Four score and seven years ago our fathers brought forth upon this nation...*

"Well, I want to take advantage of yours, Ash Morgan, so strip out of those clothes this instant. I've been a virgin way too long, and I'm ready to become your wife, in all the ways that count."

"Dang it all, Sarah Jane! You make it so damn hard—"

She reached out to cup him. "I can see that, husband." His stiff member throbbed impatiently in her hand. She smiled up at him, licking her lips in anticipation, then allowed her drawers to pool at her feet before nestling against his fullness. "Make me yours, Ash. I want you."

Torture wasn't a concept Ash dealt well with. Wordlessly he stripped out of his clothes, lifted his wife onto the bed and covered her body with his own. "I've wanted you for so long, Sarah Jane. I feel like an untried youth ready to explode. You drive me wild with need.''

She grinned, splaying her hands over his naked chest and feeling the coarse hairs beneath her palms. ''That's good. Right?''

''Very good,'' he whispered before he kissed her, thrusting his tongue into her mouth and covering her mound with his hand to find her wet and wanting. He groaned again.

With a patience he didn't know he possessed, Ash stroked every inch of Sarah Jane's flesh, first with his hands, then with his tongue, caressing her nipples, pressing kisses into her belly button, then working his way lower, ever lower, until his mouth found the womanly essence of her being.

He loved her with his mouth and tongue, stroking and probing, until Sarah Jane cried out, half in pleasure, half in pain. ''Oh, Ash! Stop! Please! I can't take any more.'' Her breathing was coming in short, hard breaths as he continued to twirl his tongue around the tender, engorged bud.

The pressure built, the ache between her thighs growing stronger, until she was bucking feverishly against him, begging him to end her torment. She was ready to fly, to soar to the heavens, and the only thing keeping her grounded was the weight of Ash's body atop hers.

''Not yet,'' he whispered. ''Not just yet.''

He kissed his way up to her breasts again, toying with the turgid peaks, positioning himself at her opening, making certain that she was ready to take him.

Sarah Jane pushed hard against his hand, writhing

and needing the exquisite torture to end. "Please! I'm ready. Do it! Do it now!"

He entered her then with one hard thrust, breaking through the barrier of her virginity, and she gasped, tears filling her eyes. Sarah Jane knew a brief moment of pain, and then there was only pleasure as the crest she was riding began to swell, taking her higher and higher to a place she had only imagined.

"Sarah Jane! You're so tight. You feel so damn good," he said, kissing her mouth before plunging in the rest of the way, sheathing himself in her warmth.

His movements became more frantic and frenzied, and she matched him stroke for delicious stroke, until finally she screamed as the pressure became too intense, and she exploded.

They reached their peak together, catapulting to the heavens, then floated gradually back down to earth.

Ash's heart swelled with pride and satisfaction that he'd brought her as much pleasure as she had brought him. The gratification she'd given him had been intense, surprisingly so, considering her untried state. It was as if they'd been made for each other—two parts to form a whole.

He felt complete. He felt as if he'd come home.

Sarah Jane felt weepy, and happy, and totally in love. "I love you, Ash." She caressed his stubbled cheek. "I think I did from the first moment I laid eyes on you."

He rolled onto his side, taking her with him. All women thought they were in love after having sex, and Ash didn't usually put a lot of stock into the declaration. But he knew Sarah Jane meant every word, and he was humbled by them. His heart ached with the knowing of it.

But did he love her in return? That was something he had yet to figure out.

"You were wonderful," he said, kissing her forehead and the tip of her nose.

She heaved a sigh of utter contentment and smiled widely. "Really? I'm so relieved I did all right." Lightning was too calm a word for what she'd just experienced, she'd decided.

He grinned. "And how did you like it? You had such high expectations, as I recall. I hope I didn't hurt you too much."

"Not too much. And the pleasure far outweighed the pain. I never realized. No wonder all those women who work in whorehouses don't seem to be bothered by their situation in life. If I could feel like that all day and all night, I'd—"

He covered her mouth with his hand. "Don't even say it. You'll get plenty of what you crave right here in our bed."

She kissed his chin. "Oh good, because I'm going to want to do this quite often. Morning, noon and night, I should think. And maybe in between."

Ash hugged his wife tightly, thinking that if there was a luckier man alive, he hadn't met him yet.

Chapter Thirteen

Sarah Jane woke to the feel of Ash's lips upon her neck. Gooseflesh erupted over every inch of her body, and desire shot through her like a white-hot poker. The hands that cupped her breasts were making her nipples tingle, and she had the strangest ache between her thighs.

But that dull discomfort was nothing compared to the way her head felt at the moment. It was pounding. Banging a kettledrum with all the force a body could muster would have been a close description.

Ash's hand moved down to touch her femininity, and she groaned, then gasped aloud, clasping his hand when she realized just what his intentions were.

What had gotten into the man? Had he forgotten all about their agreement?

"Stop that! What on earth do you think you're doing?"

"Making love to my wife?"

Tousled and stubbled, his eyes heavy with passion, an achingly sweet smile on his lips, Sarah Jane thought her husband was the sexiest man on the face of the planet. Her heart did several flip-flops.

"How are you feeling this morning, little love?" he asked, kissing her gently.

Wanting to give in to the enticement of those soft lips, but remembering the courting pact they'd made, a feeling of utter dread crept through Sarah. As hard as she tried, she could recall nothing about the previous evening, and had no clue why Ash's behavior had changed so dramatically.

"I've felt better," she finally replied, massaging her pounding temples with her forefingers. "I must have contracted the influenza. My head is banging like a drum."

He grinned knowingly. "I tried to tell you last night that you'd feel like hell in the morning after drinking all that punch, but you wouldn't listen."

The punch! How many glasses had she had? She couldn't remember. But it had tasted so good, so sweet, and it had made her feel so wonderful, so free, so—

Oh, no! "Do you know how many glasses I imbibed last evening?"

"Four is what you admitted to, but I'd say it was more like six or eight."

She shut her eyes, and the tenderness between her legs intensified. "What happened after we arrived home?" she asked, dreading the answer but needing to know for certain.

Believing Sarah Jane was playing some type of coquettish game, Ash went along with her, placing another tender kiss upon her lips. "We made love, just as you demanded. And I must say it was—"

She bolted upright, clutching the bedclothes to her chest, her eyes round as saucers. ''I don't believe you! I would never have demanded such a thing. Not after we agreed to a proper courting period.''

Ash looked affronted by the implication. ''I'm not in the habit of ravishing drunk women, if that's what you're getting at, Sarah Jane.''

''Well, apparently that's just what you did. You took advantage of me and had your way without my permission. There's a name for that, you know.'' Ash bounded out of bed, naked as the day he was born. Sarah Jane glanced beneath the covers to find that she was naked, too, and made a horrified squeaking sound.

''It's just like a woman to throw themselves at a man, then cry rape after the fact. Well, you're my wife, and there was no such thing involved. If anyone was in danger of getting molested last evening, it was me. You practically threw your naked self at me. I did try to dissuade you, make no mistake about that, but you were determined to have your way with me.''

Her mouth gaped open. Why couldn't she remember something so important? But she couldn't, not any of it. And Ash looked quite earnest. Could he possibly be telling her the truth? If so, she had made a terrible mess of things once again.

''What of our agreement to wait and get to know each other better?'' she asked. ''You were supposed to court me, to treat me with respect, as is due a wife. If I was incapacitated, as you've indicated, you should have—'' She shook her head, which made her head ache even more, and heaved an anguished sigh.

Donning his jeans, Ash sat down next to her on the

bed. The mattress dipped under his weight, and she braced the sides of her head. ''You can blame me for what happened last night if you want, Sarah Jane. But I'm telling you right now that you wanted it as much as I did. You know yourself that you've been hot for me ever since you came here. I was just—''

She gasped, covering her mouth, which felt as dry as ten wads of cotton. ''That's a horrid thing to say! You make me sound like a loose woman.'' But he was right, and she knew it. And dammit, so did he!

His brows lifted. ''Well, you did tell me last night that you envied those women at O'Connor's. You said that if you could feel like they did all the time that you'd—''

''I did not! You are lying through your teeth, Mr. Morgan.'' Her cheeks felt as hot as molten lava.

He frowned, his voice hardening. ''I never lie, which is more than I can say for you, Sarah Jane.'' Well, hardly ever, he amended, remembering Zeke's scheme to marry him off. He'd never told Sarah that it had been Zeke's idea to contact Miss Cartwright and Zeke who had written her the letters.

Fear tickled Sarah Jane's spine like a feather, and she swallowed with a great deal of difficulty. ''What's…what's that supposed to mean?'' Had he heard something from Miss Cartwright? Did he know she'd manufactured facts to suit her purpose?

''It means that you're lying to yourself right this instant, woman. You told me you loved me, and that you wanted to consummate our marriage, wanted to make love with me morning, noon and night, and now you're denying it.''

He heaved a sigh. ''I was beginning to think things

were starting to work out between us, Sarah Jane. But if there's one thing I can't abide, it's a lying woman. If we can't be honest with each other, then—''

Sarah Jane didn't want to think about what ''then'' might mean, because if Ash ever found out that she had lied... She swallowed hard, brushing the hideous thought away. She had more pressing things to worry about at the moment.

Good Lord! Had she really confessed her deepest feelings to Ash last night? She must have been really snockered, pixilated, drunk as a skunk.

''What did you say when I told you that I loved you? What was your response?'' If he'd truly confessed to loving her, she wanted to know it. She wanted him to say it to her face. Because she knew that had he admitted such a thing, she would have remembered it. She was sure of it.

''I didn't say anything. I'm...I'm not sure of my feelings just yet.''

Disappointment stabbed her breast like a jagged-edged blade. ''I see.'' She crossed her arms over her chest, hoping the pain his words caused would dissipate. It didn't, and she wondered if someone could die of a broken heart, because right now hers was shattered into a million little pieces. ''You like me enough to make love to me, but you don't admit to loving me, is that it?''

Ash scrubbed the frustration from his face with the palm of his hand. He was in dangerous territory now, and he knew it. Women put a great store by love and romance and the like. But honesty should count for something, too, he decided. ''We don't know each other that well yet, Sarah Jane. I've never believed in love at first sight and all that. Love's supposed to grow over a period of time. Get better with age, so to speak.''

"We are not discussing fine wine, Ashby Morgan. And if you believe that nonsense, then you've never really been in love."

Her ridiculous conclusion made his mouth unhinge. "I've been married twice before, so I think it's extremely foolish for you to conclude that I've never been in love."

"The number of times you've been married hardly matters a whit. I know plenty of couples who married for a variety of reasons, and who have never fallen in love. You married me and didn't even know me, didn't you? I say you fall into the category of never having been in love."

Ash stood, unwilling to debate the point further. She might just be right. He'd never felt as passionately about either one of his first wives as he felt toward Sarah Jane. But passion and love were two separate things in his mind. Love was something his parents shared—a meeting of the minds, a completeness.

It was as if they'd been made for each other—two parts to form a whole. The feelings he'd expressed last night now came back to haunt him.

"You'd better get dressed or we're going to be late for church. I promised Addy we'd leave early this morning. I'll go down and get breakfast started."

"Thank you. I won't be long," she said, relieved when he finally closed the door. Throwing back the covers, she saw the telltale sign of her lost virginity on the sheets and grimaced.

It was a bitter irony that she'd lost her virginity to the man she loved—something she'd been wanting to do since the first day she arrived—and she couldn't remember a blasted thing about it.

Well, the deed was done. She was Ash's wife now, totally and completely. She could be carrying his child at this very moment. Her hand went to her abdomen to caress it gently. It was highly unlikely he'd be able to annul their marriage now that they'd consummated it.

So why wasn't she totally ecstatic? Why wasn't she thrilled that her fondest desire had come true? The one thing she'd been wanting for weeks had finally happened, and she felt totally miserable about it.

Ash didn't love her.

Even after they'd made love, after she'd given herself to him—albeit not knowingly—after she'd confessed her feelings for him, he still didn't love her.

"Sarah Jane," she told herself, "you have really gone and done it this time." Maybe she was irresponsible and foolish as her parents claimed.

She had fallen hopelessly in love with a man who didn't love her in return, and that was about the most irresponsible and foolish thing she'd ever done!

"Gordy and me climbed all the way to the top of the apple tree, Sarah Jane," Addy said proudly, unable to contain her grin, while her cohort shook his head.

"It wasn't all the way to the top, Mrs. Morgan. Just most of the way. My mom says it's not good to exaggerate."

Sarah Jane smiled at the pair, who seemed painfully mismatched, despite their obvious growing affection for each other. She set down two glasses of milk and a plate of cookies before them. "I made these myself, so let me know what you think." She held her breath, while Addy bit into the oatmeal cookie.

The child's eyes widened in surprise, then registered pleasure. "They're good, Sarah Jane! Your cookies are good. I can hardly believe it."

"Well, you needn't sound so surprised, Adelaide."

"They're delicious, Mrs. Morgan," Gordy said, smiling up at her with slavish devotion, clearly smitten by his friend's stepmother. "Oatmeal's always been my favorite."

Addy pulled a face. "Stop being a kiss-butt, Gordy Peters. Sarah Jane's married to my daddy, so you shouldn't be mooning over her like some lovesick calf."

The boy's cheeks exploded with color, and Sarah Jane bit back a smile, feeling genuinely sorry for him. She knew how painfully honest her stepdaughter was most of the time. And after this morning's conversation with Ash, she also knew what it felt like to make a fool of herself.

"Gordy, do you know any of the boys who work at the mine?"

He wiped the milk mustache from his face with the back of his hand and nodded. "Sure I do. I know lots of them."

"I know them, too," the young girl said. "But Daddy don't want me going near the mine. He says it's too dangerous."

"Your daddy's right, sweetie. I don't want you going near there, either.'' She was glad the mine was several miles from their home, or Addy would be tempted to prove her father wrong on a daily basis.

Addy reached for another cookie. ''How come you want to know about the boys, Sarah Jane?'' she asked before taking another bite.

''I was wondering if any of them would be interested in attending some classes.'' Sarah Jane seated herself at the table. ''I'm hoping to start a school here at home, and I was thinking of inviting some of the boys to come.''

''Daddy won't like that none,'' the child informed her, talking around the cookie in her mouth. ''Uncle Zeke said my mama used to butt into mining business all the time, and he and Daddy didn't like it one bit. Women and business ain't natural, according to Uncle Zeke.''

That sounded like something the Morgan men would say, but Sarah vowed that she would prove them wrong.

Gordy nodded. ''That's what my papa's always telling my mama, too, when she tries to make suggestions at the store. She just ignores him though.''

In total agreement with Mrs. Peters, Sarah Jane smiled. ''Your mother sounds like a very astute woman, Gordy. I must make it a point to make her acquaintance soon.''

''How come you're wanting to start up a school, Sarah Jane? Don't you have enough work to do around here? Can't figure out why you'd want to do more when you don't have to.''

''I've been thinking about this for quite a while now, sweetie, and I've spoken to your father about it." Though she neglected to mention that Ash was totally opposed to the idea. "Since I'm already teaching you lessons every afternoon, it wouldn't be that much more difficult to teach others, too, if they want to learn. I'd like those boys who work at the mine to have the opportunity to be schooled, if they want it."

"I can spread the word, Mrs. Morgan, if you'd like," Gordy offered with an eager smile, but Addy was much more reserved.

"When Daddy gets wind of what you're doing, Sarah Jane, he's gonna bust a gut." And if he got mad, he might make Sarah Jane leave, and Addy didn't think she could accept that consequence, not anymore. She'd grown very attached to the woman, despite her determination not to.

Even knowing the child was probably right, Sarah felt that the school was something she was morally bound to do. Her father would have called it her Christian duty. Ash would call it meddling, among other things. "And are you going to tattle on me?" she asked, relieved when Addy grinned and shook her head.

"Nope! I think it'd be fun to attend classes with some of the other kids, even if they're all boys."

"Can I come to your school, too, Mrs. Morgan?"

"If your parents say it's all right, Gordy. But aren't you already attending school in town?"

His fawning gaze fell on the little girl seated next to him, and his look turned pleading. "Yeah, but it's not as much fun as coming here would be."

"I'll expect you to learn and not play, young man."

"Gordy's real good at learning, Sarah Jane. And I

will be, too. Come on, Gordy," she said to her friend. "Let's go climb that apple tree again, and I'll tell you all about Cinderella and the prince."

The kids had no sooner rushed out of the room than Sarah Jane's brother-in-law sauntered in, looking as if he hadn't gotten a whole lot of sleep the night before. "Breakfast and lunch are long over, A.J., but I can offer you some milk and cookies if you're hungry." She headed for the icebox and the pitcher of cold milk.

The man smiled gratefully, then straddled one of the chairs at the table. "Thanks. I'm famished." He pulled the plate of cookies toward him. "Mmm. These are good. Taste kinda like the ones Mama used to make."

Sarah Jane's heart swelled with pride. "I'm getting better."

"I never had any doubt."

"Did you enjoy the party last night? I didn't see much of you or Cynthia Rafferty. It seemed like you both disappeared about the same time."

He sucked in his breath, nearly choking on the mouthful of cookies. "Uh, we took some air."

"Really? You must have taken quite a bit to have been gone for so long. Now that I'm thinking about it, I can't recall seeing either one of you after Ash and I cut the wedding cake." Swallowing her teasing smile, she did her best to look earnest, all the while enjoying the man's discomfort. A.J. wasn't very good at hiding his feelings.

Recalling just what he and Cynthia had been doing back at her house the night before, A.J. shifted nervously in his chair. With Beulah occupied at the reception, and the house empty for the taking, he and Cynthia had strolled back there and done a little kissing and hugging, and—

When he thought about how close he'd come to taking the willing woman on her living room sofa, his heart started thudding. Only the thought of Mrs. Rafferty walking in on them, and the fact that he wanted more than just a roll in the hay with Cynthia, had kept his britches firmly fastened.

"We took a walk down by the river," he replied, seeing no way around the lie.

"I envy Cynthia for having such a fine man to court her." Sarah Jane's voice was wistful. "A woman needs to be courted properly."

"Guess you missed out on that, huh?"

She smiled. "For the most part. But I'm not complaining. I'm in love with your brother, even if he's not the most romantic man in the world."

Ash was damn lucky; A.J. wondered if he knew it. "Morgan men tend to keep their feelings close to their chest, Sarah Jane, so you shouldn't be feeling too badly if Ash hasn't come right out and said the words you're longing to hear. He's a cautious man. But I know he cares about you."

Tiny seeds of hope blossomed in her chest. "Has he said as much?"

"No. Not in so many words. But I can tell. He wouldn't be encouraging me to get married and settle down if he wasn't happy himself."

Her face collapsed like a deflated balloon. "Haven't you heard the old adage misery loves company?"

Rising to his feet, he held out his hand and pulled

her into his arms, giving her a comforting hug and kissing the top of her head.

It was how Ash found them when he entered.

"Get your hands off my wife, or I'll break every bone in your body, brother!" His face purpled in outrage, his hands balled into fists, Ash looked like an angry mountain lion ready to pounce and devour his prey.

Noting the deadly glint in her husband's eyes, Sarah Jane quickly stepped out of her brother-in-law's embrace. "Ash! For heaven's sake. A.J. was only trying to cheer me up."

Marching farther into the room, he pulled his wife away from his grinning brother. "Let him cheer up Cynthia Rafferty, not you."

A.J. threw back his head and laughed. "You're a jealous son of a bitch." He winked at his sister-in-law. "See, it's like I told you, Sarah Jane—the man's delirious."

"What's this fool talking about, woman? I don't like you two keeping secrets from me. It's not right having secrets with a man who's not your husband, Sarah Jane."

Winking at Ash, whose frown only grew deeper, A.J. said, "Thanks for the cookies and conversation, Sarah Jane. I'll be paying a call on Miss Cynthia now, so I guess I'd better be going. We're fixing to go out this evening, so don't plan on me being here for supper."

"Have fun," she responded, sighing deeply as the man quit the room, and Ash screwed up his face in disgust.

"Are you still carrying on about that courting business, Sarah Jane? I can't believe after last night that you don't think we're beyond that point.''

To Ash's utter surprise, she wrapped her arms about his waist and pressed her cheek into his chest. ''I've decided not to be mad about what happened last night. It's what I wanted, and I'm happy to have the first time over with.''

''Meaning that we'll be doing it again?'' he asked hopefully, running his hands over her back, cupping her buttocks, and feeling himself harden. Ash couldn't be within ten feet of Sarah Jane without having such a predictable response.

''I want to remember every moment the next time we make love, Ash. I'm afraid I don't remember any of what occurred last night. Though I'm sure it was glorious.'' How could it not be? From what she'd already experienced, Ash was a very skilled lover.

''Well…Addy's climbing trees, A.J.'s out visiting his lady love, and Zeke's with the widow. We've got the rest of the afternoon to make new memories. So let's not waste another moment just talking about it.''

Her eyes widened in disbelief. ''But it's the middle of the day! And a Sunday, to be exact. Won't that be sacrilegious?'' The thought of her parents entering into such a scandalous act on the Sabbath was incomprehensible. The thought of Xenobia Parker doing the act at all was—well, it just was.

''If I remember my Bible correctly, it's full of begetting and increasing and multiplying, so I'm thinking that God would approve mightily of our being together as man and wife. I know I would.

''And if we don't go upstairs right now, I'm going to take you right here on top of the kitchen table.''

She gasped, then peeked around him to gaze at the table, and her heart fluttered wildly in her chest. Fanning her heated flesh, she tugged impatiently on his hand. "Let's hurry. You've got a lot of lovemaking to make up for, husband."

Hauling her up and over his shoulder like a sack of potatoes, he grinned. "It'll be my pleasure, wife."

Chapter Fourteen

It was pure unadulterated pleasure that ran through every pore of Sarah Jane's body as she lay sated and replete in her husband's embrace. The lingering rays of sunshine showering the bed warmed her heated flesh, and she had the fleeting thought that life didn't get much better than this.

"A penny for your thoughts, little love," Ash whispered, kissing her forehead and hugging her close. "Your mysterious smile only adds to your seductiveness. You're so beautiful it takes my breath away."

His words filled her heart with joy, and she gazed up, her eyes glowing with love. "So are you, husband." She would never tire of saying that word, for she truly felt they were one now.

Bussing the tip of her nose, he said huskily, "You'd better quit looking at me like that, or we're never going to get back downstairs to make dinner."

"Maybe we should just spend the rest of our lives right here in bed," she suggested, stretching like a contented feline.

"Who'll work the mine if we do that? Who'll make dinner? Tend to the house? Take care of Addy?"

Her lower lip jutted out. "Spoilsport."

Hating to leave her husband's embrace but knowing she must, Sarah Jane reached for her blue woolen robe and donned it. Having had time to mull over Ash's comments concerning honesty and their life together, she'd decided now that they were officially husband and wife, in all the ways that mattered, she wanted no more secrets between them.

She still wasn't brave enough to confess her ruse regarding Miss Cartwright and how she had duped him into marrying her, but she wanted to tell him about her plans for opening the school at the mine.

Being candid and honest was the best thing to do. And now that they'd been intimate in their feelings, she was sure he'd look upon things differently, maybe even offer to help her.

With his hands behind his head and a satisfied smile curving his lips, Ash looked peaceful in repose, and she hated to disturb him. But she couldn't wait. The school was too important to her, and she was eager to get started.

"Ash?"

"Hmm?"

"Remember a few weeks back when we spoke about my idea for the mine school?"

Remembering very well, Ash groaned and eased off the bed, reaching for his pants and shirt. The determined glint in Sarah Jane's eyes didn't bode well for his peace of mind. "We'd decided that it was a foolish idea and that we weren't going to talk about it anymore, as I recall," he fabricated, avoiding her eyes by making great pretense of searching for his boots.

"Now you know very well that's not what we concluded at all, Ashby Morgan. I'm still of a mind to open up a school for those boys, and I want to do it right here at the house."

His head popped up and he shook it adamantly. "Absolutely not! This is one subject I'm not going to give in on, Sarah Jane. The mine is not an area for you to meddle in. You're likely to cause problems, and—" And Zeke would have a conniption if Ash were to give in to Sarah Jane's demands. After Adelaide's unending interference, the old man would likely quit on the spot, blood relation or no.

And Ash didn't think it was his place to get involved in schooling employees, at any rate. That was the responsibility of the parents and the individuals themselves. A boy who wanted to learn was going to find a way, no matter the obstacles.

"Just forget about it, okay? I don't want you bringing this subject up again. It's closed as far as I'm concerned."

How totally unfair! She should have known he'd be unreasonable and stubborn about it, just like always. She felt like stamping her foot—on his head!—but she didn't. Instead, she replied, "But why? It's the right thing to do, and you know it. Why are you being so stubborn?"

Fully dressed, he approached her with an implacable expression, gently smoothing the deep groove between her brows with his fingertip. "Maybe someday, when and if I can afford it, I'll build a school at the mine and hire a teacher. I'll have to think long and hard on it though, because it's not something I feel comfortable doing.''

She opened her mouth to object, but he kept on. ''However, it's definitely not going to be now. Do you understand, Sarah Jane? I don't want you interfering in my business.''

Disappointment filled her. ''Yes, but—''

''No buts about it, woman. That's the way it is. Now promise me you'll forget all about this school idea of yours.''

Things were so good between them right now, she didn't want to ruin it. But how could she promise such a thing? It went against what she believed.

To do nothing about righting a wrong was wrong in itself.

Her father preached that a person had a moral and social responsibility to others. She'd been raised on the doctrine, and she couldn't very well toss aside those teachings just because Ash wanted her to. It wasn't fair of him to ask that of her.

Not that anyone would ever accuse Ashby Morgan of being fair! Stubborn, impossible, arrogant, but never fair.

''I—I'll drop the idea for the time being.''

''Good.'' Relieved that the matter was settled once and for all, he planted a quick kiss on her lips. ''Now, let's go downstairs and see what we can rustle up for supper. All this activity has worked up quite an appetite.''

Though she smiled and agreed, Sarah Jane knew she wouldn't be able to keep her promise not to interfere, and crossed her fingers behind her back.

She wasn't lying, she told herself. Not really.

* * *

As she'd done so many times in the past, Sarah Jane allowed her heart, not her head, to rule her behavior. Despite her husband's vehement objections, she proceeded with her plans to open a school for the mine workers. She was certain that once it was fully operational Ash would see for himself the progress she was making with the young minds, and then he would surely change his.

Housed in a back room of the barn, which had been a toolshed years ago and no longer used by the Morgans, Sarah's school consisted that first week of Addy, Gordy, Georgie Ann—who wanted to learn arithmetic because she "couldn't cipher worth beans"—and a young breaker boy who'd been injured when the coal he'd been sorting cut his fingers severely and he'd had to take a few weeks off to recuperate.

Tom Jennings was a promising lad with a quick mind and an eagerness to learn. Each time he answered a question correctly and Sarah Jane saw the look of pride and accomplishment on his face, she knew the risk she was taking was worth it.

By the end of November the number of students in Sarah's school had grown to ten, but it was obvious from the size of Georgie Ann's stomach that she'd be one student who'd soon be leaving them.

"This baby's dropping like a stone, Sarah Jane," Georgie Ann remarked as soon as the students had cleared the barn for the day. "I doubt I'll be able to attend classes much longer."

Sarah Jane patted the woman's large belly and nodded. "You look like a ripe watermelon that's ready to burst. I think from here on out it would be wise if you remained at home until after the baby's born. Walking back and forth from your place every day can't be good for you, especially since the weather's turned so cold. I'll come over and tutor you, if you like.''

Clutching one of Sarah Jane's books to her chest, Georgie Ann's face registered disappointment. ''I'm so glad I had this opportunity to learn, Sarah Jane. I know I chided you when you first mentioned opening up the school, but I'm glad you did. I just hope Ash and Zeke don't find out what you're doing and make you shut it down.''

Locking the shed with a padlock she'd purchased from Gordy's father, Sarah Jane, worried about the very same thing, heaved a frustrated sigh. ''I live with that fear every day, but I'm quite willing to do so if everyone is benefiting from my instruction. And I think they are.

''Addy's comportment has improved dramatically since she's been around other children, and she's developed a real love of reading. And the oldest Walker boy, Joey, told me this morning that he'd like to go on to college one of these days.

''Hearing comments like that just fills my soul with pride and pleasure. It's gratifying to think that I might actually be making a difference in that boy's life.''

''Hard to believe your husband hasn't gotten wind of things yet. Robby said just this morning that Ash had been complaining about the sickness rate among the younger boys. He was thinking about calling in a doctor to see if there was some kind of epidemic going on.''

There had been, Sarah Jane thought. An epidemic of learning.

Why didn't Ash realize that what she was doing was important and necessary? If only she could make him understand and change his mind. But she knew his mind was already made up. Every time she broached the subject, he ignored her. And so she continued to deceive him, feeling guilty about it all the while. Especially when she lay in his arms, safe, sated, and so much in love that it hurt.

When the women reached the cozy kitchen, they hung their heavy woolen coats on the wooden pegs by the back door. Georgie Ann headed straight for a ladder-back chair to take the weight off her cold, swollen feet, while Sarah Jane put a copper kettle of water on the stove to heat for tea.

Sharing a cup of tea after class with her best friend had become a daily ritual, and one she was loath to give up now that Georgie Ann was to begin her confinement. Having the young woman to share her burden with had lightened it somewhat.

"There'd have been no reason for subterfuge if Ash had been reasonable about the school from the beginning. And I can't be held responsible just because those boys have a burning within them to learn. I can't tell you how many thank-yous I've received from their mothers, who want more for their sons than the hard, dangerous life of a miner."

"Well, with the Thanksgiving holiday approaching next week, you'll be shutting down the school for a while anyway, right?"

"Yes. Tomorrow's class will be the last until after the first of January, though I wish I didn't have to close, even for a short time. But with the holidays coming it seems only practical. And since it's going to be my first time to cook Thanksgiving dinner, I'm going to need the extra time to prepare, especially since you won't be around to help me.''

The pregnant woman patted her hand reassuringly. "You'll do just fine. I'm going to write out my recipes for candied sweet potatoes and corn bread stuffing, and there ain't nothing to roasting a turkey. The big fat tom does all the work hisself. You just have to baste it every once in a while."

Sarah Jane looked skeptical. "My cooking skills have improved dramatically, thanks to you, Georgie Ann, but I'm still a bit apprehensive at the prospect of cooking for such a large group of people. Zeke's asked Etta to join us, and A.J.'s planning on inviting Cynthia and her mother."

Sarah Jane chewed her lower lip nervously. "Can you imagine having Beulah Rafferty scrutinizing every bite? I'll be a nervous wreck."

"That woman fancies herself a great cook, but there's a persistent rumor that it was her cooking that finally did in her husband. She claims it was his heart, but Zeke's fond of saying that Sam Rafferty died of acute indigestion."

Laughing, the blonde shook her head. "As if I didn't have enough problems already, now I'm going to have to act as referee between those two, if Beulah shows up. Which is a big *if*, knowing how she feels about Zeke."

"Oh, she'll show all right. Beulah Rafferty wouldn't miss the opportunity to pick up a little gossip. So you'd best be careful not to mention anything about the school in front of her. She's got a mouth as wide and fast as the Monongahela River.''

"You needn't worry on that account. I have—" At the pained expression on Georgie Ann's face, Sarah halted in midsentence.

"Uh-oh." The woman grabbed her swollen abdomen, squeezing her eyes shut and taking a deep breath.

Her brows drawn together in concern, Sarah's voice filled with fear. "What? What's wrong? Is it the baby?" Good Lord! What if it was? She didn't know anything about babies. What on earth was she going to do? Nothing she'd learned at the Cartwright School had prepared her for delivering a baby!

Georgie nodded, drawing her lower lip between her teeth. "I—I'm afraid it is. You'll need to go for help.''

Unable to decide if she was more horrified at the prospect of staying with her friend or going for help, Sarah Jane opted for the former and shook her head. "I won't leave you alone like this. Something dreadful could happen while I was gone, and then I'd never forgive myself. Come on," she urged. "Let's go upstairs and get you into bed."

"I'm—I'm not sure I can make it." With Sarah Jane's help, Georgie Ann stood, and in the next instant a large pool of water formed at her feet. Staring down at the liquid, the pregnant woman's eyes filled with fear and apology. "I'm in for it now, I'm afraid. My water's broke."

"Is that bad?" Sarah Jane's eyes widened as she stared down at the mess all over the pine-planked floor.

"It means the baby's coming."

At that moment, the front door slammed shut and Sarah Jane, believing it was Ash, breathed a sigh of relief. Thank the good Lord! Help was at hand, she thought. Then she heard Addy's excited voice and all hope fizzled.

"It's snowing, Sarah Jane! It's snowing! Come out and see."

Occupied with Georgie Ann's plight, Sarah Jane hadn't noticed that a light snow had begun to fall, until she glanced out the window and saw the fat white flakes drifting to the ground. Under normal circumstances she would have been thrilled by the sight. Now, however, wasn't a good time for inclement weather, and she groaned in frustration.

"Botheration! I can't believe this is happening. Things seem to be going from bad to worse."

"Just get me somewhere where I can lie down, Sarah Jane," Georgie Ann said, rubbing the small of her back to ease her discomfort. "I'll do the rest. Women have babies all the time. How hard can it be?" She moaned loudly, giving Sarah Jane a pretty good indication. Though Georgie Ann tried to appear brave, she knew her friend was in a great deal of pain.

Wrapping her arm about her, she shouted for Addy to come and help. When the child arrived and saw what was happening, her eyes grew round as saucers. "What's wrong with Georgie Ann? She ain't gonna die, is she?"

"No, sweetie. Georgie's going to be just fine. But I need your help. Please run upstairs and gather up some sheets and blankets, then bring them to your daddy's study. Can you do that?"

Grasping the seriousness of the situation, much to her stepmother's very great relief, the young girl nodded, complying without further question.

Sarah Jane had Georgie Ann lie down on the leather couch in Ash's office, until she could figure out what else to do with her. By the pained sounds she was making, it was highly unlikely that the pregnant woman would make it up the stairs to one of the bedrooms.

"Put more water on to boil, Sarah Jane," Georgie instructed as soon as she fell back onto the sofa. "You'll need to sterilize scissors or a knife to cut the cord, and—*yeow!*" She screamed at the top of her lungs as the contraction hit her, then breathed deeply, clutching her taut belly.

Her face perspiring profusely, Georgie Ann remained as practical as ever. "I'm going to need help getting out of these clothes. Do you have an old nightgown I could put on?"

"Don't do anything drastic," Sarah Jane said. "I'm going upstairs to gather the things we'll need. I'll be right back."

True to her word, she was back in less than five minutes, along with Addy, who'd been instructed to place the sheets beneath Georgie Ann's body as best she could to absorb the blood and cushion the child's arrival.

"How come that baby's coming out now, Georgie Ann?" the young girl asked as she worked. "Aren't you supposed to wait for the doctor to come? Sarah Jane just learned how to cook. I don't think she knows nothing about delivering babies."

"Thanks for your vote of confidence, Addy," her

stepmother said. "Now, you'd best move out of the way." Setting the basin of warm water on Ash's desk, she wrung out a washcloth and placed it on the woman's forehead.

"Guess we'll both be getting a fast course in childbirth today, sweetie. But if you don't want to stay and watch, I'll understand. It's not going to be pleasant, and Georgie Ann's likely to yell like a banshee before all's said and done."

Addy didn't budge, though it was on the tip of her tongue to ask what a banshee was. Her stepmother's frazzled state made her think twice, and she said instead, sounding very grown-up, "I'll stay. Just my luck you'll go and do the same thing as Georgie Ann when it's time for you to have a baby. I'd better learn in advance how to take care of you."

Sarah Jane was touched by the sentiment. "A very sound idea, but that's not going to happen for quite a while. Your daddy and I haven't been married long enough to have a child."

Through her pain, Georgie Ann listened to the young woman's naive explanation and managed a small smile. She'd learned from experience that God and babies had minds of their own when it came to getting pregnant, and she wondered if Sarah Jane realized that those bouts of nausea she'd been complaining about for the past week were probably an indication that God had taken matters into his own hands, with a little help from Ash.

By the time Ash, Zeke and A.J. arrived home, Robert James Freeland II had been born. His shock of dark hair, healthy set of lungs and creamy complexion proclaimed him to be Georgie Ann's son. His stubborn refusal to give up on life was a good indication, too.

Sarah Jane and Addy were in awe as they gazed at the perfect bundle of humanity snuggled in his mother's arms. "A.J.'s gone to fetch your husband and mother, Georgie Ann," Sarah explained, brushing away strands of sweat-matted hair from the tired woman's face. "I know Robby's going to be proud that you've given him a son. Why, he'll probably burst all of the buttons on his shirt." She smiled softly at her friend.

"Mama was hoping for a granddaughter, but Robby wanted a son, so I know he'll be strutting around here like a rooster." Her eyes shone with pride that she'd been able to fulfill her husband's fondest wish.

"Your baby don't have much hair, and he sure is red." Addy scrutinized the newborn closely, looking somewhat concerned. "He's kinda homely, but I like him."

"Adelaide Morgan, you know my son is quite gorgeous!" The new mother flashed the child a grin, then sobered.

"I don't know how to thank you, Sarah Jane, and you, too, child, for everything you did. You were both so levelheaded and calm throughout the whole ordeal. And me screaming my fool head off the entire time."

Addy had thrown up once, Sarah Jane had felt like doing the same a time or two, but neither of them mentioned that to Georgie Ann. Instead, they smiled proudly at each other, knowing the experience had brought them closer together.

"A woman who's giving birth deserves to shout the house down, in my opinion, so you needn't apologize."

"Would you like to hold little Robby?" Georgie Ann asked.

As the woman held the child out to her, a warm flush crept over Sarah Jane. Her arms had been aching to hold the baby again. "I'd love to, if you're sure. I wouldn't want to hurt him."

"Babies are tough, silly. You won't hurt him a bit."

Taking the child and cuddling him to her breast, every maternal instinct Sarah Jane possessed rose to the forefront. Grazing her fingertip down the baby's soft cheek, she whispered, "He's wonderful! And so very perfect."

She hoped life held more for Robert James Freeland II than working in the coal mines. From what she'd seen of the young miners, they were boys who'd already turned old before their time. She hated to think that this little baby would one day turn out the same way. All the more reason, she decided, to continue teaching.

Ash entered at that moment and pulled up short at the sight of his wife holding the child. He sucked in his breath at the perfect picture and felt his insides tighten and his heart expand. He hadn't given much thought to having more children, but seeing Sarah Jane holding the infant, he wondered what it would be like to have a son to call his own—a son with blond hair and bright blue eyes who looked just like his mother.

Hearing the door click shut, Sarah Jane looked up

and presented her husband with the most tender of smiles, and Ash felt the jolt clear down to his toes. "Come meet Georgie's new son," she said.

"I helped to deliver him, Daddy. Sarah Jane said I did a real good job, too. I ain't never gonna have me one of those, I can tell you that. Georgie Ann screamed her fool head off the entire time."

"Those were shouts of joy, Addy girl," the woman replied, making Sarah laugh, for she knew how hard Georgie Ann had struggled to bring her son into the world.

"Giving birth is a lot harder than I thought it would be," she admitted, gazing down at the child and kissing the top of his head. "But it's well worth any amount of pain, I've decided."

Ash released the breath he didn't know he was holding and smiled.

Chapter Fifteen

"**Y**our turkey dinner's delicious, Sarah Jane." Cynthia Rafferty smiled down the long candlelit table at her hostess. A lovely arrangement of bittersweet and yellow chrysanthemums graced the center of the mahogany table.

"It's clear to everyone here that you've gone to a lot of work. Thanks for including Mama and me in the festivities. It's especially nice to share this special day with people we like." She cast a sidelong glance at A.J. and smiled softly.

"The bird's a bit dry," Beulah said, making a face of displeasure as she chewed. "But that's to be expected, considering this is your first time to cook a turkey, Sarah Jane. Cooking a proper Thanksgiving dinner takes years of practice. I'd be happy to offer you some instruction if you'd like."

In actuality the turkey was quite moist, and Sarah Jane was unsure of how to respond to the woman's unjust criticism. Poor Cynthia looked mortified by her mother's thoughtless remark, and Sarah Jane wanted to put the young woman at ease. Smiling, she replied,

"How kind of you to offer, Mrs. Rafferty," and noted that her brother-in-law seemed grateful for the effort.

Knowing the older woman's proclivity for saying whatever popped into her head, A.J. had debated long and hard on whether or not to invite Cynthia and her mother to Thanksgiving dinner. But Sarah Jane had convinced him that if his intentions toward Cynthia were serious, they would have to put up with her mother sooner or later.

At the far end of the table Zeke listened to the opinionated woman and his eyes narrowed into thin slits, his anger evident by the steady tapping of his fingers against the tabletop. "I think Sarah Jane's done a fine job of cooking this dinner," he said, winking at his niece, who smiled gratefully in return, but then gasped when he added, "This here bird's a lot moister than some dried up old hens I know."

It was as obvious as the pinched look on Beulah Rafferty's face to whom the old man was referring, and A.J. wanted to smile. But it wouldn't do to alienate his future bride or mother-in-law, though the unkind woman had it coming. Zeke, with his irascible ways, was just the man to put her in her place.

Age not only gave folks wisdom, it gave them gall.

At Zeke's barb, Beulah let loose with an outraged bellow and was about to say something rude when Sarah Jane decided to interrupt before a major battle erupted and ruined the meal she'd spent days preparing.

She had mentally steeled herself for Mrs. Rafferty's outspokenness and wasn't nearly as bothered by the woman's comments as Zeke seemed to be. And she suspected that the older man's motives were somewhat self-serving. The animosity between the older couple had been palpable throughout the day.

"Thank you so much for your helpful comments, everyone. I'm delighted the dinner turned out as well as it did. Ash and I are happy we're able to share our holiday with such fine friends and relatives."

"You missed your calling, Sarah dear," Etta said with a sympathetic smile, reaching out to pat her hand. "You should have gone to Washington and joined the diplomatic core."

"Well, I, for one, am glad she didn't." Ash held up his wineglass for a toast. "To my wife, a woman of vast and amazing talents, not the least of which is cooking." As he gazed upon his wife's proud, flushed face, Ash was suddenly hit by a thunderbolt. He loved her. He loved Sarah Jane!

And he was proud of her, too. In the short time they'd been married she had learned to cook quite respectably, had helped transform Addy into a suitable young woman, allowing the child to blossom under her tutelage, and she had given her body and heart to him unequivocally, asking nothing in return.

She had also kept her promise about the school, and for that he was most grateful. In time, when she had children of her own to care for, she would forget all about educating the young mine boys.

Sarah Jane smiled widely at him, a smile that seemed to say that she wasn't the only one with amazing talents. Remembering their previous night's love-making and the delicious, stimulating activity in the bathtub, Ash nearly fell off his chair.

"Speaking of talent," Beulah began, dumping three tablespoons of sugar into her tea, then stirring it repeatedly, banging the spoon against the sides of the china cup until Sarah Jane wanted to scream, "you are the talk of the town these days, young woman."

A feeling of dread crept through Sarah Jane, quickly replacing the warmth of moments before. Mrs. Rafferty was about to reveal her secret regarding the school. Then Ash, who was looking at her with some unfathomable emotion shining in his eyes, was going to strangle her with his bare hands. "I—"

What would she say? That she had gone behind her husband's back, gone against his wishes to follow her own instincts?

"Everyone's been talking about how you delivered the Freelands' baby all by yourself. I must say that I am quite surprised that you were able to carry it off."

Relief poured out of her so rapidly she felt somewhat faint. "I had a tremendous amount of help in the form of Miss Adelaide Morgan."

"Really?" The older woman looked down her long nose at the child, who smiled smugly back at her with a milk mustache riding her upper lip.

"Me and Sarah pulled that baby right out of Georgie Ann. He was bloody and full of…crap," she said, wiping her mouth with the back of her sleeve before flashing a quick apologetic smile at her stepmother for cursing. "And we had to cut that rope thing growing out of his belly button with scissors. I thought Sarah'd puke her guts up for sure when she had to do that."

"Well, my goodness!" The woman paled and clutched her throat, and Ash, who should have castigated his child for her outrageous dinner conversation, sat grinning like a hyena.

"Thanks for the thrilling rendition, kid," A.J. said, chuckling. Reaching under the table, he patted Cynthia's knee and was rewarded with a sharp intake of breath. "Guess we'll know who to call whenever we need help from now on."

Smiling somewhat hesitantly, Sarah Jane said, "I'm not sure if anyone still has an appetite after Addy's colorful recitation of events, but if you do, Etta's brought several of her delicious pumpkin and pecan pies, and I can personally vouch that they are the best I've ever tasted."

"They are, without a doubt." Zeke tossed a sideways glance at Beulah and smirked. "No one can outcook my Etta." Leaning over, he kissed the woman seated next to him, and she beamed brightly.

"Why thank you, Ezekial," she said, truly touched by the gesture, though somewhat surprised. Zeke wasn't normally demonstrative in front of other folks.

"Humph! I'm sure your opinion is slightly colored, Mr. Morgan. There are others at this table who can cook equally well as Mrs. Dobbins, as I'm sure you know."

Tipping back his chair so that it rested on its hind legs, Zeke interlocked his fingers across his chest. "Well now, if you're talking about our Sarah Jane, then I guess I'd have to agree with you."

Beulah's spine stiffened against the back of the Queen Anne chair. "I was talking about my own considerable ability in the kitchen, Mr. Morgan." She looked to her daughter for confirmation, and Cynthia nodded dutifully, but not before a big sigh escaped her lips.

"Mama's a fine cook." She was certainly adept at cooking her own goose, she thought, sorry that the woman couldn't enjoy the day and the company without making it into some type of competition between her and Etta Dobbins.

The widow didn't seem at all inclined to participate. Zeke, on the other hand, was another matter.

"A woman who knows how to cook like Etta is a rare find. Yes, indeed." Turning slightly in his seat, he said to the older woman, "Etta Dobbins, will you marry me?"

The startled group of diners sat momentarily stunned.

Sarah Jane and Addy clapped their hands in excitement.

Ash and A.J. looked at their uncle as if he'd lost his mind.

Etta burst into tears and nodded. "Yes, Zeke, you old fool. I will marry you. And it's about time you asked. I'd almost given up hope."

Before anyone at the table could offer their congratulations, Beulah took matters into her own hands, declaring venomously, "Oh, Zeke's real good at asking, but when the time comes for him to actually do the deed...well, that's another story."

Zeke flashed his old flame a hostile stare but kept his mouth shut, much to everyone's relief.

This was a Thanksgiving Sarah Jane wasn't likely to forget anytime soon, she decided, wondering what distressing events she could look forward to in the ensuing weeks until Christmas.

*   *   *

Early Monday morning Ash and Zeke were once again seated on the old wagon, heading down to the mine to begin the day's work.

The wind was biting, slapping their faces like an angry, harsh hand as they snuggled deeper into the warmth of their heavy sheepskin coats. The maple and hickory trees had lost nearly all of their leaves, and except for a few of the oaks, which clung to their color with tenacious resolve, the landscape appeared brown and barren.

Ash decided that it was the perfect time to discuss his uncle's rather unorthodox marriage proposal to Etta. Zeke had spent the remainder of the Thanksgiving holiday with the widow at her home, and there hadn't been an opportunity for him to talk to his uncle about it until now.

"Well, you sure as hell took everyone by surprise, old man," Ash said, clucking his tongue and urging the mules to pick up their pace. "You coulda gotten the same result by firing off a cannonball into the middle of the holiday festivities. I thought Mrs. Rafferty was going to jump across the table and have at you. If looks coulda killed, you'd be dead by now."

The old man rubbed his whiskered chin. "I had me a little too much wine that evening. And that damn Beulah was just getting on my nerves something fierce, egging me on till I lost my fool mind."

"So you proposed to Etta in retaliation?" Ash arched a brow, waiting and wondering what his uncle was up to. He knew Zeke had always prided himself on remaining a bachelor. Of course, the old man had no qualms about dragging others into the state of matrimony.

Not that Ash was complaining. Marriage to Sarah Jane definitely had its rewards. For a naive young woman untutored in the ways of love, his wife had become an apt pupil and he a zealous teacher. He was so eager to take her to his bed each evening that he found himself watching the regulator clock on the mantel after supper, wishing the seconds and minutes away, so they could retire to their room.

"Not exactly," Zeke confessed when his nephew's eyes widened in question. "But kinda. Oh, I love the old gal, don't get me wrong. And I guess I'm gonna go through with marrying her. Etta's put up with me all these years, and I owe her for that.

"There's worse things than being hitched." He grinned. "But I figure by now you already know that." The old man struck a match and lit his cob pipe, puffing hard to get it going in the frigid morning air.

"I've got no complaints. I admit to being worried at first, because Sarah Jane's kind of headstrong and all, but she's coming around, just like you said she would."

"Looks like your brother's fixing to marry Cynthia Rafferty."

"Did he say as much?" A.J. hadn't mentioned a thing to him about his plans.

The old man shook his head. "Nope. He didn't have to. I know all the signs. The man practically drools every time the woman walks into the room. He's like a lovesick calf.

"And you know what that means? It means we're gonna have to put up with that Beulah Rafferty at every family gathering." He pulled a face. "This is God's way of punishing me for all my past sins."

Ash threw back his head and laughed. "Well, by God, it's about time someone did. That old gal hates you. What on earth did you do to her anyway? I don't recall you ever said."

Zeke shifted uncomfortably on the bench seat, and the ruddiness of his cheeks had nothing to do with the cold. "I ain't proud of what I done, but it's over with now. Ain't no use beating a dead horse into the ground, if you get my drift."

Ash's expression grew knowing, his gaze boring into the old man like a drill bit. "You took advantage of poor Beulah Rafferty then dumped her like yesterday's garbage, didn't you?" He shook his head. "I'm surprised at you, Uncle Zeke. You taught us boys better'n that."

The man hung his head in embarrassment. "I never meant for things to go so far, but you know what it's like when you're young. And Beulah was a good-looking woman back then. After all was said and done, she expected me to marry her. But I already knew how demanding she was, what her temper was like, and I didn't love her like a man should love a woman he's going to marry, so I took a trip and waited for things to cool down."

"You took the coward's way out and ran off, you mean?"

"Yep. I did. And I ain't saying I'm proud of my behavior. But things turned out all right for her. She was married to Sam Rafferty before I returned. No one's ever accused Beulah of letting any grass grow under her feet. Marriage was what she was after, and marriage was what she got. Just not to me.''

''How'd you know that you didn't leave her in the family way?''

''I made sure of that before I took off. I'd never leave a woman in a lurch. That ain't the Morgan way.''

Zeke's code of morality and approach to life was different than most, but Ash wasn't about to condemn his uncle for his youthful indiscretions. God only knows he'd made mistakes in his own past, like marrying Wynona before he was dry behind the ears. And he and Adelaide hadn't exactly been a match made in heaven.

His mama'd always said that it took a man a lot longer to season than it did a woman. Ash figured she'd been right about that.

Fifteen minutes later, Ash pulled the mule to a halt before a large wood-framed building known as the breaker, and he and Zeke parted ways.

Aptly named, the breaker was where the coal was dumped, broken and washed, before the children known as breaker boys got hold of it. There, they sorted through the crushed rocks and eliminated the slate and stone that wouldn't burn, pulling out only pure bituminous coal, which would later be placed into railcars for shipment.

Turning to stare at a group of youngsters playing baseball on the culm heap, Ash felt a twinge of guilt that he might be robbing those boys of their childhood and a different way of life, just as Sarah Jane had accused him of doing.

But he knew deep down that most boys who

worked at the mine did so because their parents either needed the extra money and demanded it of them, or they wanted to follow in the same footsteps their fathers had taken at the same age.

An arduous path that led to neither riches nor good health.

Maybe he should reconsider Sarah Jane's suggestion and open that school she was always harping at him about. He could work the boys in shifts, allow them a few hours off each day to attend classes, and it wasn't likely that all of them would want to go to school, at any rate. For some the thought of school was far worse than sitting hunched over a pile of rocks all day performing the tedious task of sorting.

About to enter the large building, he stopped at the sight of Tom Jennings running toward him. "Hey there, boy! Where're you going in such an all-fired hurry? We've got rules around here about running."

A big smile lit the boy's dirty face. "Sorry, Mr. Morgan. I forgot." The exuberant child then pulled out a paper from inside his oil suit and held it up proudly. "I got me an A on the history test. Mrs. Morgan said—" Suddenly remembering who he was talking to, and the fact that the school was supposed to be kept secret, he shut up tighter than a clamshell.

Taking the paper from the boy's outstretched hand, Ash frowned deeply when he recognized his wife's handwriting. She had complimented the child on his improvement over the past few weeks.

Weeks! Not days. But weeks!

Dammit, Sarah Jane! She had defied him, all the while acting sweet, serene and sexy as hell to distract him.

He'd been played for a fool, he thought, and fought hard to keep his temper in check and his voice calm. "How long has Mrs. Morgan been teaching you, Tom?"

The child swallowed. "Uh, I meant my mom. She's been teaching me, Mr. Morgan. Don't know why I—"

He stared intently at the child. "Tom, you know I wouldn't like it if you lied to me, don't you?"

The boy's big brown eyes grew even larger. "Yessir! But it was supposed to be a secret. I didn't mean to tell, Mr. Morgan. Please don't be mad at me. I just wanted to get some learning in.

"I cough all the time from the coal dust, and my hands are scarred from where the rocks cut into them. I just wanted to learn so I could do something else when I grow up. I don't want to die young, like my brother did."

Ash squeezed the boy's shoulder, remembering how tragic Pete Jennings's death from miner's asthma had been and how hard Tom had taken it. "I'll handle things from here, Tom. You needn't worry. Is school still in session?"

He shook his head. "No, sir. Class is stopped until after the new year."

"How many of the boys attend class with you?"

"There's ten people altogether, but not all come from the mine. There's your daughter, a friend of hers from town, and a pregnant lady, too. But I hear the lady's gone and had her baby and might not be coming back for a while."

Georgie Ann! Ash felt as if he'd just been sucker-punched, and by a slip of a woman he called wife. A woman who had used his own daughter and neighbor against him.

At the child's worried frown, Ash patted the boy's shoulder. "Go on back to work now, son. Nothing more will be said about this."

Looking relieved, Tom headed inside to break the bad news to his fellow classmates, while Ash headed home to break the bad news to his wife.

Chapter Sixteen

"Sarah Jane! Where are you, woman?"

Ash's harsh voice blew up the stairs like an ill wind—a tornado would be more precise—making Sarah Jane moan loudly as she lifted her head from the washbasin, wiping her forehead with the back of her hand.

She'd been throwing up for the past ten minutes and felt as if her insides were about to fold in on themselves. Of course, today hadn't been the first bout of nausea she'd succumbed to, and it probably wouldn't be her last, if her suspicion proved correct.

The nausea and illness that had been plaguing her for weeks seemed a good indication that she was pregnant with Ash's child. And though she was delighted at the prospect, the images of Georgie Ann in the torturous throes of childbirth still held vivid in her mind and terrified her.

Women died in childbirth. And the pain Georgie Ann experienced had been very real and difficult. Sarah Jane had never considered herself a coward. Until now.

"Sarah Jane, where the hell are you?"

Rinsing her mouth out with water, she scrubbed her face with a damp washcloth, straightened her clothing, then replied, "Upstairs in the bedroom. I'll be right down."

But he didn't wait. She could hear his boots pounding the treads, eating up the distance like a rampaging bull. In a matter of moments he burst through the doorway, wind tossed and red faced, and looking as if he had murder on his mind.

Sarah Jane gulped, then forced a small smile. "You're home early. What a nice surprise."

Slamming the door behind him, Ash took several deep breaths. He'd hoped the trip home would have cooled down his temper, but it hadn't. He was ready to spit nails, to pound his fists against the wall, to—

He sucked in air, and when he felt rational enough to discuss what was on his mind, he said, "I had a very interesting and informative talk with one of my breaker boys today, Sarah Jane. Does the name Tom Jennings mean anything to you?"

Her face paled and, feeling momentarily dizzy, she reached for the bedpost. He knew. Ash knew about the school. Straightening her spine, she prepared herself for battle. "Yes. Tom's a very bright boy."

"A very bright *student,* don't you mean?"

There was no point in lying further. She had been found out. Now that her secret was out in the open, she felt relieved. No matter how proficient she was, lying never came easy to someone with a conscience. "Yes. Tom's a student in my class."

"How could you, Sarah Jane? How could you go behind my back and do it anyway, after I expressly forbade you to go forward with the school? You totally disregarded my wishes.''

When the dizziness passed, she let loose of the post and held out her hands beseechingly. ''I tried to talk to you about it, Ash, but you wouldn't listen. You ignored me, even though I tried numerous times to explain what I wanted to do. So I finally gave up and went ahead on my own.''

''Using my own child and Georgie Ann as your accomplices?'' His eyes reflected pain, his voice bitterness.

Hers held conviction. ''They had nothing to do with it. The school was my idea, and mine alone. Addy and Georgie Ann were students, nothing more. And they shouldn't be held accountable.''

''But they kept your secret, didn't they?''

''Because I asked them to. Both felt badly about deceiving you, as did I, but I convinced them that the school would do more good than harm. If you want to blame someone, blame me. But don't take your anger out on Addy or Georgie Ann. They don't deserve it.''

With long, quick strides, he paced from the fireplace to the door and back again, looking angrier than Sarah Jane had ever seen him. His face mottled with rage, his slate-gray eyes were as cold as the snow that still dampened the ground outside.

''I'm sorry for concealing things from you, Ash,'' she said, trying to repair the damage she'd caused. ''But I'm not sorry for teaching those boys. They're like sponges, soaking up every bit of knowledge presented to them. If you could see what a difference I'm making.'' He took a menacing step toward her, but Sarah Jane held her ground, unwilling to be intimidated.

"A marriage is supposed to be based on trust, not on deception and lies. How can I ever trust you again, Sarah?" Shaking his head, he added, "It's not enough that you lied, but you went and made me the laughingstock of the mining community."

She reached out, placing her hand on his arm and felt the muscles bunch before he pulled away, as if her touch revolted him. "I'm sorry. I didn't mean to humiliate you or make others think less of you. I just wanted to make a difference in those boys' lives, and I think I have."

"At what expense? Did you give even the slightest thought to what it might do to our marriage? I thought things were finally getting good between us. I thought we had finally made a commitment to each other. I thought—"

Hell, now was not the time to confess his feelings for her. If she knew how much he loved her, she would use it against him, use it to manipulate and have her way. Just like all women were prone to do.

Tears brimming in her eyes, Sarah Jane slumped onto the bed. "I'm sorry. I shouldn't have gone behind your back, but I felt it was important."

His look was incredulous. "More important than me? Than us?"

"Of course not. I—"

He shook his head. "Save it. I'm not up for any more of your excuses. I have to get back to the mine."

His continued arrogance and unwillingness to listen fueled Sarah's anger. And though she felt genuine

remorse for what she had done, Ash had only himself
to blame. He'd forced her into the deception by his
own stubborn refusal to heed her suggestions, to pay
attention to feelings and needs that were important to
her, to see her as anything but a wife and mother.

Well, he would listen to her now!

"Since you're not inclined to listen to anything I
have to say, I am through apologizing or trying to
explain my motives."

He pulled open the door and looked back. "Is that
so?"

"Yes, it is. But there's one more thing I want you
to know."

He sneered. "What's that? Not another one of your
feeble attempts at explanation, I hope?"

Rising to her feet, she crossed the room and
stopped directly in front of him, staring him square
in the eye. "I'm pregnant! Put that in your pipe and
smoke it, you arrogant jackanapes!" Then before he
could respond, she ducked under his arm and sailed
out of the room, leaving Ash dumbfounded and in
shock.

"I haven't ice-skated in years, A.J." Cynthia giggled as she careened toward him on the slick frozen
pond. Her cheeks were chapped red from the cold,
her breath visible in the cold morning air. "I may just
break my neck and—*ooh!*" She screamed, "Watch
out! I can't stop."

She collided with him, and he wrapped his arms
about her, hugging her to his chest. "Now you know
I'm not going to let anything happen to you, honey.
I want you all in one piece when I finally have my

way with you.'' He wiggled his eyebrows suggestively.

Smiling softly, she pressed her face into the wool
of his coat and sighed. ''You may just break my heart
instead.''

''Now, Cyn, you know I love you. And as soon as
I can get around your mother, we're going to get married. I promise.''

''I love you, too, A.J. But I don't understand why
we have to wait. Mama's never going to give her
consent. I've told you that. She's stubborn and old
and her mind's made up.'' Cynthia had lived long
enough with Beulah to know that there was no rea-
soning with the woman, and she wasn't going to allow her to ruin her future happiness.

She loved A.J. Morgan, and she intended to marry
him, with or without her mother's blessing.

Thus far, Mrs. Rafferty had proven to be a formi-
dable obstacle, but A.J. was determined to win her
over for her daughter's sake. He just hadn't figured
out how yet. ''You'll never be happy, Cyn, if you
marry me and lose your mother in the process. I know
you two have had your differences from time to time,
but you love her, and she loves you. And I don't want
to come between you.''

Putting her gloved hand in his, she led him to the
bench at the edge of the skating rink. ''You're a fine
man, A.J. I don't understand why Mama is so blind
that she can't see you as I do. I'm going to talk to
her again. Have it out with her, once and for all.''

He shook his head. ''Don't! You'll just end up
fighting, like the last time. Let me talk to her, honey.
I've been known to have sweet-talked a few women

in my day. And maybe I can work the old Morgan charm on her.''

A.J. prayed he was right. He'd fallen hard for Cynthia and, now that he'd found her, had no intention of ever letting her go. No matter what he had to do or say to Mrs. Rafferty.

"I love you, A.J. I want to be with you. If my mother doesn't consent to our marriage soon, then I think we should just go ahead and consummate our union without the benefit of vows.''

Eyes wide, A.J.'s heart started thumping. He and Cynthia had been on the brink of going to the finish line many times, but he'd always held back. Now she was giving him license to proceed, and he knew he wasn't going to be able to do it. He loved her too much.

"I'll speak to your mother as soon as we return to your house. Explain the way it is between us.''

She heaved a dispirited sigh. "I've already spoken to her. She won't listen. She doesn't think you're financially stable enough to support me in 'the style to which I've become accustomed.''' Cynthia laughed harshly. "Whatever that means. We're not exactly living in the lap of luxury, so I don't know where my mother gets her exalted ideas from.''

A.J. squeezed her hand. "She's just worried for you. And I suspect that she fears being left alone. You were all she had left after your daddy died. She raised you. And the thought of losing you is probably what's driving her unreasonable attitude. I'll talk to her, see if I can't change her mind, reassure her that you'll always be part of her life.''

"And if you can't? Then what?''

"Then I'll send Uncle Zeke over to deal with her."
He grinned wickedly. "She'll say yes just to get rid
of him."

Cynthia wished she could share A.J.'s optimism,
but she knew her mother a lot better than he did. And
bringing Zeke into the picture was not going to help.
"I thought for sure those two were going to come to
blows at Thanksgiving. I've never seen my mother so
combative before."

"I suspect she's still carrying a torch for the old
geezer, but don't ask me why. From what Ash said,
he didn't treat your mother in a very gentlemanly
manner." A.J. had been as surprised as his brother at
the old man's revelation.

She caressed his cheek. "And if I give myself to
you in a moment of passion, will you run away and
leave me brokenhearted, like Zeke left Mama?"

Drawing her into his arms, he kissed her tenderly.
"Zeke didn't love your mama, honey. But I sure as
heck love you. And one day soon I'm going to show
you how much."

"Sarah Jane!"
Ash stormed into the kitchen, pulling up short at
the sight of his "pregnant" wife standing on a wob-
bly chair, reaching for a can of baking powder. He
rushed forward, scooping her into his arms.

"Let me go, Ash! Are you crazy?" When her feet
finally reached the floor, she stiffened her spine and
jutted out her chin, indignation riding her hard.

"Are you?" he retorted. "A woman in your condition shouldn't be climbing up on chairs. You could
have fallen and injured yourself. And no more climb-

ing apple trees, either, now that you're expecting my child.''

She banged the red tin of Calumet on the counter. ''It's my baby, not yours. So don't think you'll be coddling me and dictating what I can and cannot do.''

Her cheeks glowing bright red, Sarah Jane looked as if she might burst a blood vessel, and Ash worried that she'd make herself ill. ''Now don't go getting yourself upset, Sarah Jane,'' he said, trying to calm her down. ''I admit I flayed your hide a bit hard a while ago. But I was angry. I didn't know—''

''That I was pregnant?'' she finished. ''Well, at least you listened to that speech, didn't you, Ash? Too bad you never listened to any of the others I gave. It might have saved us both a lot of grief.''

Plowing agitated fingers through his hair, he let loose a sigh and gazed upon her flat stomach. ''Are you sure about the baby? I don't want to get my hopes up and then find out it's not true.''

The tenderness on his face, the longing in his voice, weakened her knees. ''I'm not positive, because I haven't seen the doctor yet. But I've been tossing up my breakfast each morning, and my breasts are tender to the touch. I feel different, not my usual self. And I'm tired all the time.''

Filling two cups with coffee, she placed them on the table, then sat down beside him. ''You seem pleased at the prospect of having another child. I wasn't sure you would be.''

''Hell yes, I'm pleased! I love kids. Oh, I know I haven't been much of a father to Addy, but I'm trying to change for the better. And I'm hoping for a son. I guess every man wants a son to carry on his name and all. But that doesn't mean to say that I don't love Addy. I love her like crazy. I just wish I'd been a better father, that's all.''

Touched by his confession, she reached out and clasped his arm. ''Addy loves you, Ash. All little girls love their daddies. There's a special bond that exists between them. Don't you know that?''

There was wistfulness in her voice and sadness in her eyes when she spoke. ''What of your parents, Sarah Jane? Have you heard back from them since you wrote?'' She rarely spoke of her family, and he sensed there was a problem.

She shook her head, sipped her coffee and forced the tears back. ''No. Not yet. I'm sure they're busy. Papa has his church. And my mother's always busy with dozens of charitable events and social engagements.'' They were still angry at her. She couldn't blame them.

He arched a brow. ''Too busy to write their own daughter?''

''I was somewhat of a disappointment to them. They probably haven't reconciled to the fact that I moved away so abruptly.''

Her comment confused him. ''But surely they gave their consent to Miss Cartwright before allowing you to marry and make the trip here?''

''Of course,'' she replied quickly, hoping he attributed her flushed cheeks to the hot coffee. ''It's just that—well, we didn't see eye to eye on a great many things, and I left with a lot of unresolved issues still between us.'' That was certainly true, though she doubted they realized the extent of her hurt, and wondered if they even cared.

Reaching out, he took her hand in his. "I'm willing to forgive you about the school, Sarah Jane, if you promise that you'll never lie to me again. Lying's about the most awful sin there is, and I don't want any more lies to come between us. Will you promise me that?"

Feeling guilty that she was unaware of his own deception in marrying her, he vowed to tell her the truth. But not today. Not when he'd been so self-righteous and critical of her behavior. But he would tell her and soon.

Tell him, Sarah Jane. Tell him about Miss Cartwright.

But she couldn't. Ash would never forgive her. Not now. Not after the school incident. Not after what he'd just said.

"I won't let anything come between us, Ash, except for this baby." She patted her stomach, hoping to divert his attention. "When I start ripening it's likely to prove an obstacle to getting close." She grinned, and so did he.

"Don't you worry about that, little love. I'm very dexterous when it comes to lovemaking."

"So I've noticed."

His tone grew serious. "I've been doing a lot of thinking about the mine school, Sarah Jane, and I've decided that you can continue on with your classes after the winter holiday is over." It was a small enough concession to make after all the happiness she'd given him. And seeing how joyful she was made him realize that he'd come to the right decision. He only wished he'd come to it sooner.

With a squeal, she jumped up from her chair,

knocking it backward to the floor in her haste to wrap her arms about his neck. "Oh, Ash! I'm so happy. Thank you. Thank you so much! You don't know how much this means to me." She kissed him then, starting at his cheek, then working her way to his lips, and soon gratitude turned to much more.

When his heart returned to its normal beat, Ash pulled her onto his lap. "I want you to be happy, Sarah Jane. I know we've had our differences, but I—"

She caressed his cheek. "I love you, Ash. I think I loved you from the first moment I saw you standing at the train station."

"I love you, too. I know I haven't always acted like a loving husband should, but I've come to care for you so very much."

Her eyes filled with tears. "Are you just saying that because of the baby? You don't have to, you know. I'd still love you anyway."

He tweaked her nose, then kissed her. "Of course not. I'm happy about the baby, Sarah Jane, but it's you I want."

"Will you always love me, no matter what?"

Her worried expression sent a chill of foreboding up his spine, but he shrugged it away. He would love her forever and ever. No matter what. "I will. You can count on it."

She heaved a sigh, then placed his hand on her abdomen. "I hope we have a son who looks just like you."

"And here I was hoping for a little blond boy."

"Really?" She smiled, then her expression sobered. "Addy doesn't know about the baby yet. Do you think she's going to feel threatened? We've grown so close these past months. I don't want anything to jeopardize my relationship with her, and I don't want her to think that this baby is going to come between the two of you, either.''

Ash didn't know quite how to respond. Until this very moment, he hadn't considered what his daughter's reaction might be. But Sarah Jane had. She was always thinking of the welfare of others, and he loved her all the more for it.

''I think we should tell her together. But not until you've seen the doctor and are sure that your suspicions are correct. No sense getting her hopes up. I have a feeling that Addy's going to be as excited as we are about this child.''

''I hope you're right. I love that little girl like she was my own flesh and blood.''

''You've been good for her, Sarah Jane. And I've never thanked you properly.''

She smiled seductively. ''Well, if you're not in any hurry to get back to work...''

He wasn't.

Chapter Seventeen

Seated by the fireplace in the parlor two weeks later, Sarah Jane and Addy were poring over recipe books for the upcoming Christmas holiday when a sharp knock sounded at the door. Before either of them had the opportunity to answer, they heard the front door open, and then slam shut.

Sarah Jane had just risen to her feet when Georgie Ann appeared in the doorway. "Surprise! I'm back!" Though her cheeks were chapped red from the cold, her smile radiated sunshine, and Sarah was delighted to see her.

Rushing forward, she said, "Oh, how I've missed you, Georgie Ann! But where's the baby? Don't tell me you left Robby at home?" She pursed her lips in disappointment. "I was so looking forward to holding him again."

"You just saw Georgie Ann last week, Sarah Jane," Addy pointed out from her sprawled position on the floor. Shaking her head and rolling her eyes, as if she just didn't understand grown-ups, she greeted their visitor with a wave before going back to the task at hand.

Draping her wet coat over the back of a green-and-red-plaid wing chair to dry out, Georgie Ann moved to the fireplace to thaw her backside, which felt like a frozen icicle. The fire was warm and welcoming, and she began to melt immediately. "It's starting to snow again," she said by way of explanation, rubbing her hands briskly together, "so I didn't want to bring Robby out. He's home with Mama."

At the mention of snow, Addy rushed to the window and grinned widely. A light snow was falling and just beginning to blanket the ground. "More snow! Oh, Sarah Jane, can I go outside and play? *Please?* We can finish looking for recipes later. I promise."

"It's *may* I go outside, sweetie. And the answer is yes, providing you bundle up. I don't want you coming down sick before Christmas. I've got enough to contend with at the moment."

The child raised her brows. "Oh, you mean—?" She smiled slyly. "Guess you'll be wanting to tell Georgie Ann yourself, huh?"

"Tell me what?" The dark-haired woman plopped down on the sofa, gazing at Addy and Sarah Jane, an expectant look on her face.

Sarah Jane couldn't contain her smile. "Ash and I are going to have a baby."

"Well, shoot, Sarah Jane, everyone knew that except you. You were puking to beat the band before I birthed little Robby, so I'm not real surprised to hear you're in the family way. Have you seen the doctor yet?"

Disappointed that her news was not a surprise, Sarah Jane inclined her head and smiled nonetheless. "He confirmed it only last week. Ash is walking on air. He's thrilled about becoming a father again."

She glanced toward the doorway the child had exited. "And how's Addy taking it?"

"She's tickled pink. She told us that she wants a little sister to fuss over and that she'll be madder than a wet hen if I give her a baby brother. But I know she's only teasing."

With pride in her voice, Sarah added, "Etta's teaching her how to knit, and she's wants to make a blanket for the baby. Isn't that sweet?"

Smiling wanly, the new mother said, "I'm happy for you, Sarah Jane. Truly I am. It's just—"

Something was dreadfully wrong. Georgie Ann wasn't acting at all like herself, and Sarah Jane worried that her friend might be ill. "Whatever's the matter? You seem out of sorts. Aren't you feeling well?"

"I'm just so darn tired all the time," Georgie Ann confessed, toying with the folds of her skirt and heaving a dispirited sigh. "Little Robby keeps me up half the night with his screaming. And his father still expects me to wait on him hand and foot.

"There're days when I just don't feel like getting outta bed. Having a baby is a lot harder than I thought it would be, is all."

Moving to the sofa, Sarah sat down next to her friend and reached for her hand. "I'm sure what you're feeling is normal. Things will get better as soon as the baby's a bit older and starts sleeping through the night, you'll see."

Tears filled Georgie Ann's dark eyes, which

alarmed Sarah Jane. The Georgie Ann she knew wasn't prone to hysteria or self-pity, and she'd never seen her cry before. "I feel like a bad mother, Sarah Jane. Sometimes I just want to bury my head under the pillow, 'cause I can't stand hearing my baby cry. He cries all the time. Mama said he's colicky and will probably do this for a good while yet."

"Oh, sweetie, I'm sorry!"

"I begged Mama to come over today and sit with Robby, so I could get out of the house for a little while and come visit you. I've missed our time together. Do you think that was bad of me?"

She rushed to reassure her. "Of course not! You're exhausted. I can see by the purple smudges under your eyes that you haven't been getting enough sleep. And you look like you've lost weight, too."

"I haven't been eating too well," she admitted.

"I'm sure you must be lonely cooped up in the house. This inclement weather we've been having hasn't helped matters in the least. I should have visited more often, but I thought you'd rather not have company until you had time to adjust to the baby's schedule. I can see I was wrong."

"You're always welcome in my home, Sarah Jane, you know that. And I'm sorry for ruining your announcement with my own selfish problems. Robby says I need to grow up and quit acting like a child."

A look of pure disgust crossed Sarah's face, and she wished Robby Freeland was in front of her at that very moment so she could knock some sense into him. "Men! They're such insensitive clods. They just don't know when to keep their mouths shut, do they?"

The woman finally smiled. "I guess not. Else we women wouldn't have anything to complain about."

Sarah poured two cups of hot tea from a white porcelain pot decorated with tiny purple violets and handed her one.

It was so good visiting with Georgie Ann again, she thought. She'd missed their daily chats and apparently so had her friend. It made Sarah Jane feel all the more guilty for having let her best friend down just when she needed her the most.

Hoping to take Georgie Ann's mind off her troubles, she changed the subject. "I guess since you've been cooped up at home you haven't heard about A.J.'s ultimatum to Mrs. Rafferty, have you?"

"Well, of course, I have. Mama said it was all the talk when she went into town the other day to fetch groceries. I guess A.J. let the old hag have it."

"According to my brother-in-law, he was very diplomatic. Or tried to be. Fortunately for Mrs. Rafferty, A.J. is far more even tempered than Ash." Her husband would have lit into the woman like an angry bear. Having tasted his wrath a time or two, Sarah Jane knew exactly what he was capable of, and she didn't care to experience it again.

"When A.J. informed Beulah that he and Cynthia were planning to get married, he said she threw a hissy fit. But he calmly informed her that if he and her daughter didn't marry right away, he was going to compromise Cynthia and create an ugly scandal. And that Beulah would never be able to hold her head up in Morgantown again, because he intended to let everyone know that it was all her doing that Cynthia had become a ruined woman."

Georgie's eyes widened, and she leaned forward, not wanting to miss a word of the juicy revelations. "I hadn't heard that part. What did Beulah say? She must have been furious."

"A.J. said that she broke down and cried, and that the real reason she didn't want him marrying Cynthia was because she hated Uncle Zeke and wouldn't have anyone with Morgan blood in her family. Except Ash, of course, because he was financially well situated, unlike A.J., and could take proper care of her daughter." Sarah rolled her eyes in disbelief that anyone could be so shallow.

"She said that? To his face?"

"Yes. But I thought A.J. handled it very well. He told her that it would be just revenge against Zeke if Beulah's daughter was to marry a Morgan. Sort of like coming full circle, after the unkind way she'd been treated. And that he was in the process of looking for a farm, and that once they were settled they wanted her to come visit just as often as she liked."

"Good grief!" The young woman clutched her throat, clearly dismayed. "A.J.'ll be sorry he said that. That old busybody will be moving in with them permanently, trying to run their lives. They'll never have a moment's peace."

"A.J. doesn't care. He confided that if that's the only way he can get Beulah's blessing, then so be it."

"When's the wedding going to take place?"

"The Saturday before Christmas. Which is why I've been poring over these recipes." She patted the pile of cookbooks on the piecrust table next to her. "I'm in charge of the reception. But it's going to be a small affair, thank goodness! Just family and a few friends. You and Robby are invited, of course."

Georgie Ann clapped her hands, her eyes glowing with excitement. "I just love a party! I'll have Mama make me a new dress. And I can help you with the food preparation."

"That would be wonderful."

"Oh, Sarah Jane, thank you! I feel so much better about things since we talked." She leaned forward and hugged her.

"That's what friends are for. And someday I might need you to be there for me." Sarah patted her tummy, fear entering her eyes, and Georgie Ann suspected immediately what had put it there.

"You're scared about having this baby, aren't you?" she asked, clasping her friend's hand. "Your face is as white as that snow outside the window."

Taking a deep breath, Sarah Jane nodded. "I'm very excited about having a baby, Georgie Ann. Please don't get me wrong. But I keep remembering how difficult your labor was, and I'm not sure I can handle it. And...and I don't know what kind of mother I'll be."

That scared her most of all. She had only her mother's example to follow, and she definitely did not want to be like Xenobia Parker, a woman who couldn't express her emotions, who couldn't tell her only daughter that she loved her.

"Posh! You'll be an excellent mother. Just look at what wonders you've accomplished with Addy. And don't be silly. Of course, you can handle the pain. Oh sure, it hurts when the baby's coming out, and before that when the labor begins. But the painful memories disappear once your child's born.

"Mama says that God gives a woman pain during childbirth, so she'll appreciate the gift of giving life all the more. And he makes her forget about it afterward, so there's no unpleasantness attached to the baby."

"I hadn't really thought about it like that." It was a comforting notion, Sarah decided.

"I'd go through it all again, because the end result is worth it. I wouldn't give up my baby for anything, even with all the complaining I've been doing." Suddenly Georgie Ann looked down, aghast at the dark stain spreading over her bodice. Patting herself with a linen napkin, she said, "Goodness me! I'd best get home. My breasts are leaking like a sieve, which means it's time to feed my baby."

"Guess God didn't figure out how to stop that from happening," Sarah Jane said, grinning, and Georgie Ann laughed.

"Robby's fond of saying that God has a strange sense of humor. He may be right."

Sarah Jane was to think about that in the days and weeks ahead.

With her lower lip caught between her teeth in concentration, Addy moved the wooden rolling pin back and forth across the large square of sugar cookie dough. "I ain't—I mean I've never made Christmas cookies before, Sarah Jane. I hope they turn out."

Frowning at the lump of brown gingerbread dough on the table before her, Sarah Jane replied, "That makes two of us, sweetie.'' If she never saw another gingerbread man or sugar cookie cutout, it wouldn't bother her in the least. She'd been baking nonstop for days in preparation for the upcoming wedding reception and Christmas holiday, though it felt more like months. She probably had enough sweets to open her own bakery shop.

''How're my two girls doing?'' Ash asked upon entering the kitchen, the smells of cinnamon, nutmeg and vanilla assaulting his senses and making his stomach grumble.

The windows were clouded with condensation; Addy had drawn a face in one of the panes, and he smiled at the childish effort. The domestic scene touched him deeply. Addy and Sarah Jane cooking together...who would have ever thought?

''I've got some interesting news, but I don't know how you're going to react to it, Sarah.''

With cookie cutter in hand, she glanced up from her task, and said, ''If it requires making more Christmas cookies and confections for Saturday's wedding, I don't want to hear it.'' Then she placed the cookie cutouts on a tin baking sheet.

Ash reached toward the pile of baked gingerbread men and his wife slapped his hand. ''Hey! I just wanted a taste.''

''Those are for guests. Now what's the news?'' She was tired, her feet and back ached, and she felt as if she would collapse at any moment. What she needed was a strong tonic to invigorate her blood. She'd read about the Peruvian Syrup for iron-poor blood in the last issue of the *Farmer's Almanac* and intended to ask the doctor for some the next time she saw him.

"Zeke and Etta have decided to tie the knot alongside A.J. and Cynthia."

Her mouth dropped open, then she fell onto the chair and burst into tears. "But that means I've got to make more food, and—" She held the sides of her head as if it was about to explode and wailed.

"Daddy!" Addy said, quite furious that her father had upset Sarah Jane. "You're not supposed to just blurt out stuff like that. Don't you know how tired Sarah Jane is because of the baby?" She shook her finger at him. "Shame on you!"

His daughter's chastisement made Ash study his wife more closely. She'd stopped crying and had now returned to decorating the cookies. She did look a bit tired, but the doctor said that was to be expected. Sarah Jane's mood swings were caused by her pregnancy, and he'd learned not to take her frequent outbursts too seriously.

"I'm glad you're protective of your stepmother, Addy. That shows a great deal of maturity."

"I wish you'd quit talking about me as if I wasn't here." Sarah Jane wiped her forehead with the back of her sleeve before looking up at her husband. "I'm sorry I reacted so horribly. I couldn't help myself, as I'm sure you know by now."

Smiling softly, he moved to wrap his hands about her waist, kissing the back of her neck. Gooseflesh erupted everywhere, making Sarah draw in her breath sharply.

Would she always feel that tingle in her spine, that trickle of excitement that went clear down to her toes?

Yes, she decided without hesitation.

"I can tell Zeke and Etta to postpone their wedding, if you think it'll be too much for you to handle, love."

She shook her head, her cheeks tinged pink with embarrassment. "Don't be silly. I was just a bit overwhelmed at the news. It makes perfect sense for them to get married at the same time A.J. and Cynthia do, as long as Cynthia doesn't mind. Has anyone bothered to ask the bride how she feels about sharing her special day?"

When Sarah Jane turned toward the stove, Ash filched a cookie and bit into it. "Mmm, these are good. Your cooking sure has improved, love," he said, winking at his daughter, who grinned in response.

"So, what was Cynthia's response?"

"She said it was fine with her. Beulah had a conniption, of course. But A.J. was able to calm her down. Don't know how that brother of mine can handle that aggravating woman." Ash shook his head in bewilderment. "She drives me nuts."

"Wait till you meet my mother. You probably won't like her, either." His mysterious smile gave her pause, but she shrugged it off, turning her attention to her stepdaughter.

"Addy, besides Gordy, is there anyone else you'd like to invite to the wedding party? I've been thinking that it's time you developed some female acquaintances."

The child shrugged, staring down at the toes of her scuffed shoes. "None of the girls in town like me. So I guess not."

"I'm sure that's not true, sweetie. Gordy seems to think they do. And if you act a little friendlier toward them, they might include you in some of their activities. Think about it and let me know. If you decide that you'd like to invite a couple of the girls—maybe the Hobart twins?—I'll send their mothers a note.''

The Hobart girls were well mannered and rather on the shy side, and Sarah thought that they would complement and tone down her stepdaughter's boisterous personality and vice versa. And they didn't seem at all mean-spirited or catty, like some of the girls she'd observed at church.

Leaning back in his chair as he gazed upon his wife, Ash was once again astonished at the level of sensitivity she displayed toward his child. Sarah Jane had told him only last night of her concern that Addy had no female friends, and that she wanted to encourage her to socialize more. She hadn't wasted any time in putting her thoughts into action, and for that he was extremely grateful.

Addy was maturing into a lovely young woman, and he had his wife to thank for it. His daughter's hair, which had grown almost shoulder length, was shiny and combed neatly into two braids now. She dressed appropriately for a young girl her age, and she smelled as sweet as roses most of the time, thanks to the scented soaps Sarah had purchased for her as a gift. Her speech had also taken on refinement, and she hardly ever cursed anymore, which was nothing short of miraculous.

Thinking back to how his daughter had looked and behaved before Sarah Jane had arrived, Ash was stunned by the transformation. He would be forever grateful to Miss Dorothea Cartwright for sending him such a wonderful wife.

* * *

In Philadelphia, Miss Dorothea Cartwright had just left the Walnut Street residence of the Reverend and Mrs. Parker, after having finally discovered—much to her very great mortification and displeasure—the whereabouts of their daughter, Sarah Jane, her most wayward and absentee student. And the bane of her existence these many years.

Apparently, Sarah Jane's letter to her parents, which had been written some time ago, according to the reverend, had been misdirected by the postal service and had only just reached them a few days ago.

Not one to be made a fool of, Dorothea fully intended to get to the bottom of things and let Sarah Jane know in no uncertain terms just what she thought of her outrageous behavior—her outrageous *criminal* behavior—in falsifying documents, rifling through mail, and pretending to be someone she was not.

Her successful escape out the bedroom window of the dormitory had also set a dangerous example for the other students. One she intended to rectify immediately.

Dorothea had a feeling that Ashby Morgan of Morgantown, West Virginia, would be very interested and shocked to learn that his wife had married him under the falsest of pretenses, and that she, Dorothea Cartwright, a woman of impeccable reputation and rigid standards, had been used most cruelly by Sarah Jane in an effort to perpetrate this ruse.

Taking small, precise steps as a proper lady was wont to do, even if she was rushing to accomplish a very important task, she hurried down the sidewalk crowded with holiday shoppers and headed directly for the train station to purchase a ticket for her destination.

She would spend the upcoming Christmas holiday with her sister's family in Virginia, then venture on to West Virginia to confront her disobedient, incorrigible and headstrong former student.

Sarah Jane Parker needed to be made an example of, and Dorothea knew she was just the woman to accomplish that task.

Chapter Eighteen

Leaning back against the plump cushions of the sofa as she gazed upon the gaily decorated Christmas tree, Sarah Jane heaved a contented sigh, then took another sip of frothy eggnog, which tasted deliciously decadent.

It was indecent to feel so happy. But she did.

The wedding reception had gone off without a hitch. In fact, she had received nothing but compliments on the food and decorations, including praise from Beulah Rafferty, which had taken her totally by surprise.

The woman wasn't known for her generous nature or effusive comments, but Sarah Jane suspected that Beulah was slowly learning to mend her ways. The older woman had much to gain if she did, and a lot to lose if she didn't.

A.J. had made it clear that as the future grandmother of his and Cynthia's children she would be expected to set a sterling example for them. Of course, she had agreed wholeheartedly, even promising to curb her tendency to gossip. No one, however, believed she would.

Looking absolutely adorable in green taffeta and white lace, Addy had relished her role as Cynthia's maid of honor, and Sarah had been very grateful to her sister-in-law for bestowing such a distinction upon the young girl. Ash, too, had looked resplendent in his formal attire as he stood up for his brother as best man.

Best man. A fitting term, for her husband was the very best of men.

"I think that's the loveliest Christmas tree I've ever laid eyes on," she said to her husband, staring in wonder at the ten-foot blue spruce standing proudly near the front window, the top of the tree nearly reaching the high ceiling. "Thank you so much for cutting it down and helping Addy and me to decorate it this afternoon. We couldn't have managed without you."

Rubbing her small stockinged feet, which were propped up on his lap, Ash smiled, feeling mellow and quite happy himself. A.J. and Zeke were finally married off, he was going to be a father again, and he was so much in love with his wife that it scared him. He'd learned from his past marriages that happiness was fleeting, and he couldn't bear to think that his and Sarah Jane's happiness might not be destined for a lifetime.

"Life is what you make of it," his mother had always counseled. Ash intended to enjoy and treasure every moment he shared with Sarah Jane.

"You and Addy did all the work of making the cranberry and popcorn garlands and the pretty paper cutouts," he said finally. "I merely supervised the production."

"We never had a Christmas tree when I was a child," she confessed, marveling at the lighted flickering candles and pretty store-bought red and green glass ornaments that Ash had brought home from town. Paper snowflakes that she and Addy had cut from white paper hung from the branches. "Papa said it took away from the real meaning of Christmas and wouldn't let Mama put one up. But I don't think that's true, do you?"

He indicated he didn't with a shake of his head, then said, "When my mother was alive we'd always put up our tree on Christmas Eve, so I'm glad we're continuing that tradition this year. This is the first tree we've had in a very long time, so I guess that makes it extra special."

Christmas just hadn't seemed the same after his mother died, and neither he nor A.J. had felt like bothering with the traditional festivities, though he could see now that he'd been remiss in denying Addy the joy. She'd loved every moment of the tree trimming this year.

The snow fell silently and determinedly beyond the frosted glass windows. The fire crackled softly in the hearth, the pine logs popping every so often, clear reminders that winter had arrived.

"It's so quiet around here with A.J. gone on his honeymoon and Zeke living at Etta's house. I'm not sure I'll ever get used to it."

"You won't get a chance to get used to it, love," he reminded her. "Don't forget A.J. and Cynthia will be moving in with us once they return. My brother's still trying to work out the details of purchasing that farm over in Clarksburg. He's talked to Georgie Ann's brother-in-law Floyd about a loan.

"I hope you don't mind that I invited them to stay here for a while."

"Don't be ridiculous! Of course I don't mind. They're family, after all, and we have plenty of room. And I welcome the chance to get to know Cynthia better. We seem to have a great deal in common." From the few times they'd shared tales of their up-bringing and how their respective parents had needed to control every aspect of their lives, Sarah Jane knew they were kindred spirits.

Cynthia was so sweet natured that one couldn't help but like her. A.J. had chosen well.

"And we're both married to the Morgan brothers, after all," Sarah Jane added with a grin.

"Lucky girls," he said, but his eyes were twinkling.

There were dozens of gaily wrapped boxes under the tree, and Sarah Jane couldn't quite contain her childlike enthusiasm as she wondered how many were for her. But it was the bestowing of presents that was really the most fun. She had bought Ash a new robe, a pocketknife and several other small items. For Addy she had purchased four novels, two shirtwaists and skirts, and the baseball and bat she'd been wanting.

"I hope Addy likes all her gifts come morning. I can't wait to see her face when you bring in her special surprise."

"*Shh!*" Placing his finger to her lips, Ash cautioned silence. "My daughter has the biggest ears of anyone I know. If you even breathe a word, she's likely to hear. And I want her to be surprised.''

"My lips are sealed.''

"Not too tight, I hope.'' Lifting her across his lap, he began to kiss her senseless. When her eyes were glazed over with passion and she couldn't form a coherent thought, he pulled back. ''Now that I've got your attention, love, I want to give you one of your presents early.''

His wicked grin made her gasp. ''Ashby Morgan! Shame on you! I think you'd better wait for…for *that* until we retire for the evening. What if Addy were to come down and—''

He chuckled. ''It's not what you're thinking. Though I'm quite anxious to give you *that,* too.''

"Well, what is it?'' she asked. ''I'm dying to know. Though it wasn't necessary to get me a present. I have so much already. I feel blessed with you, Addy, and now the baby on the way. I can't think of anything else I could possibly need.''

"What's the one thing you've regretted since getting married? The one thing you said you would change if you could?''

She thought for a moment, then a nervous twittering began in her stomach that soon turned into a bona fide rumble of fear. ''You mean about my parents?'' She had told him once that she wished she and her parents had parted on better terms. What she hadn't told him was that they'd never really parted officially, never really said goodbye.

He was looking inordinately pleased with himself, and that worried her. ''I was going to wait and surprise you after the new year, but I decided that with the baby coming, it might not be a good idea to cause such a shock to your system.''

His surprise obviously had something to do with her parents and a feeling of foreboding filled her. If what she thought was correct, if Ash was bringing her parents to visit, then she was going to be in a great deal of trouble.

Please let it be anything but that, she prayed, unwilling to take the chance of ruining her marriage, even for the sake of mending fences with her family.

''My parents?'' she asked in a small voice, holding her breath, hoping she'd guessed wrong.

Unable to hide his excitement, he squeezed her cold, clammy hand and explained, ''I wrote your mother and father, inviting them to come for a visit. I sent them two train tickets with directions on how to get here. I received a telegram from them the day before yesterday. They're coming!

''Merry Christmas, love,'' he said, kissing her cheek.

A sickly smile crossed Sarah Jane's face, and it was all she could do not to bolt out the door and run for her life. As much as she wanted to see her parents, to explain everything that had happened and why, to do so would mean exposing her lies and deceit to Ash.

And if there was one thing her husband had made perfectly clear in the time they'd been married, it was that he wasn't going to stand for any more falsehoods or fabrications.

She swallowed with a great deal of difficulty. ''Merry Christmas,'' she replied, thinking that God really did have a sense of humor. And she had some-how become the butt of the joke.

''Adelaide Morgan!'' Sarah Jane looked down at the puddle beneath her feet and cringed at the liquid spilling over the toes of her brand-new red leather shoes, a Christmas present from Ash. ''I told you to keep an eye on your puppy. Theodore has had another accident in the house.''

Addy's Christmas surprise was proving to be an even bigger one for Sarah Jane. Though she adored animals, especially puppies, she did not like them pid-dling in her clean house. The realization that she was starting to sound more and more like her mother and Miss Cartwright didn't faze her a bit.

''Bad puppy!'' Addy scolded halfheartedly. ''Teddy's sorry, Sarah Jane,'' she said, holding up the squiggling, pink-tongued dog for her inspection, and allowing him to lick her stepmother's arm as a display of his contrition. ''He's just nervous being away from his mommy. Daddy said it won't take him long to get housebroke.''

The scrappy terrier was cute, and Addy had fallen in love from the first moment she set eyes on his eager-to-please face, so Sarah hoped Ash was right. ''Take Theodore outside and let him do his business there. He has to learn not to piddle indoors.''

While Addy did what she was told, Sarah Jane bus-ied herself in the kitchen, making the final prepara-tions for her Christmas dinner of baked ham, scal-loped potatoes, cloverleaf rolls and buttered carrots. Fortunately, she had lots and lots of cookies left over for dessert.

Zeke and Etta would be here soon to spend the holiday with them. It had been decided the night before that they would stop by Beulah's house on the way and invite the woman to share in the family festivities, since A.J. and Cynthia were in New York City on their honeymoon.

Zeke had been less than enthusiastic about the idea, but Sarah couldn't bear the thought of anyone spending Christmas Day all alone and Etta, bless her heart, had backed her up.

She'd made plenty of food, so Beulah's attendance wasn't going to prove a problem, unless, of course, she and Zeke got into another argument.

Now that Zeke was married, she hoped some of Beulah's animosity toward him had lessened. The old man had promised to behave himself, though she distinctly remembered a similar promise had been made before the now infamous Thanksgiving dinner fiasco.

Placing the last rose-patterned china plate on the green linen-covered dining room table, she looked up to find Ash entering the room. "Merry Christmas," she said, pleased he'd chosen to wear her gift. "You look quite handsome in that blue wool shirt, I must say. That color does wonderful things for your eyes."

Those very eyes glittered wickedly, and Ash moved forward to wrap his arms about her, patting her tummy. "And how's my son doing today? Growing by leaps and bounds, I hope."

Her stomach was still relatively flat, so she had no idea how big the baby would be when it finally reached full term. "Your son could very well turn out to be a dainty little girl," she reminded him, and turned in his arms to kiss his chin, hoping she could give him the son she knew he wanted.

"Well, if that's the case then we'll just have to hurry up and make another, won't we? Why don't we start right now? It seems like ages since I've made love to you." He nuzzled her ear, inserting the tip of his tongue into the whorl.

Her cheeks warmed, and her heart began to pound. "I'd hardly call three days ages." Though it felt like that to her, too. "In case it's escaped your notice our guests will be arriving at any moment, and your daughter is just outside the back door with her new puppy. So behave yourself."

He glanced at the regulator clock hanging on the wall and frowned. "It's hours till bedtime, but I might be able to wait, if you promise you won't be too tired tonight."

A wicked gleam entered her eyes, and she smiled. "I won't be too tired, if you volunteer to help me wash the dishes afterward."

"I see that I married a manipulative siren," he countered, before giving in to a smile. "All right. I'll help. But you had better make it worth my while, woman. If any of my men find out that I'm doing women's work, I'll be laughed out of the mine."

"Oh, there's no need to worry on that account. It'll definitely be worth your while. I have a little surprise in store for you."

She had yet to wear the diaphanous nightgowns she had purchased from Mrs. Hodak. The timing had never seemed appropriate, but Sarah intended to rectify that tonight.

* * *

Propped against the down bed pillows, the kerosene lamp on the nightstand flickering gently, Ash held his hands over his eyes as instructed and wondered what mysteries his wife had in store for him. He couldn't quite decide who was more excited at the prospect: he at receiving the surprise, or she at presenting it.

"Can I peek now?" What sounded like a hairbrush banged down on the dresser, then a rustling of paper and finally a drawer slamming shut.

"Not yet! I'll just be another moment. I'll let you know when I'm ready. Now don't peek and spoil the surprise."

"You've got my interest up, love."

She giggled, then said saucily, "I hope more than your interest is up. Okay, you can look."

Uncovering his eyes, his gaze fell upon the vision standing at the foot of the bed, and his mouth dropped open. Sarah Jane wore the sheerest, most provocative nightgown he'd ever seen—and he'd seen quite a few on the women down at O'Connor's. But this one was far more revealing.

"Where did you get that?" Blood thickened and pooled in his groin.

"Don't you like it?" She pirouetted, holding the sides of the gown out as she twirled. "I bought it especially for you."

"Hell yes, I like it!" He bounded off the bed to take a closer look. Her full breasts were clearly visible through the lace that attempted to cover her bosom but wasn't quite succeeding. The black material was so thin, so incredibly transparent, that he could detect the slight swell of her tummy, the triangle of light blond hair between her thighs.

He swallowed. "That's some nightgown!"

Smiling seductively, she floated toward him like an angel. "Mrs. Hodak said it came all the way from Paris, France. Guess those French ladies aren't very modest."

"Lucky for French men," he said, pulling her to his chest for a kiss. "Of course, you know you won't be wearing this creation very long."

Sarah wondered what Ash would think if he knew who the gowns had been intended for originally. His association with Lula Mae Tucker had dissolved completely. Since the day of their marriage, he'd spent all of his evenings at home, and there'd been no further unpleasant encounters with the prostitute. In fact, she'd heard a rumor that Lula Mae had left town— moved on to more profitable pastures, as it were— after hearing of A.J.'s marriage to Cynthia.

She'd learned an important lesson about men, marriage and women of easy virtue: if a wife gave her husband a little bit of the forbidden fruit at home, there'd be no need for him to stray and taste the apple elsewhere.

"You're so beautiful, Sarah Jane. I'm the luckiest man alive." Ash dropped to his knees, carefully lifting the hem of the nightgown to expose his wife's belly. Then he placed tender kisses upon it, worshiping her and the unborn child within. "I love you both so much!"

She cradled his head, tears blurring her vision. "You're going to make me cry, then I won't be the least bit sexy or do this gown justice."

He carried her to the bed and laid her down upon the sheet. "You don't need pretty gowns to do you justice, love. You'd be beautiful in a burlap sack. And I like you best naked anyway.''

Feigning disappointment, she thrust out her lower lip and asked, ''You mean I wasted all of your money on this lovely gown?''

He removed the gown in question and tossed it on the floor. ''I'd rather gaze upon your flesh, upon these pink-tipped beauties, than a scrap of black lace.''

She wrapped her arms about him. ''You make me feel beautiful, though I'm sure in a few months I won't feel that way at all. My body's going to be—''

He smothered her words with a kiss. ''Your body's going to be beautiful, no matter how big the baby grows inside of you. Never think otherwise. You'll soon be the mother of my child, and there can be nothing lovelier than that.''

Like a spark to dry tinder, his words fueled her desire. Pushing him onto his back, Sarah Jane moved down the length of him, allowing her long hair to trail over his body like a silken whip, and he writhed beneath the onslaught.

''What? What are you doing?'' he asked, his voice thick with passion.

''I want to give you pleasure, Ash. I want to give you the same pleasure you give me.'' Taking him into her mouth, she tasted the saltiness of him, heard his sharp intake of breath, as she continued to explore and love him with her mouth and tongue.

He groaned aloud. ''Where did you learn how to do that?'' He took a deep breath. ''You'll unman me if you don't stop, love. A man can only take so much torture.''

She smiled, tossing her hair back over her shoulder,

a glimmer of triumph in her eyes, before straddling him and exploring his chest with her hands and lips, running her fingers through the thick mat of dark hair. "I can see why men like to be in this position of superiority. It gives one a certain sense of power." With a mischievous grin, she wiggled a bit, and he cursed beneath his breath. "I can see you like that," she said.

"I like it too well. But why are you torturing me? I thought you liked all your presents."

"I did. This is your reward for choosing so well." With that, she lowered herself upon him and rode the crest of her passion, taking him with her on a journey to the stars and beyond.

They peaked together, their breathing labored, their sweat-slick bodies glistening as they slowly descended back to earth to relax in the aftermath of their heated lovemaking.

Pulling Sarah into his arms, Ash nestled her against his chest and kissed the top of her head. "I'm the luckiest man alive to have found you."

Thinking what lay ahead, tears filled her eyes. "I hope you'll always feel the same as you do now."

"I will," he whispered without hesitation.

She wished it could be true.

Chapter Nineteen

The snow had been falling for ten days straight with no sign of letup in sight. The new year had arrived on the shirttails of a blizzard, and Sarah Jane wondered if they were destined to spend the remainder of the winter indoors.

School was closed until further notice. Ash and A.J. were home early most days, because the roads were nearly impassable. The coal that had already been mined was piling up because nothing could be shipped by rail.

Two factors made the forced isolation bearable: Addy was still enthralled with her new puppy and kept herself occupied playing with Teddy, and Cynthia had proven to be a delightful companion and conversationalist. Sarah Jane had grown inordinately fond of the woman.

"I had no idea how stimulating New York City could be," her sister-in-law said as she finished wiping the grime from the dining room windows with a solution of ammonia and water. "It's way too crowded for me to ever consider living there, but the entertainment and museums..." The young woman's eyes widened with wonder. "It's just so alive. I've never really experienced anything like it before."

Cynthia's confinement in Morgantown must have been similar to her own at Miss Cartwright's, Sarah Jane thought, but perhaps a bit more lonely. It didn't seem she had many friends, which was yet another similarity between them.

"I've never been to New York City, but Philadelphia has some very interesting museums and historic treasures. It's considered the cradle of liberty, after all. Of course, my time to enjoy those sights was rather limited."

"Because of your stay at Miss Cartwright's?"

She had confided most of her unhappy childhood circumstances to her sister-in-law, having found a sympathetic ear and an understanding heart. "The woman was a martinet. We had to toe the line or else. Most of our excursions outside of school were strictly for educational purposes. We rarely did anything just for the pure pleasure of it. Miss Dorothea Cartwright was not a frivolous woman, as she so often reminded her students."

Polishing the legs of the mahogany table with a soft cloth generously laced with beeswax, while Sarah Jane dusted the crystal stemware in the china cabinet, the redhead made a face of disapproval, and said, "I don't understand why your parents forced you to stay at that school for so long. You were rather old to be incarcerated like that. I mean, it sounds almost like a prison."

Sarah Jane found it difficult to keep the bitterness out of her voice. "It was like a prison. At least, to me. I suppose my parents thought it would serve me well to learn everything I could from Miss Cartwright. They had aspirations that I would remain at the school and teach. Of course, they never bothered to consult me about what I wanted to do with my life, never took into consideration how miserably unhappy I was.''

''What's going to happen when they finally arrive? How are you going to deal with them?''

Having taken Cynthia into her confidence about her reasons for marrying Ash, and his subsequent well-meaning but misguided benevolence in bringing her parents to her, she shrugged, placing the wineglasses back inside the cabinet. ''I don't know. If they mention anything to Ash about—'' She looked over her shoulder to make sure they were alone. ''If he finds out that I married him under false pretenses, I fear my marriage will be over.''

Covering her face with her hands, she suddenly burst into tears. ''Oh, why did I have to be so stupid?''

Cynthia moved quickly to her side and wrapped a comforting arm about the pregnant woman's thickening waist. ''Because you were desperate to escape, that's why. No one can blame you for that, least of all Ash. Now stop crying. It's not good for the baby when you get upset.''

''It's not going to be good for the baby when he doesn't have a father to tuck him in at night and play ball with him, and—'' She started to wail again.

''Sarah Jane Morgan, that will be quite enough! I know we haven't known each other all that long for me to be lecturing you, but I think someone needs to.

And since Georgie Ann isn't able to get over here because of the snowstorm, then I guess the task falls to me.'' She led her into the parlor, where they seated themselves on the couch before the cozy fire.

''First of all, this weather is making everyone depressed and out of sorts.''

Sarah Jane heaved a sigh. ''I'm looking at it as a reprieve,'' she admitted, wiping her eyes and nose with the edge of her apron. ''If it keeps snowing, my parents won't be able to arrive anytime soon. Maybe not at all,'' she added hopefully.

''The only sensible thing for you to do, dear heart, is to tell Ash the truth about everything before your parents arrive. It's really the only recourse you have left, Sarah Jane.''

Blue eyes widening, Sarah Jane replied, ''Tell Ash the truth? But—but he'll hate me. He'll never forgive me. Not after I promised to be absolutely truthful with him from here on out. You have no idea how upset he was after the school incident.''

Cynthia couldn't keep from laughing. ''Forgive me, but—you must stop being so melodramatic. You remind me of Addy. Ash isn't going to hate you. The man is so in love with you that he can hardly see straight. The way he looks at you is indecent. And don't even bring up that baby. He turns into an utter fool whenever it's mentioned.''

Sarah Jane tried hard not to be insulted, for she knew her sister-in-law was only trying to help. ''A.J.'s just like him,'' she pointed out.

''Yes, I know.'' The new bride smiled happily. ''I can't wait to get pregnant.'' She patted her stomach. ''I'm so terribly jealous of your having a baby.''

"Would it surprise you to know that I was quite jealous of you when we first met?"

The redhead's eyes widened. "Jealous of me? Why?" Then it dawned on her. "Surely you didn't believe—? Oh, Sarah Jane, how could you?"

She smiled ruefully. "I'm afraid I did. You seemed so upset when Ash announced that we were getting married that I naturally assumed you had designs on him."

"I was upset because I knew my mother was going to take the news badly and make my life miserable. Which she did, by the way. Mama had done everything in her power to get Ash and me together, but the spark just wasn't there. I knew, and I think Ash did, too, that we would never be more than friends.

"But I confess it's a boost to my ego knowing you were jealous. As pretty as you are, I'm really quite flattered. But you had and have no cause to worry. Ash is totally in love with you. And there's just no getting around the fact that you're going to have to come clean and confess."

"I guess Miss Cartwright was right about one thing," Sarah Jane said with a dispirited sigh.

"What's that?"

"She always warned me that my 'propensity for telling falsehoods' was going to get me into a great deal of trouble one of these days."

"You are going to be in a great deal of trouble, young man, if you do not find me a suitable means of transportation to get to Morgantown! I have pressing business there, and I do not wish to be kept waiting."

Dorothea Cartwright tapped her umbrella impatiently against the train station's wooden planks as she addressed the stationmaster. Her cheeks were chapped from the cold, and her nose was actually running. She dabbed at it discreetly with her handkerchief.

Pushing back his dark green visor, Virgil Purdy scratched his head, trying his hardest to remain professional, as he had been taught. He had a lot of experience in dealing with bossy women. His cousin Beulah Rafferty was about the bossiest, most opinionated female he knew. Cantankerous, even! If he could handle Beulah, he sure as heck could handle this irate customer, he decided.

"Can't do nothing about the snow, ma'am," he attempted to explain, despite her pinched-mouth expression. "It's been coming down like this for days. You were lucky your train got through. The snow's five or six feet in some places. The roads are impassable. And even if I had a way to get you to Morgantown, I couldn't. There'd be too much liability for the railroad. We're concerned for your safety, ma'am."

Her displeasure hung in the air like a thick fog, and Virgil swallowed. "I reckon you'll just have to cool your heels here in Fairmont till there's a break in the weather. Sorry, but there's nothing more I can do."

Not one to be thwarted by anything as inconsequential as a blizzard, the older woman leaned closer to the cage that separated her from the man, her eyes narrowing. "I insist that you drive me to Morgantown, Mr.—" she glanced quickly at the painted sign hanging above his head "—Purdy. Or I shall be forced to report you to your superiors."

"I ain't got no superiors in Fairmont, ma'am, so

that's gonna be a mite hard. I suggest you go on over and settle yourself down on one of those benches by the coal stove, same as the other folks have done. As soon as there's a break in the weather, we'll get you on your way.''

With a loud harrumph, Dorothea drew herself up to her imposing five-foot eight-inch height. She was tall for a woman, and used it to her advantage whenever possible. ''Provincial and inept!'' she declared, then turned on her heel and did as instructed.

Eyeing the motley group of traveling companions with distaste, she moved to an unoccupied bench and wiped it with her handkerchief before sitting down.

Perhaps, Dorothea thought, feeling her toes begin to thaw, Sarah Jane Parker had unknowingly created her own punishment.

West Virginia was a living hell, in her opinion!

She was going to tell him. She was going to tell Ash everything, just as Cynthia had suggested. Her sister-in-law was right. It was her only recourse, Sarah Jane decided, descending from the upstairs master bedroom three days later.

Honesty was always the best policy. Whoever had made up that adage was no doubt correct. She would be honest, and Ash would forgive her. Her husband loved her. She loved him. It would work out.

It had to!

As if conjured up by her thoughts, the front door opened and Ash came in, wearing a big smile on his face as he stamped his boots to remove the caked snow. ''Hello, love,'' he said, discarding his heavy jacket and hanging it on the hall tree.

"I'm glad you're home early, Ash. There's something we need to talk about."

"I've got something to tell you, too, Sarah. Good news!" He was beaming from ear to ear. "We've hit a very rich seam of coal. The best one yet. Zeke thinks this could be our ticket to expanding the mining operation. Isn't that exciting?" He wrapped his arms around her waist and twirled her about.

"Yes, very!" She matched his grin with one of her own and kissed his cheek. "Congratulations! That's wonderful. I know how hard you've been working."

"The work's not over yet. I'm afraid it's really just beginning. That's why I came home early. I've got to pore over the books. See if there's enough money to buy additional equipment, hire more workers.

"But that's enough about me. What was it you wanted to tell me? There's nothing wrong, is there?" He looked her over from head to toe. "You're feeling okay, aren't you?"

She wouldn't spoil his good news. It wouldn't be fair. Not when he was so happy and proud. Tomorrow would be soon enough to confess her transgressions.

"I feel fine. Wonderful, even. I'm not tossing my food back up anymore, and my appetite has returned full force. I ate a huge breakfast this morning. Georgie Ann said I was going to grow as fat as her mother, if I wasn't careful."

"So what did you want to talk to me about?"

She shook her head, crossing her fingers behind her back. "It's nothing. I was just going to ask what you wanted for dinner. I was thinking about frying up some chicken."

"That sounds great. Call me when it's ready." And

then he disappeared into his office, leaving Sarah Jane feeling more nervous and depressed than she had been already.

The following morning Sarah Jane was determined to make a clean breast of things. She had hardly slept a wink all night for worrying, and now she had overslept.

Ash was already at the breakfast table when she entered the kitchen. The aroma of coffee made her stomach grumble, which was a good sign. A week ago the smell had made her violently ill.

"I made coffee and a pot of oatmeal," her husband told her. "You looked like you needed your rest, so I didn't wake you."

She leaned over and kissed his cheek. "That was sweet of you." Glancing about, she asked, "Where's Addy? Has she eaten already?"

He nodded. "I told her she could spend the day with Zeke and Etta. She's been cooped up in the house for weeks, and needed a little diversion, so I took her and the pup into town early this morning."

That was true of everyone, Sarah thought. They all needed some diversion. Now that the weather had finally cleared and the snow had melted somewhat she could resume teaching on Monday, and things could finally get back to normal.

"I thought it would be nice since it's Saturday," Ash continued, "if you and I spent some time alone together. With the holidays, the blizzard, and now the new coal seam that's likely to take up a great deal of my time, we haven't had much time to just sit down and talk, discuss plans for our future." He was thinking about adding on to the house, maybe include a sunporch so Sarah could use it as a schoolroom. And he wanted more bedrooms for all those kids they were planning to have.

His intuitive comment made her hands sweat, and she almost dropped the mug of coffee she was handed. "What about A.J. and Cynthia? We won't really be alone." She took a sip, hoping the warm liquid would soothe her frazzled nerves.

"The lovebirds are heading to Clarksburg today to sign the final papers for the purchase of the farm. They'll be leaving soon, and then we'll be all alone." He wiggled his brows suggestively. "We may just head back upstairs and go to bed."

She smiled softly. "That sounds promising. But first, there's something we need to discuss."

"Not the dinner menu again?"

"No. I—"

The sound of a wagon laboring up the driveway halted her in midsentence.

Ash rose to his feet and said, "Someone's coming. Wonder who it could be at this time of morning."

"My parents?" Her heart began thudding as she followed him to the front of the house, not ready for the confrontation she knew was inevitable.

He shook his head. "No. The trains from Philadelphia were all delayed because of the storm, so your parents are presently stuck in Washington, D.C."

"You knew they were on their way here and didn't tell me?" *Good heavens! Could things get any worse?*

Smiling ruefully, he replied, "Guilty as charged. I

was trying to surprise you again, but it's just not working out like I thought."

Ash pulled aside the lace curtain and gazed out the parlor window, his forehead crinkling in confusion as he caught sight of the tall woman with the dour expression.

"Do you recognize our caller?" she asked, standing on tiptoe and trying to peer over his shoulder.

"Nope. But from the looks of her, the starch-stiff way she's dressed and all, I'd venture a guess that she's not from around here. Looks too citified."

Fingers of panic began to march up and down Sarah Jane's spine like a full contingent of army regulars as she pushed aside her startled husband and looked for herself. Recognizing the mystery woman instantly, she gasped.

"Do you know her, Sarah Jane? Sarah Jane, what's wrong?" Ash had never seen his wife looking so distraught. "Why are you looking as if you might faint? You're scaring me, woman."

Dropping the curtain back in place, she turned toward him, her face as pale as clotted cream. "We need to talk, Ash. Now. Right this moment. There's something very important I've got to tell you. Our whole future depends on it."

He wrapped his arm about her waist to steady her, growing increasingly worried at the fear he saw on her face. "Who is that woman, Sarah Jane? Tell me."

As the woman approached the front porch, Sarah Jane swallowed. "It's Miss Cartwright. Miss Dorothea Cartwright from the Cartwright School in Philadelphia."

"Miss Cartwright? What the hell's she doing here?

I didn't send for her." Even though he'd thought a
time or two about writing to the woman, he'd never
followed through. Now he was glad. He wouldn't
have wanted Sarah to think that he'd been checking
up on her.

"She's come about me."

"You? I don't understand. Miss Cartwright's the
one who sent you to me."

At that moment two things happened: A.J. and
Cynthia descended from the second floor, and a loud
knock sounded at the door.

Cynthia took one look at Sarah Jane's face and
rushed toward her. "What's wrong, dear heart? You
don't look well. You should be sitting down."

"I'll answer it," A.J. said, heading for the door.
He returned a few moments later with a somewhat
amused expression on his face.

"There's someone here to see you, Ash. Says her
name's Dorothea Cartwright. I told her to wait in the
hallway."

Sarah and Cynthia exchanged meaningful looks,
then Cynthia patted her hand. "It'll be all right.
You'll see."

"What's going on?" A.J. wanted to know.

"I haven't told Ash yet," Sarah told her sister-in-
law, her face growing paler by the minute. "I was
about to when—"

"Told me what? What the hell's going on around
here? Will someone please tell me?"

Ash and A.J. stared at their wives, who said nothing, then both men turned at the sound of the visitor's
approach.

"I'll be happy to tell you what is going on, Mr.

Morgan. I am Dorothea Cartwright from the Cartwright School of Finishing and Comportment in Philadelphia.

''That woman you call wife—'' she pointed a bony
finger in Sarah Jane's direction, not bothering to hide
her antipathy ''—is an impostor.''

Chapter Twenty

"An impostor? What the hell—heck are you talking about, Miss Cartwright?" Ash's angry glare burned into the woman to such a degree that she took a step back, fearful of becoming scorched. "This woman's my wife. The very wife you recommended, I might add. I'll not have you barge in here and sully her reputation in any way."

She lifted her chin imperiously. "I did not recommend Sarah Jane Parker to be your wife, Mr. Morgan. She took it upon herself to do so, forging my signature on correspondence, misrepresenting herself and my endorsement."

Ash's mouth dropped, but he snapped it shut quickly.

"Your wife is a fraud. If I was so inclined, I could have her arrested for what she's done."

Sarah Jane gasped audibly and grasped Cynthia's arm, squeezing tightly. The woman patted her hand reassuringly.

Exchanging a dismayed look with A.J. before turning to look at his wife, who was shaking like a leaf in a high wind, Ash was relieved that his brother and sister-in-law were standing close by her side, giving Sarah Jane the support that he wasn't able to provide at the moment.

Damn Dorothea Cartwright's hide!

And Sarah Jane's.

She had lied to him.

Again.

Was there no end to the woman's machinations?

Heaving a sigh of pure disgust, his eyes narrowed as his gaze returned to the malevolent woman. The spiteful look she wore said more graphically than words that she was quite capable of carrying out her threat, but he wasn't about to give her the satisfaction of knowing he'd been duped. This was a family matter that he was determined would remain in the family.

''I'm afraid you've come a very long way for nothing, Miss Cartwright, though I appreciate your concern. Sarah Jane has already confided the circumstances that brought her here. We are happily wed, despite the lack of good judgment on her part.''

Sarah Jane sucked in her breath and said nothing.

The older woman's eyes widened. ''She has? That doesn't sound like the Sarah Jane I know.'' She turned toward her former student and continued, ''I'm glad you've matured a bit, young woman. But what you did was wrong. I hope you realize that now. You could have destroyed my reputation, and the school that I've worked long and hard to establish. I can't allow my students to undermine those efforts.''

Taking a deep breath, Sarah Jane stepped forward, wondering why Ash had lied to protect her. She wasn't brave enough to look at him, fearful of what she might see in his eyes: anger, hurt, disappointment. Hate? All the things she'd caused by her selfish acts.

"I know what I did was wrong, Miss Cartwright, but I was desperate. I'm sure you were unaware of how very unhappy I was at being forced to remain at your school."

"I was aware. But it was your parents' desire that you remain there, though I told them on several occasions that I thought they were making a big mistake by insisting you do. We prefer that our students are happy in their environment."

Sarah Jane's mouth fell open. "You did? You do? But—but I thought it was your idea that I stay." As punishment, she wanted to add, but didn't.

"As much as I needed the tuition money your parents provided, Miss Parker, er, Mrs. Morgan, it was not worth all the aggravation that your habitual scandalous misbehavior caused. I wanted nothing more than to wash my hands of you, as I'm sure you were well aware.

"But that decision was not mine to make. It was your parents' wish that you remain at the school and become a teacher, under my tutelage. They felt your headstrong tendencies would get you into trouble if you were left to your own devices. I can see now that they were correct in that assumption."

Suddenly realizing that she was being remiss in her manners, Sarah Jane ushered the freezing woman farther into the room and took her wrap. She offered her some hot coffee, which she accepted gratefully.

"The circumstances that led me to behave the way I did were unfortunate, Miss Cartwright," she said after everyone was settled comfortably on the sofa and chairs. "But I can't honestly say that I am sorry for running away as I did."

The woman tsked several times, but didn't interrupt.

"Marrying Ash Morgan is the best thing that's ever happened to me. I now have a daughter by my husband's previous marriage, and a child on the way." The headmistress's eyes widened in surprise, but she didn't comment or tsk again. "And I'm very much in love with my husband.

"You have not met my brother-in-law, A.J., or his wife, Cynthia, but as you can see, I am surrounded by a wonderful family. Something I did not have the six years I was left alone at your school."

Looking stunned by the revelation, Ash opened his mouth to speak, but then closed it again, remembering that he was already supposed to be privy to that information. He cast his wife a thoughtful look.

"Your mother and father care about you, child. I don't think they meant any harm."

Sarah Jane sighed. "I realize that now. I've matured, and I think I understand what motivated their behavior. But nonetheless, it was wrong of them not to have consulted me in what I wanted to do with my life."

"You say you are with child, Sarah Jane, and so you will know soon enough what it is like to be a parent. I have never had children of my own. But I've raised enough of them over the years to know that it's a lofty responsibility. One does one's best, then hopes it's enough."

Dreading the question but knowing she must ask,

Sarah Jane took a deep breath. "Do you intend to press charges against me, Miss Cartwright?"

The woman looked from Sarah Jane to Ash, mulling over the question, then finally shook her head. "After being in this miserable state for less than a week, I have formed the opinion that you've been punished enough.

"And I also believe that you have matured enough to make Mr. Morgan a proper wife. I shall let the matter rest."

"Thank you, Miss Cartwright." Sarah released the breath she'd been holding, as did Ash, and she chanced a peek at him to find that he was gazing intently at her, a curious look on his face.

She offered a small smile, knowing that this incident was far from over. She still had her husband to face, and she dreaded that confrontation most of all.

After Miss Cartwright was safely on her way back to Philadelphia, and A.J. and Cynthia had left for Clarksburg, Sarah Jane and Ash were finally alone. Though not in the way Ash had originally intended.

They remained in the parlor—Ash staring into the blue and gold flames of the fire as if mesmerized, Sarah Jane gazing out the window at the leaden gray sky, which matched the feeling in her heavy heart at the moment.

The silence between them was deafening to the point where she just couldn't take it anymore. She turned to face him, mustering what was left of her courage. "I know you probably hate me now, Ash, but I want you to know how very sorry I am for having deceived you. I'll understand if you want to—'' She swallowed, blinking back tears. ''If you want to dissolve our marriage.''

He turned and looked at her, his face a mask of pain. ''I don't want to divorce you, Sarah. I love you. But what you've done has disappointed me. I thought we had an understanding.''

A kernel of hope sprouted in her breast and she moved toward him. ''I wanted to tell you. I tried several times, but I was afraid that you'd send me away if you knew what I'd done. I fell in love with you from the first moment we met, and I just couldn't bear the thought of not living my life here with you and Addy.''

Reaching out, he took her hand and led her to the sofa. ''I know you don't understand why I've been so adamant about there being honesty between us, Sarah Jane, and perhaps it's my fault because I wasn't more forthcoming about things in my past.''

She shook her head, her face a mask of confusion. ''Your past? I don't understand.''

''I was quite young when I married for the first time, as was my wife, Wynona. I thought I was in love. I didn't really know about love back then. I didn't really know about it until you came into my life, Sarah Jane.'' He squeezed her hand.

''Wynona married me under false pretenses. She lied when she said she loved me. She was, as it turned out, in love with a married man and carrying his child. I was a convenient escape, a way for her to salvage her reputation and appease her parents.''

Sarah Jane gasped, her eyes filling with tears again. ''I'm so sorry. I—I can see why you must have thought me like her. I lied to you so many times.''

He heaved a sigh. "You're nothing like her, Sarah Jane. You're warm, kindhearted, generous to a fault. Not the least bit malicious, and a whole lot more impetuous. And I knew from the first moment I laid eyes on you that I was lost."

"Oh, Ash." Her heart was full to bursting she loved him so much.

"I'm sorry about your unhappy childhood. I never would have brought your parents here had I known. I thought I was doing the right thing. But after hearing about the callous way you were treated, now I'm not so sure."

"It doesn't matter. It's time we faced each other, confronted the past and made amends. The hurt I've borne has festered into something ugly. I love them both. I just don't understand what motivated them to abandon me the way they did."

He scooted closer to her and wrapped his arm about her shoulder, looking for just the right words. "I think Miss Cartwright was right when she said that they were only doing what they thought was best. I'm sure they loved you and still do. I hope you will find it in your heart to forgive them."

"Will you ever find it in your heart to forgive me?" she asked in a small voice. "I know I don't deserve your forgiveness for all the trouble I've caused, but I promise—"

He held his finger to her lips and smiled. "Please, no more promises. Except one. Just promise to love me with all your heart and soul, as I love you, and never leave me."

"I promise. But you must promise me something, too."

His brow arched, and he smiled mischievously. "To make love to you every morning and every night?"

She grinned. "Well, there is that. But I was thinking more along the lines of no more surprises. From now on, let's be totally honest and open with each other."

He had the grace to look chagrined. "Since we're being totally honest, I have a confession to make."

"You? What could you possibly have done?"

"Remember the letters you received at the school, the ones intended for Miss Cartwright?"

She smiled softly. "Yes, they were lovely. I—"

"I didn't write them. Zeke did. It was his idea, not mine, that I find a wife."

"Zeke?" Her eyes widened, then she threw back her head and laughed. "We are a pair, aren't we?"

"A good match, I think."

"Okay. From here on out, no more surprises, no more lies, no more—"

"Excitement?" He arched a brow. "This is beginning to sound rather dull."

"It is, isn't it? Don't worry," she informed him with a kiss. "I had my fingers crossed behind my back."

He kissed her long and hard, then said, "I love you, Sarah Jane. I always will."

"I love you, too."

He peeked around her back. "Your fingers aren't crossed. That's good." With that, he picked her up and carried her toward the stairs. "Of course, there's only one true test of making sure that you're telling me the truth."

"There is?"

"This test could take most of the day? I'll want to make certain it's accurate."

"And will you be up for it, Mr. Morgan?" she asked, nibbling his chin.

"Most assuredly, Mrs. Morgan."

She peeked behind to make sure his fingers weren't crossed, and breathed a sigh of relief.

Epilogue

Seated on the white-haired gentleman's lap, Addy smiled adoringly at her new best friend, the Reverend Seth Parker, who had arrived with his wife, Xenobia, just two days before and been eagerly welcomed into the family by the young girl.

"Grandpa Seth, do you want me to read you some of the small women book? It's really good. Sarah Jane gave me my very own copy for Christmas."

The minister smiled warmly at the child and nodded, and Sarah Jane couldn't keep tears from clogging her throat. She remembered sitting on her father's lap countless times while he read to her. They'd always been close, always shared a love of reading and learning, until he and her mother had made the decision to ship her off to boarding school.

"I think your father is quite smitten with little Adelaide," her mother said, an indulgent smile curving her lips.

They were standing in the doorway of the parlor, observing the child and older man.

"He always did have a soft spot for little girls.

He'll probably act quite foolish when your baby finally comes, Sarah Jane, especially if it's a girl.'' Her mother's eyes sparkled with happiness. ''I can't believe my daughter is actually going to have a baby and that I'm going to be a grandmother.''

It was on the tip of Sarah Jane's tongue to ask her mother why. Why now was she suddenly so involved, so interested in Sarah Jane's life? Why had she sent her away to begin with? Why hadn't she been a more caring, affectionate mother? Why had she been so indifferent to her only daughter?

But she decided against it.

Since her parents' arrival there'd been no discussion of past events or the circumstances that led her to marry Ash. It was obvious they felt awkward about her sudden departure from the Cartwright School and even more confused about what had motivated it in the first place. But they'd made no mention of it, and neither had Sarah.

Ash had advised her to let sleeping dogs lie and make a new beginning. Dredging up the past wouldn't serve any purpose, he'd told her, especially since they didn't seem to realize that they'd done anything wrong. Sarah Jane knew he was right from the moment she laid eyes on them.

Upon entering the Morgan home, Xenobia had declared with an exasperated shake of her head that her daughter had always been headstrong and impulsive, and that she was so relieved that Sarah Jane had found a strong man to take care of her and curb her impetuosity.

Ash had nearly choked on her words, for he'd learned the hard way that no one was going to curb or tame his wife. He'd declared out loud that he wouldn't want it any other way. Sarah Jane had rewarded him amply for his loyal declaration.

As if conjured up by her thoughts, Ash approached and wrapped his arm about her. "How's my beautiful wife doing?" Nuzzling her ear, he grinned when Sarah Jane's mother got an appalled look on her face and went to join her husband on the sofa. "I think I've shocked your mother."

"Probably. She's never been known for being demonstrative."

"How are things going? You seem tired."

"It's been difficult keeping things bottled up inside, but I think you're right. I'm going to try to put the past behind me and concentrate on our future."

"That's my girl." He kissed her hard, and they heard Xenobia's sharp gasp.

"Don't mind them, Grandma," Addy said to the older blond woman, sounding very grown-up. "Daddy and Sarah are always smooching and hugging. That's how come she's got that baby inside her tummy. Sarah Jane told me all about how it happens. Do you want to hear?"

Xenobia Parker paled and looked as if she might faint, the reverend swallowed his smile, while Sarah Jane rushed forward, a panicked look on her face.

"Addy, I think you should take your grandparents out back and show them Teddy's new doghouse."

"That's a splendid idea," her father said with a wink, and Sarah Jane's heart began to soften.

"Okay. Come on, Grandpa, Grandma. I promise I won't let Teddy pee on your shoes." With bemused expressions, the couple followed their new grand-daughter out of the room.

As soon as they had disappeared, Sarah Jane began to laugh. She laughed so hard that she had to hold her sides, fearing she might do exactly what Addy had promised Teddy would not. "I just love that little girl to pieces," she said when she'd regained her composure. "If anyone can get through to my parents, it'll be Addy. She says what's on her mind, and they need a good dose of that."

"She's getting more like her mother every day." At her confused expression, he added, "I mean you, Sarah Jane. You're Addy's mother now. She told me last night that she wants to start calling you 'Mommy.'"

"Oh, Ash!" Tears of joy filled the young woman's eyes. "Really? I'm so thrilled."

Taking her hand, he led her to the sofa. "You don't think my daughter is going to allow the new baby to get one up on her, do you? And she loves you so much, Sarah Jane."

Smiling, she heaved a sigh of pure contentment. "I'm so happy. Sometimes I have to pinch myself to believe that I'm part of this wonderful family."

"Which is growing by leaps and bounds, by the way. A.J. told me last night after everyone had gone to bed that Cynthia's expecting."

Sarah squealed, clapping excitedly. "I'm so happy for her, for both of them. I can't wait to see Cynthia and A.J. tonight so I can tell them so." A.J. and Cynthia had taken up residence at their new home this morning. The farm was located only twenty miles from Morgantown, so she and her sister-in-law would be able to visit frequently.

"The way A.J. tells it Beulah's taking most of the credit. Go figure. That woman annoys me."

"Well, she'll be here tonight, along with Zeke and Etta, so you'll have to behave yourself."

"I'm planning to, but you'd better talk to Uncle Zeke. He's fixing on spiking the punch at your parents' welcome party."

"My parents don't imbibe, so this should be an interesting evening."

"Life's gotten a whole lot more interesting since you came into mine."

She scooted over and sat on his lap, wrapping her arms about his neck. "I'm not too much for you to handle, am I?"

He patted her abdomen. "Well, there's a bit more of you to love, but I think I'm up to the task."

"If you're *up* right now," she said, casting a meaningful look at his lap, "we might sneak upstairs for a while."

Gathering her into his arms, he stood, wearing a huge grin on his face. "I never thought you'd ask."

* * * * *

One small spark ignites the entire city
of Chicago, but amid the chaos, a chance
encounter leads to an unexpected new love....

THE HOSTAGE

As Deborah Sinclair confronts her powerful
father, determined to refuse the society
marriage he has arranged for her, a stranger
with vengeance on his mind suddenly appears
and takes the fragile, sheltered heiress hostage.

Swept off to Isle Royale, Deborah finds herself
the pawn in Tom Silver's dangerous game of
revenge. Soon she begins to understand the
injustice that fuels his anger, an injustice
wrought by her own family. And as winter
imprisons the isolated land, she finds
herself a hostage of her own heart....

SUSAN WIGGS

MIRA

"...draws readers in with delightful characters,
engaging dialogue, humor, emotion
and sizzling sensuality."
—*Costa Mesa Sunday Times* on *The Charm School*

On sale mid-April 2000 wherever paperbacks are sold!

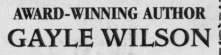

**Harlequin®
Historical**

Edgewood, Texas

A brand-new series from bestselling author

CAROLYN DAVIDSON

Available now
THE BACHELOR TAX (#496)
When rancher Gabe Tanner proposes to the town
spinster to avoid the dreaded tax, he never guesses
he'll fall in love!

Coming in May 2000
TANNER STAKES HIS CLAIM (#513)
Straitlaced sheriff Wesley Tanner falls for the new
saloon singer. Can he convince Angelena that they
could make beautiful music together?

And in November 2000 keep a lookout for
Anna Tanner's story, appearing in our in-line
Western Christmas Collection.

**Harlequin Historicals
The way to past *should* have been.**

Available at your favorite retail outlet.

Romance is just one click away!

online book **serials**

➤ *Exclusive* to our web site, get caught up in both the daily and weekly online installments of new romance stories.

➤ Try the Writing Round Robin. Contribute a chapter to a story created by our members. Plus, winners will get prizes.

romantic **travel**

➤ Want to know where the best place to kiss in New York City is, or which restaurant in Los Angeles is the most romantic? Check out our Romantic Hot Spots for the scoop.

➤ Share your travel tips and stories with us on the romantic travel message boards.

romantic reading **library**

➤ Relax as you read our collection of Romantic Poetry.

➤ Take a peek at the Top 10 Most Romantic Lines!

Visit us online at

www.eHarlequin.com

on Women.com Networks